W9-AAX-749

BETHANY HAGEN

JUBILEE

Manor

The conclusion to
LANDRY PARK

DIAL BOOKS
an imprint of Penguin Group (USA) LLC

DIAL BOOKS

Published by the Penguin Group
Penguin Group (USA) LLC
375 Hudson Street
New York, New York 10014

USA/Canada/UK/Ireland/Australia/New Zealand/India/South Africa/China
PENGUIN.COM
A Penguin Random House Company

Library of Congress Cataloging-in-Publication Data
Hagen, Bethany.
Jubilee Manor / by Bethany Hagen.   pages cm
Sequel to: Landry Park.
Summary: "Madeline struggles to unite her own gentry class and the impoverished Rootless, but when the Rootless are suspected of murdering gentry heirs, Madeline finds herself at odds with the boy she loves and the very people she is trying to lead"— Provided by publisher.
ISBN 978-0-8037-3949-9 (hardback)
[1. Science fiction. 2. Social classes—Fiction. 3. Love—Fiction. 4. Murder—Fiction.] I. Title.
PZ7.H1233Ju 2015
[Fic]—dc23   2014041700

Printed in the United States of America

1   3   5   7   9   10   8   6   4   2

Designed by Jennifer Kelly
Text set in Minion Pro

To

who didn't get to see this book published

JUBILEE
Manor

ONE

It was the shouts that caught my attention.

I had been looking over the menu for tonight's dinner—roast goose and lobster—when I heard the noise come from outside, where the gardeners had been rolling heavy solar heaters into place and shoveling snow off the wide gravel walks. Curious, I went through the ballroom to the patio doors, hoping to find the source of the commotion.

For the first time in the month since I'd stood up to my father at Liberty Park, the estate bustled with activity. On my way through the ballroom, I passed servants carrying fresh bundles of flowers, neatly pressed linens, crates of long white candles for the candelabras and chandeliers. I made a quick mental note of the progress as I walked, trying to calculate how much more still needed to be done. The dinner my uncle and I were hosting tonight was to welcome the Rootless and the gentry together, to try to demonstrate goodwill on both sides. How well the Rootless would adapt to sharing a table with their oppressors remained to be seen, but I felt hopeful that tonight would be a turning point.

Tonight was important.

The men were gesturing emphatically to one another, and I could hear them arguing even before I opened the glass doors that led outside. A rush of cold damp air hit me, cutting through the filmy silk dress I wore. "What's going on?" The frigid air made my voice unusually sharp. I took a breath and changed my tone to something softer, more polite. "I heard the shouts. Is everything okay?"

One of the men, the head gardener, touched his hat respectfully. "Good afternoon, Miss Landry. There's really nothing going on here, just an unexpected complication."

But I'd already stepped out onto the patio, shivering, snow soaking through my thin slippers, and now I could see what the men were concerned about: an ugly red stain in the snow, right on top of where the platinum atomic symbol was inlaid into the stone.

"We were clearing off the patio," he said, "and we noticed a heap of snow in the middle. We started shoveling and found this."

"It looks like blood," someone said.

"It looks like a *lot* of blood," another added.

I came forward to examine the stain more closely. It did indeed look like blood, a vivid crimson that eerily matched the color of my hair. Darker in the middle and surrounded by bright splatters, the stain was large and deep. When a gardener used his shovel to scrape away a section, the snowmelt lingered in scarlet puddles on the patio.

The wind picked up again, ruffling my hair, and the scent of something metallic and salty blew with it. "Do you think this means that someone is hurt? Have any of the servants reported injuries?" I asked.

The head gardener shook his head. "None of the staff has been hurt. And it would be difficult to hide a wound that produced that much blood."

"Could it have been an animal?" I asked. "Maybe a fox or a wild dog cornered something." I felt a flutter of fear as I thought of my cat, Morgana, who habitually wandered outside.

"But then where's the rest of it? No carcass, no bones. Not even a trail showing where it had been dragged off." The gardener shook his head, and I relaxed a little. "No. Whatever bled here was *carried* off and then great pains were taken to cover the blood back up. A person did this, Miss Landry."

I took quick stock of the patio. Four gardeners, two solar heaters, and assorted shovels, spades, and ice picks. Muddy bootprints were everywhere, mostly leading from the south side of the property where they'd been clearing the garden, and one leading from the east side, where the gardening shed abutted the carriage house. Ignoring the head gardener's noise of protest, I walked around the blood and down the steps, the snow scraping against my bare legs as I sank in up to my knees. At the bottom, I could see no footprints other than those that clearly belonged to the gardeners. There was no disturbed snow on the lawn, no trace of blood anywhere else. It was as if whatever—no, *whomever*—had bled into the snow had then simply vanished.

I trudged back up to the gardeners. "How long since the patio's last been cleared?" I asked.

"The night of your debut," the head gardener said.

That made sense. That was the night before I'd confronted Father and everything had changed. "So it's been a month," I said. "Could this have been here since then and no one noticed?"

He shook his head. "Someone would have seen it, surely. And besides, it snowed last night, and the snow piled on top of the stain was freshly disturbed. It must have happened today."

The thought made me intensely uncomfortable. Mere hours ago, someone had spilled what appeared to be torrents of blood right outside the ballroom of the most important estate in the entire city, and no one had noticed. Had someone been mutilated? Killed?

Please let no one have been hurt, I begged the fading sky. *Please, please, please, no more, no more blood, no more pain.*

I thought back to my father, bloodied and hands knotting in pain, when he'd been rescued from the Rootless mob at Liberty Park.

And along with the thought came a stab of fear—a rapier prick of fear really—sharp and small and gone in an instant.

"Should we tell your uncle?" the gardener asked.

4

I shook off the images of violence and savagery that crowded at the edges of my mind. "I'll get him," I said. I left the gardeners shuffling uncomfortably and went back inside to find my uncle, my slippers leaving wet footprints on the floor.

I hated having to disturb Jack with anything tonight. The events at Liberty Park, along with the shocking and painful revelation that Jack was actually my father's assumed-dead brother, had left the city in chaos and had naturally left the gentry uneasy. There was so much work to be done and tonight was a new beginning. He needed to focus and prepare as much as possible.

And, if I admitted it to myself, there was another reason I felt reluctant to tell him about the mysterious discovery. Something had been different about him in the past four weeks, a fanaticism that nestled inside his rumbling words. It made me wary, but we were so close to achieving all that we'd worked for, so close to actual change, that I felt reluctant to give the small anxieties in my mind any credence.

Jack was in my father's study when I found him. He was reading, as he often did these days, having been deprived of access to books when he lived in the Rootless ghetto. He snapped the book shut when he saw me. "Madeline. How are the preparations for the dinner coming along?"

For a moment, his resemblance to Father was overwhelming, and something tightened in my chest. "There's something on the patio you need to see," I said.

He got to his feet, leaving his cane leaning against the desk. We walked back through the ballroom, where servants rolled tables laden with fresh flowers and empty silver platters in from the kitchen elevator. Savory scents and sweet smells wafted up from downstairs, and already Crawford, the butler, was laying out bottles of wine from the cellar. The sun was dipping low outside. I would have to go upstairs soon to change and have Elinor fix my hair.

Jack opened the doors and we both stepped outside, me wishing that I would have thought to get a cloak and him showing no sign that he even noticed the cold. The creases in his face deepened as his eyes lit upon the blood, and they grew deeper and deeper as he interviewed the gardeners, listening to the same answers I had heard not five minutes ago.

"Should we alert the constables?" I asked when he finished.

He stared at the western horizon, where oranges and pinks and purples mingled together and glanced off the sparkling snow. "The guests will be here in a couple of hours. And we're not even sure that a crime has been committed."

"But surely the police could identify it as blood for certain? And maybe there's somebody in the city who's been hurt and the constables are looking for any possible leads, and—"

Jack held up a hand. "I'm not ignoring this, Madeline. But we have important work to do here tonight and I don't want it interrupted by something that's probably inconsequential."

"They could come and take a couple of pictures, maybe a

sample and then leave," I insisted. "In and out before the party even starts."

Jack met my gaze, determined gray eyes on determined gray eyes, and I managed to keep the eye contact until he finally exhaled and shrugged. "Fine. We'll call the constables. But I will make it clear that they need to be quick. My people will not take kindly to seeing the police roaming the estate, not after all the violence of the past year."

"I understand," I said. "And thank you."

He nodded at me. "Finish clearing everything else," he told the men. "But save the patio until after the constables have looked at it." He looked at me one last time before leaving. One by one, the men filed off the patio, grabbing their shovels and picks.

I stood there for a minute longer, my breath steaming, absorbed by the bloody snow. It seemed like a portent, like a warning out of a fairy tale, but for what? Things couldn't be better right now. The Rootless and the gentry would meet tonight, converse and mingle and actually learn about one another. My father had been removed from power. And David—my cheeks warmed as I thought of Captain David Dana and his bright blue eyes and sharp smile.

And I had David. Things were good.

I went upstairs, where I found Morgana curled into a silver ball on my bed. I rubbed behind her ears for a moment, glad to see her alive and clearly unharmed, and then started to change for dinner.

Elinor had already laid out my gown, a flowing chiffon of mint green with a wide sash and a short train. I wanted something understated, something that wouldn't seem too opulent to the Rootless, but also something that wouldn't seem cheap or boring to the gentry, who already didn't trust me after what happened in Liberty Park. I wanted to show them that I was still a Landry, that I still had a foot in their world, and that trying to help the Rootless didn't negate any of that.

As Elinor pinned up my hair, sliding antique hairpins into the mass of waves with almost unnerving focus, I watched the blue lights of the constables' cars flash across the windows. I wondered what they would make of the stain, and if they would try to analyze the blood or search for someone who was missing or hurt, and if they could find any other clues as to who did it.

I tried to shake the worries and fears out of my thoughts, but they clung to me like wet leaves, cold and unwelcome. What if someone was truly hurt? What if they were still hurting?

Stop, I told myself. I was overreacting, on edge from the violent events this winter. Jack seemed to think it was nothing, and if that wasn't the case, then the constables would be able to help. I had to focus on making tonight a success.

With a murmured *thanks* to Elinor, I rose from my vanity and went downstairs. The evening was beginning, whether I was ready for it or not.

TWO

Jack and I stood in the foyer to welcome the guests, my gown affording very little protection from the gusts of freezing air that circled through the house whenever the front doors opened. The Rootless contingent was the first to arrive, and I felt some dismay at their small number—less than twenty in all.

"So few," I murmured to Jack as they filed in through the door, looking uncomfortable and wary. "Did we invite more?"

"I invited them all," Jack said. He licked his lips as he looked down at the floor. "I am sure the reasons for refusal are varied."

There was something he wasn't saying. Rather than ask, I waited—a tactic I'd learned from my father.

"Many of them feel that we should not move forward with a formalized agreement with the gentry," Jack finally said, and his quiet voice made it plain that this was a difficult admission for him. "Only a handful see the wisdom in working together. Some have even gone so far as to suggest that I've had a gentry agenda all along, being both a Landry and a son of the Uprisen."

The Uprisen was the small influential group within the gentry that set legal policy and government agendas behind the scenes; only the oldest and wealthiest families counted themselves members. My ancestor Jacob Landry had been the founder of the Uprisen, and my entire life I'd been groomed to take a seat at the table with the other eleven families. So had Jack—before he'd faked his own death and forged a new place for himself among the Rootless.

"Things were easier when my identity was unknown," he said.

"I can imagine."

The group finished coming in, and we greeted them, me signaling to the servants to circulate among the guests with hors d'oeuvres and small flutes of champagne, which the Rootless seemed reluctant to take. Instead, they clustered together at the far end of the foyer, looking to Jack for reassurance.

A scowling man with slouching shoulders and darting eyes hung near the back. I was surprised to see him: Smith, the angry revolutionary who had once yanked me through a window by my hair. Jack had helped the other Rootless find gentry-style clothes, tuxedos for the men and gowns for the women, but Smith had refused. He still defiantly wore his Rootless clothes, patched brown pants and a tattered gray shirt.

He, of all the Rootless, was the most resistant to working with the gentry. Why had he even come?

Eyeing Smith, I moved across the marble floor to speak with the Rootless, to encourage them to make themselves at home. Most of them smiled at me, most of them shook my hand and thanked me for standing up for them in Liberty Park, but not him. He moved right past me as if I didn't even exist.

"I thought there was going to be dinner," Smith said to Jack, glancing around the foyer with barely contained revulsion.

"It's traditional for guests to mill in the foyer before dinner starts," Jack said pleasantly. "It gives a chance for conversation." What Jack didn't mention was that he didn't want anybody to see the constables packing up their things and leaving the patio. Better to keep the guests safely ensconced until he was certain that they had gone.

Smith walked closer, but he didn't bother lowering his voice. "You're turning into one of them," he said. "Why are we even here? Alexander Landry has been driven out and you have control. Can't you force the Uprisen to change?"

"Not without a fight," I broke in. "If you push them, there will be more violence, maybe even war—"

"A war that we would win," Smith said over me.

"—And that war would only hurt your own people and your own cause," I continued.

"She's right," Jack said. "After all, without Alexander to lead them, the gentry may feel it's in their best interest to negotiate. We have our proposals, our demands. We will ask for the gentry to switch to a safer power source—wind or solar—and they will see the irrefutable logic in that." His voice did not ring with confidence, and Smith's curling lip indicated that he noticed this.

"At the very least," Jack amended, "we try this first."

I turned to Jack. I didn't like the way he said *try this first*, as if this attempt at diplomacy was something to be scratched off a list, a perfunctory task to attempt before moving on to the real solution. And I worried that for people like Smith, the real solution would always be one of rubble and ashes.

Of blood.

But before I could say anything else, he stepped close to Jack and said, "The time for negotiation was two centuries ago. I don't want their money or their handouts. I want a world where the gentry are no more. Now, do you have the spine to see a plan through or not?"

"Smith, now's not the time."

"No, it wouldn't be. Not in front of your new friends," Smith snarled.

He stalked off and Jack cleared his throat. "He can be a little hotheaded," he said mildly.

"A little?"

The door opened once more and I turned, hoping to see David, and only barely masking my disappointment when I saw it wasn't him. The Wilder family looked faintly uncomfortable with the Rootless nearby, but when Jack stuck out his hand, Mr. Wilder shook it, only hesitating a moment. I beamed at him. The stigma against touching the skin of a Rootless person was so strong that I'm embarrassed to say it had once prevented me from helping a very sick girl. If someone as important as Clarence Wilder was willing to shake hands with the leader of the Rootless, that was a very good sign.

Mr. Wilder looked up and met Jack's gaze as he shook hands. "Thank you for inviting us," he said. His gaze slid over Jack and me, and I knew he was remembering the countless times he'd shaken hands with my father, the times he'd kissed my mother's cheek and patted my head. Landry Park without my parents—especially my father—was still a strange thing to the gentry. It was still a strange thing to me.

"It's good to see you again, Clarence." Jack's familiarity was surprising to me, but it shouldn't be—after all, he'd been the heir to Landry Park once, and men like Mr. Wilder used to be his peers.

Philip, the Wilders' son and heir, gave me a tight hug. He smelled like fresh laundry with just a whiff of Scotch. Although I'm not a demonstrative person, I hugged him back. We'd spent a lot of time together over the last year when our fathers had taught us how to run our estates, and I liked to imagine that we were friends.

"Where's your sister?" I asked him. Marianne wasn't the type to miss a party.

"She's coming later, but she's probably still off with Mark Everly. We were both planning on going over to his house this morning, but I ended up staying home instead—he's got a cold and I wasn't interested in catching it."

"So he won't be here tonight?"

"Marianne will have to come alone; what a hardship." He rolled his eyes, but his voice softened when he added, "We're expecting an engagement any day now. Speaking of missing guests, where's Captain Dana? And Miss Westoff?"

"Cara is upstairs with my cousin Ewan. They'll be down any moment. And Captain Dana will be here shortly." *I hope.*

Philip straightened his cuffs, silver links gleaming against the white fabric, the fabric striking against his dark skin. "So, the idea is that we're supposed to mingle with these people?"

"The idea is to find common ground," I said. "They're the same as us. They just don't want to live in fear or pain any longer. I think we can all relate."

Philip's mouth quirked. "I guess. But what do I even talk about with them?"

"Use your natural charm. There are two girls our age over there."

"Now *that* is common ground." He winked at me and then whisked a couple of champagne flutes off a silver tray, walking over and presenting them to the young Rootless women. They accepted with giggles.

When Jane Osbourne came in, I didn't wait for her to walk

over to greet me. I met her right at the door, unable to keep a smile from my face. Jane's mother was one of the Uprisen, and Jane and I had been close friends since we were girls. She was one of the few sensible people I could number among my acquaintances, and she and I had spent many dances and dinners in quiet conversation while the others socialized and drank. She gave me a warm hug and looked around the room.

"I can't believe you managed to get Rootless and gentry together in the same room." Her genial expression flickered as she caught sight of Philip charming the Rootless girls.

Jane has feelings for Philip, I realized, and then my heart squeezed a little for her. Philip was a charmer and a flirt. I knew a little of what it was like to love someone like that.

"I asked him to be a gentry ambassador," I said, recognizing that look. Philip was a bit of a flirt, but he was talking to those girls at my behest, so I felt partly responsible for Jane's discomfort.

"Oh, of course," Jane said, equanimity restored in an instant. "I'm glad to see that at least a few of the guests are off to a friendly start."

"Please, help yourself to some drinks and food. I'm on greeting duty."

Jane nodded, her dark curls bouncing gracefully against her long neck. *Philip better notice what he's missing*, I thought as she walked off with her parents. I liked him, but Jane was undoubtedly the best girl in this city.

More gentry arrived, but still no David. I discreetly pulled my tablet out of my deep dress pocket and checked to see if he'd called or messaged. He hadn't.

The other families managed a modicum of politeness, but when they entered the house, Arthur Lawrence and his three oldest boys refused to shake Jack's hand. I felt heat rise to my cheeks—the Lawrences were cousins on my mother's side, and I couldn't help but feel ashamed of their rudeness.

"Mr. Landry," Uncle Lawrence said. "Here you are. Alive. Shaming the gentry just as you did as a boy."

"And here you are, Arthur," Jack rumbled, "as old and as blind as ever."

Uncle Lawrence gave a thin-lipped smile. He was indeed old, but that didn't make him any less formidable. His spine was still straight, his eyes still clear, and his words still sharp. Even the ebony and silver walking stick he carried was more for show than for use.

His boys—Tarleton and Frank—sauntered past without a word. The heir, Stuart, stopped briefly in front of me but didn't bow or kiss my hand or any of the other conventional greetings. "So you're with them now?" he said, jerking his head toward the clump of Rootless. Thankfully, he kept his voice low. "I heard about what happened in the park. How you let them take your father and hurt him.

"I'll tell you what. I promise if you marry me, I'll forgive all this." He gestured to Jack and the Rootless in the foyer. "I'll even move here to Landry Park."

It was no secret that Uncle Lawrence wanted one of his boys to marry me, to bring the power of Landry Park into his vast empire of wealth and land. What I wanted to tell Stuart was that if all went to plan, the estates would no longer be the seat of all the money and influence and that the Landry name would no longer be a byword for unadulterated control. That marrying me would be pointless, because the game of acquiring good gentry blood and more money would be finished.

"I'd rather hang myself," is what I said instead.

Stuart snorted incredulously. "I can't believe we're related."

You took the words right out of my mouth.

Harry Westoff was the last to arrive and he arrived alone. His wife had flown off somewhere warm and sunny, and now that half the city knew that she had been the one who so brutally beat Cara—her own daughter—almost a year ago, it seemed like she would stay there indefinitely. Scandals may burn themselves out eventually, but the word was that the constables had officially charged Addison with assault, and that she would be arrested if she returned. Despite being thoroughly under the gentry's thumb, the police did still carry out the letter of the law occasionally, especially when the evidence was so irrefutable . . . and when the victim was also gentry.

Mr. Westoff greeted Jack in his usual half-polite, half-condescending way and shook his hand, but I noticed that both men had white knuckles and red palms by the end of the handshake. "I take it my daughter is here with your son?" he asked Jack.

Jack nodded that it was so.

"And dear Madeline," Mr. Westoff said, coming over to me and kissing my hand. "How wonderful for you to host us all here . . . together. I bet your father must be so proud."

His barbs found no purchase in me. I had thrown away any hope of Father's approval when I stood by Jack.

I heard a throat being cleared dramatically and looked up to see Cara gliding gracefully down the stairs, her pale pink dress whispering against the marble as she walked. Next to her, Ewan looked strong and handsome in a pressed tuxedo. With his red hair and pale skin, he looked as much a Landry as I did. I couldn't believe I'd never seen it before, that I had never guessed we were related.

"Hello, Papa," Cara said, dismounting the stairs and coming toward us. Ewan stayed next to her, his hand on the small of her back, a detail Mr. Westoff didn't miss. "Did you miss me?"

"Ah, Cara. One always misses what is dear to the heart."

Cara batted her long eyelashes, her face folding into an expression of saccharine adoration. "I am so *happy* to hear that I am still so important to you, Papa."

"Hello, Mr. Landry," Mr. Westoff said to my cousin. His voice was the model of politeness, but he didn't extend a hand to shake, and neither did Ewan. They met eyes and Ewan lifted his chin slightly, as if to signify that he wasn't about to kowtow to his girlfriend's father.

Mr. Westoff smiled. "How interesting. Like looking at the

dark side of the moon. You look and act exactly like a Landry but the—" here he made a motion indicating the healing sores peeping out from Ewan's hairline "—kind of ruins the effect. If you'll excuse me, sweeting." He made a short bow and went to join my uncle Lawrence, who was currently scowling at the Rootless side of the room.

"So," Cara said, acting as if the tense exchange with her father hadn't occurred. "Your party is off to a great start."

I wanted to protest, but she was right. So far, Philip was the only one brave enough to cross the wide expanse of empty marble that separated the murmuring gentry and the Rootless. An uneasiness permeated the air, a tension rife with misunderstanding and prejudice. We needed to move into the ballroom and start the buffet. Plenty of food and drinks would help people loosen up and start talking.

"I should go make sure everything is ready," I said, more to myself than to Cara, thinking of the dark bloodstain and the constables.

"Good idea. In the meantime, I'll do your job for you and get these people talking." Cara grabbed Ewan's hand and looped his arm through hers. Together, they strode out into the crowd, Cara loudly greeting the other Uprisen heirs and Ewan nodding at his people on the far side of the foyer.

"Looks like Cara Westoff knows how to work a room," Jack said quietly.

"She always has," I conceded. Jack raised an eyebrow at

me and I realized that I sounded overly critical. I cleared my throat and tried again. "If anyone can coax these people into conversation, it would be her. In the meantime, I'm going to pop into the ballroom and see if we're ready to begin."

"Please make sure the constables have finished their business. Our guests are uncertain enough without the police poking around."

I started to leave, but then I turned back to my uncle. "Do you think maybe we could invite everyone to see the library and some of the other rooms? Many of them have never been inside the house before, and maybe an informal tour would help set them at ease, give them something to talk about."

Jack nodded. "Marvelous idea." He strode over to the Rootless, offering to show them around in his booming voice. I saw Philip offer his arms to the two girls who, despite their pale skin and air of weakness, were very pretty. I noticed Jane glancing in their direction and then quickly away.

Cara saw Philip joining Jack and announced that she and her friends were accompanying them for the tour. And like that, the younger gentry were intermingled with the group of Rootless, awkwardly to be sure, but Cara and Ewan made such a compelling pair that it was hard not to feel inspired. Only the gentry adults were left in the foyer, holding their drinks and staring at the large, jostling group going down the hall.

Satisfied that the mood was improving, I slipped out of the foyer to make my way down to the kitchens.

Downstairs, the rich smells of roasting meat and melted butter hung heavy in the air, and the cooks were busy whipping up bowls of desserts and rolling out pastry dough. After getting our head cook Martha's assurances that the food was ready to be carried up, I went upstairs through the butler's staircase and peeked into the ballroom.

Tables were already laden with cold fruit and piles of rolls, croissants, and small cakes. The kitchen maids had brought up chafing dishes of whipped potatoes, creamy soups, and dark, roasted asparagus. Rolls of sushi were laid out in unnervingly precise rows, dollops of wasabi and ginger ringing the edges.

I felt a wave of pride. This was the first large dinner I had ever planned by myself, and it was all coming together. I strode over to the doors, where there was no sign of the constables or their blue-lit cars and where the patio had dutifully been cleared by the gardeners. Only the slickness on the platinum symbol betrayed the presence of snow not an hour ago, but otherwise everything looked dry and warm thanks to the solar heaters.

I went through the butler's entrance again, but this time I stayed on the first floor, making my way to the main hallway to meet up with the others and tell Jack that we were ready. And then I felt my waist seized from behind.

THREE

I turned to find myself staring into a sharp-featured face with a wolfish grin and eyes the color of the Cherenkov lanterns outside. My breath caught even before Captain David Dana bent to lower his lips to mine, and once he did, I felt like I would never breathe again. His lips were soft and warm and they tasted faintly of cloves or maybe cinnamon. His hand slid around the back of my neck while his other arm tightened around my waist. He parted my lips with his, and my knees grew weak, unable to support my weight.

"You're late," I murmured against his mouth.

"I like to make an entrance."

"Sneak in is more like it."

He drew me in even tighter, my skirt tangling around his legs. "I wanted to see you first," he said in a low voice. "I *needed* to see you first."

"David," I said. I wasn't sure what else to say. No one had ever challenged me like David, inspired me like him, and sometimes I worried that it was all too good to be true, that something would drive us apart.

"You don't have to say anything," he said. "But I will. I missed you."

I flushed, happy. "I missed you, too."

The grin came back, wider than ever. "Good. Now I suppose we should get back to your party."

I never wanted to leave this dim hallway, never wanted to be without David's arms around me, but I knew he was right, we needed to rejoin the others. I started walking, and David let me, but he kept his arm firmly around my waist. Fluttering filled my chest. I'd never had a boyfriend before. I'd never even wanted to have a boyfriend before. And this is what it felt like, to have someone want to see you and want to touch you. To claim you at that same time that you claimed them.

It was all so new. And so wonderful.

"So exactly how much did you miss me?"

"I was only with my father at Victory Lodge for a few weeks," I said, trying to keep my voice light. He had no idea how much I had missed him, how I had spent every night staring at the stars outside my window and wishing he were with me. He had been the sole anchor of my thoughts, keeping me from drifting into desperation and worry as I sat by Father's bedside and watched him labor for breath. My anchor as I stared at the pale skin that was healing too fast, as I listened to the doctors and nurses marvel at his impossible recovery. As

23

I wondered if the same genetic engine that drove his healing existed within my own body.

A low sigh escaped at this last thought.

"I'll take that as a confirmation that you went nearly mad with longing." He opened the intricately carved door to the main hallway. It was empty, but I thought I heard voices coming from the library.

"Is your mother here?" I asked.

Something tightened in David's face, something momentary and unreadable. "My mother's decided not to come. She and I have . . . ah . . . disagreed about certain current events." He said it flippantly, but the tension in the hand pressed against my side showed that this was anything but a trifling argument for the two of them. I knew how close David and his mother were.

"It's more to do with my father than the Rootless, isn't it?"

He set his mouth. "She loves him. The Rootless hurt him. I think for her, it's as simple as that. The centuries of history and suffering are completely irrelevant."

This made me sad. In a strange way, I had kind of liked Christine and her sharp sophistication, her keen perception, even though her affair with my father had lacerated our family's delicate semblance of normalcy. Even though her affair with my father had nearly destroyed my mother.

"Jude's here, though," David said, changing the subject. "He'll be happy to see you."

I didn't answer. The last time I had seen Jude, I'd told him that I was choosing David over him, even though it had been Jude whom my parents had wanted me to marry.

"Will you be happy to see him?"

"I . . . yes. Yes, I'll be pleased."

"Madeline." We stopped. We were outside the library now and I could hear the others talking inside, Jack's voice over it all. "He's my best friend. I know things are . . . *unsettled* . . . between the three of us at the moment, but it's important to me that we all get along."

"I like Jude," I said. "I've always liked him. But I worry that he feels a bit betrayed by the two of us."

"He's not like that," David said earnestly. "I promise. It's already forgiven and forgotten."

I doubted it.

"So things will be okay, then? Between us all?"

He seemed so hopeful, so eager, that I didn't want to trouble him with my anxieties. "Yes," I smiled. "Yes, it will be like it was. Before the debut."

He laced his fingers through mine. "Not exactly like before."

My tablet chimed inside my dress pocket, and I pulled it out to see a news alert about the Eastern Empire.

The Empire, a powerful federation of allied states that had invaded America two centuries before, loomed over us all. There had been a fierce skirmish two months ago, a salvo from the Empire-controlled part of the continent that both David and Jude had beaten back. No one pretended that the Eastern hostilities were at an end, but since the battle, things had been restricted to military exercises and diplomatic posturing.

However, I knew—as did David—what most didn't: that the Rootless were secretly allied with the Empire, which was an exceptionally dangerous thought. The angriest people in the world coupled with the most powerful. Their alliance had to be kept at bay, or America risked being torn apart by war.

I put my tablet back, trying to file that worry away for another time. The dinner was enough to fret about for now.

Once we made it to the library, it was clear that some degree of progress had been made. The tour and the drinks and the incessant rounds that Cara and Ewan had made had blurred the lines between the two discrete groups. Even though the Lawrence boys still regarded the entire crowd with scorn, Sai Thorpe and Jane Osbourne had joined Philip Wilder in talking to some of the younger Rootless. Other Rootless trailed near Jack, who made a point to engage the gentry in conversation, making sure to bring his people in at every turn. And happily, Smith was nowhere in sight. Probably off skulking in dark rooms, trying to find more evidence of gentry opulence.

"Impressive," David said. "They're actually talking with one another. I can't believe it."

"It's mostly thanks to Cara and Ewan," I admitted. I knew my strengths and chatting up a room full of people was not one of them.

Jane spotted us and invited us over to where she stood with Philip, Sai, and a few others. I noticed Jude was with them, square-jawed and broad-shouldered in his tuxedo. My heart caught, but in a different way than it did with David. With Jude, it was as if I was seeing someone I hadn't seen for a long time, a childhood friend perhaps. We had a certain connection, one that wasn't romantic, but that was powerful all the same. I wondered if it was because we shared so many of the same traits. I recognized much of myself in Jude . . . which wasn't always a good thing.

As we started to cross the floor, the lights around us shut off without a sound, plunging the entire library into shadowed darkness, lit only by the fire on the far side of the room. I noticed a chill seeping in through the walls and windows almost immediately. There was a silence to the house that I rarely heard.

As murmurs of consternation began to manifest among the guests, I made my way over to Jack, jostling though darkened silhouettes, David trailing behind me. I looked outside the double doors of the library, seeing no other lights, save a candelabra in the hall and a Cherenkov lantern at the end.

"I think the power's gone from the whole house," I said when I reached him. "There's no warm air blowing through the vents, and I don't see anything but lantern light or candlelight when I look down the hallway."

He nodded and pressed his fingertips to his mouth. The

firelight threw the deep lines of his face into shadow. "Interesting," he said.

"What?"

"Normally, if there was some sort of malfunction with one nuclear charge, the backup charge would kick in automatically. Unless somebody did this on purpose and removed both at the same time." He shook his head. "Without the heaters, it will get impossibly cold in here. Perhaps it would be best to ask our guests to leave."

First the blood from nowhere, now this. It was hard not to feel that the universe was karmically against this party somehow.

I sighed. "I'd rather not have our first attempt at bringing them together go down as a disorganized disaster. Let's invite the others to join us in the library—we can use the fireplace to keep warm—and then have the kitchen bring whatever food is already prepared in here. Maybe it will be kind of cozy."

"And I can go get some more candles for light," David offered. But as Jude approached us, also offering to help in whatever way he could, the lights went back on as suddenly as they shut off, revealing confused but relieved guests. The library seemed emptier, as if a few had already slipped out and made their way back to the foyer to rejoin the other guests, but those who remained seemed upbeat enough, and the warm blasts of air that began blowing from the brass grates allayed my fear that everyone would be shivering violently while they tried to eat Martha's award-winning bouillabaisse.

28

"Huh," David said, looking around. "Well, that was an easily solved crisis."

"And an unusual one," Jack said. "I think I'll have Ewan step down into the basement and make sure that nothing is amiss with the charges. While he does that, shall we proceed to dinner as planned, before anything else goes wrong?"

We had made our way back into the foyer when Ewan rejoined us from the basement. From the moment I saw him pushing through the crowd, I knew something was wrong.

"The charges were intentionally removed," Ewan said as he reached Jack. He was smart enough to speak so that only Jack, David, and I could hear him, but I noticed several of the guests trying to eavesdrop. "The first one was replaced correctly—that's why the power's on again—but the backup one wasn't slid all the way back into the station."

"As if someone was in a hurry," I said.

"Or didn't really know what they were doing," Ewan added. "But they knew enough to wear gloves. I found a pair abandoned by the basement door."

"But why?" David cut in. "It seems like a lot of trouble for ten minutes of mild confusion."

Jack examined his cane for a moment. "I think we'd do our best to forget about it," he said. I started to interrupt but he held up his hand. "What matters is that everything is working properly again and that we can proceed as planned. It was probably meant as a prank by one of our young people, and nothing foils a prank more than ignoring it."

"I just don't like the idea of someone intentionally interfering with the charges," I said.

"I don't either. But what else can we do?"

Jack was right. Taking a deep breath, I smoothed my gown and walked to the front of the foyer. The conversation quieted and heat crawled up my cheeks as all eyes turned to me. "Everyone, if you'll join me in the ballroom, we are ready for dinner."

I placed my hands on the gleaming handles of the ballroom doors, ready for the music and food and drinks to wipe away the earlier parts of the night. At least the power outage had given the guests something shared to talk about, and that was always a good thing. I turned the handles and opened the doors, expecting to see my ballroom brilliant and gleaming and ready.

A sharp intake of air came behind me, and I knew without looking that it was from Cara. I got as far as taking a step into the room before I realized why she had gasped.

Marianne Wilder lay stone dead in the middle of the floor.

FOUR

Her arms were spread wide and her body was twisted, as if somebody had dropped her from their arms without caring how she landed. Her dark brown eyes were open but slightly cloudy, her long braids spread around her head like an inky halo. Her skin was ashy and strange, and her face was sunken somehow. She wore a day dress of saffron-dyed wool, mottled with dried bloodstains. And all around her were smears of red—blood, it looked like—but the sharp scent of new paint was unmistakable.

"Is she . . . ?" Cara asked, but her voice revealed what she already knew.

Something in my stomach twisted and my eyes burned, and I forced myself to breathe, to try to speak, but my throat hurt too badly to utter a sound.

And then a thick keening came from behind us, the sound of a man whose heart had been torn out and devoured. Clarence Wilder shoved his way past me and then fell to his knees next to his dead daughter, Philip close behind him. They both started crying in deep unbelieving sobs, Mr. Wilder grabbing at the limp fabric of Marianne's dress.

At the sound of her father's wailing, my own tears came, pricking and spilling, laced through with the bitter pangs of shock. Marianne. Philip's sister. A girl who had never been mean to anyone, a girl whose sweet prettiness had made her such a sought after prize despite the Wilders' modest fortune. Who would do this? And *why?*

And the blood from this afternoon . . . it had to have been hers. But then how long had she been dead? Where had her body been all that time?

Jack made his way beside me, and I felt a prickle of fear when I saw his face, completely shocked and completely horrified. I had only seen that expression on his face once before, and it had been as he'd stared up at his youngest son shivering underneath the gibbet cage. I wanted Jack to be certain and decisive and to know what to do. But he was as appalled and confused as the rest of us.

"God help us," he said, his breathing ragged.

We needed to do something. Take charge, take control. What would Father do if he were here?

"We need to call the police." My voice sounded strange. Distant. How could I still be looking at this and be able to talk, be able to think with Marianne sprawled on the floor, except she wasn't Marianne any longer, she was something else, something other. My stomach knotted violently, and I put the back of my hand to my mouth and turned around.

David and Jude were right there. Jude put his arms up to my

bare shoulders to steady me and then dropped them quickly. "What do you need me to do?" he asked instead.

"Get the police," I said, feeling as if I might be sick with every exhalation. Now that I had noticed it, the smell of fresh paint had become overwhelming. It was all I could smell and think about, and every breath stank of it, stank of this horrible moment and of finding Marianne's body cold on the floor.

Jude bowed quickly and left the crowd, taking his tablet out of his pocket as he did so.

"The Wilders," I said numbly to David. "Someone should . . ." He was off before I finished, making his way over to the grieving men in quick and graceful strides. He knelt beside them both, putting his arms around them and murmuring low words, rocking back and forth with them, and never had I felt so in love with this charming boy I still barely knew, this boy of sharp edges and hidden compassion.

Meanwhile, Jack had turned, too, his face once again composed. "Ladies and gentleman, I'm afraid that I must ask you to enter the library once again. I'm certain the police will want to question all of us in order to bring a close to this unspeakable crime—"

"Was this your plan all along?" Harry Westoff demanded. "Lure us here and then slaughter us?"

"Are you going to kill *all* of our daughters?" Mr. Glaize added. "Or maybe you'd like our sons, too?"

"Now wait," Jack said, raising his hands. "This is a tragedy, but surely you see—"

"Here's what I see," Uncle Lawrence said. "I see the leader of the Rootless gathering us here with our enemies, playing games in the dark, and then murdering one of our own, leaving her broken body for us all to find."

And just like that, everything the night had accomplished, the scant but hopeful beginnings of a new life, crumbled to the ground. The gentry guests fused together into one outraged clump, their voices growing more and more enraged, turning their backs to the rest of the room. I could hear shouts—about the police, about the military, about control. The Rootless kept silent, faces stony and defensive, anger flashing in their eyes.

I went to David and the Wilders, and I knelt with them, ignoring the train of my dress as it dragged in the paint. I wrapped my arms around Philip as he cried—he cried so bravely, in a way that guys my age rarely did, openly and without shame. He grabbed at my wrists, and I rocked with him, meeting eyes with David as I did.

He mouthed something at me, something I didn't quite catch, and then he pointed his gaze meaningfully at the paint, and I followed his look with my own, and I saw it. The misshapen circle around Marianne wasn't a circle at all, but a clumsily drawn atomic symbol, complete with smaller circles to represent the electron cloud around the nucleus. It was eerily representative of the Landry family crest, except for one thing: a giant red slash through the middle. It was so much like the warning scrawled onto the front of the house last year. *We are rising.*

A message for us, for the Landrys. For the gentry.

I shivered.

I heard voices and then a swarm of navy-coated constables came in, eyeing the Rootless with dislike, but keeping their distance for now. Instead they came into the ballroom. I helped Philip to stand, but David couldn't persuade Mr. Wilder to leave Marianne, and in the end, it took three constables to lift him to his feet and move him away from his daughter's corpse. Someone brought a chair and he sat, shell-shocked and ashen, and Philip moved next to him, tears still flowing freely from his eyes.

"The security cameras," I said to David and Jack as the constables took over the scene with their pictures and measurements and forensic samples.

"Yes, of course, the constables will look at those, too," Jack said distantly.

"I want to look at them now," I insisted. "I was in the ballroom half an hour ago and it was empty. No sign of anyone. But then the power went out."

"They used the power outage to hide from the cameras

while they were moving the body," David said. "If we can see who went down into the basement to cut the power . . ."

"It won't be that easy," Jack said. "This is the work of someone who put a lot of thought into this."

And he was right. In my father's study, we leaned over the control panel for the security cameras, scanning the footage. And when we finally found it, it was unbearably disappointing. A figure in a black mask that covered everything but his or her eyes ducked into view and quickly ducked back out. The person wore a heavy black coat, which made it hard to tell if the figure was male or female.

A constable appeared in the doorway. "If you don't mind," he said. "We'll need to ask some questions now."

"So it begins," Ewan said under his breath.

"What?" I asked.

"They'll question everyone and they'll come to the inevitable conclusion that the Rootless did it, even though they won't have proof. It always happens this way."

It was true that the constables didn't have the strongest record when it came to impartial justice. Last year, they had raided the Rootless ghetto countless times, trying to find the person who attacked Cara and vandalized our house, even though Cara's attacker turned out to be gentry . . . and her own mother, at that.

One by one, we were brought into the drawing room, where a kitchen maid had thoughtfully brought up coffee, tea, and some of the elaborate cocktails that had been meant for the dinner party. The food had been moved into the library and the guests were encouraged to eat, but it seemed, understandably, that food was on no one's mind. Not while a body was being examined only a few rooms away.

When it was my turn to be questioned, I poured myself a cup of hot black coffee and sat in the blue damask chair opposite the constable, a youngish man with premature silver salted in his dark hair.

He introduced himself as Inspector Hernandez and, stylus poised, he asked me a few routine questions—name, age, how long I'd lived in the house—*Madeline Landry, seventeen, all my life.*

While he talked, I found myself glancing at my lap—pools of green chiffon, my hands folded in the middle. If I looked at him, if he gave me one more compassionate glance, I knew I would cry again. So as he quietly went through his list of questions, I kept my eyes down, noticing the smallest of details. Like that my skirt now had smears of red paint streaking up the sides.

The inspector's voice brought me back. "You saw the blood on the patio, correct? What time was that?"

"About four thirty in the afternoon," I replied. "I heard the gardeners talking about it and I went outside to see what was wrong."

"And you noticed nothing unusual up to that point?"

I shook my head.

He sighed. "The security camera above the patio was smashed with a rock—the feed stopped early this morning, so I'm assuming that's when it happened. I'd hoped maybe you'd heard . . ."

Again, I shook my head.

"At any rate, it's good thinking that you called the police to document it."

"Yes," I agreed, although I was remembering how reluctant Jack had been to call the police. He'd said he didn't want to upset his people, but had that been all? Had he had suspicions even then that something like this might happen?

"Walk me through your night," the inspector said.

I started with the blood, and then worked my way through getting dressed, greeting the guests and checking on the ballroom, trying to be as precise as possible when it came to times.

"And there was nobody else in the ballroom, you are quite certain of that? Not hiding in a corner or under a table?"

"I was alone, I'm sure of it."

"So you leave and then what?"

I remembered David's lips hot and urgent on mine. I flushed. "Captain Dana found me in the hallway. We decided to rejoin the others."

Inspector Hernandez raised an eyebrow. "Did you rejoin them right away? Or did you linger for a moment or two?"

I'm sure that I flushed even deeper. "We, ah, spoke for a few minutes in the hallway."

He wrote something down. "I don't want to embarrass you," he said kindly. "I'm just trying to establish where everybody was tonight."

I cleared my throat. "We weren't alone together very long. It was only moments after we got to the library that the lights went dark."

"And was everybody in the library when you got there?"

"Well, I didn't have enough time to really see before the lights went out, but yes, I think everybody was there." But even as I said it, I remembered that it wasn't quite true. Smith. I hadn't seen Smith in the library and I remembered feeling relieved, hoping he'd left and gone home and taken his toxic hostility with him. . . .

"What is it?" the inspector asked, peering into my face. "Is there something you've remembered?"

"A man," I said slowly. "Smith is his name. He's a Rootless, a friend of my uncle Jack's. He was here early on in the evening and very unhappy. He doesn't believe the gentry and the Rootless should mingle. He thinks the gentry are basically too corrupt to expect any sort of peace between our peoples."

Inspector Hernandez raised his eyebrow. "And he was missing before the power went out?"

"I think so. I'm pretty sure."

"Interesting." Another note on his tablet. "Your uncle didn't mention that he wasn't in the room. In fact, he specifically listed him among those present in the library during the outage."

"Did you see him?"

The inspector was already shaking his head as he swiped his finger across the screen to slip back through his notes. "Nobody here by that name. Granted, it was difficult getting names out of any of the Rootless, and he could have easily left after the body was discovered. I am aware that not every Rootless is a fan of the police." His tone wasn't disdainful. It was almost sympathetic, which made me like him a little bit. It was a rare constable who felt compassion for the Rootless. Maybe the investigation would be more impartial than Ewan thought.

"But my uncle said that he was definitely here during the power failure?"

The inspector glanced down at his screen again. "That's right."

The beginning of a frown tugged on my mouth, but I fought to keep my face placid. I moved on. "The blood in the snow . . . how soon until you can tell if it's Marianne's?"

Inspector Hernandez slid his stylus into his breast pocket. "A day, maybe two. In the meantime, please don't hesitate to contact me personally if you remember anything else, anything at all. I'm here to make sure that whoever did this to Miss Wilder is brought to justice."

I stood to leave.

He opened his mouth as if to speak, then hesitated. "I am not sure if I should mention this, but is there anybody you can think of that might have a grudge against you or your uncle? The crest with the slash through it, dumping her body in your ballroom on the night of a party—it's very personal."

"If you want to document all the people who are angry with the Landrys," I said, suddenly feeling incredibly tired, "you'll be working for a very long time."

He inclined his head, a gesture of both agreement and sympathy.

We shook hands and I left, taking my untouched coffee with me.

FIVE

Midnight. The stars glinted in the night sky above us, accompanied by a thin sliver of a moon. Cara, Ewan, David, Jude, and I had gone up to the observatory while the constables removed Marianne's body and the maids set to work scrubbing the floor free of paint. Nobody could fathom going to sleep or going home, but nobody wanted to be near the ghastly scene, either.

The men had somehow found tumblers of Scotch, and Cara and I each held a steaming cup of hot tea and brandy, although I hadn't taken a sip of mine. I wandered from window to window, watching the constables load their equipment back into their cars. A long black vehicle was at the front door, its back doors open and waiting. I looked away. I didn't want to see Marianne's body again, even though it hardly mattered; it would forever be burned into the back of my eyelids, her blank eyes and tangled braids and paint-splattered limbs.

The silence was almost unbearable, but the thought of talking was equally so. Not for Cara apparently, because she murmured, "I feel like we're already at a funeral."

"Have a little respect," I snapped, an unexpected anger

surging in my chest. "A girl died today. Our *friend* died today."

"Madeline," Jude said, touching my arm. "I'm sure she didn't mean anything by it."

David—who still hadn't said anything—paced, drinking his Scotch in long, practiced gulps. He set the empty glass down on a table near the telescope. "There's not going to be any real justice. I can already feel it. The constables are going to blame the Rootless like they always do, and the gentry will clamor for Rootless blood all while the real killer walks free. . . ."

"How do you know that the killer isn't Rootless?"

They all stared at me.

Ewan lowered his glass. "What are you trying to say?"

"I'm not—I'm not trying to say anything necessarily. I just don't think we can rule anyone out at this point."

"My people had nothing to do with this," Ewan said. A warm color was creeping up his neck. "This was the work of a lone maniac. *Not* of the Rootless."

"You have to admit it looks suspicious," I said. "The charges—something only the Rootless really know about— were removed to cut the power, and then a dead gentry girl is found on our ballroom floor. And the symbol, the atom with the slash through it—doesn't it all seem like someone who is angry with the gentry? With my family?" Looking into Ewan's gray eyes, I corrected myself. "With our family?"

"Exactly," he said. "Someone who is angry with our family. You *or* me, your father *or* my father. That means that it could be anyone from anywhere, gentry or Rootless or someone from the middle class or even someone from the Empire."

"This feels like something personal," Jude spoke up. "The fact that she was dead before she was put in the ballroom, the paint— this is someone who wants to send a particular message."

Like Smith. I took a drink of the tea and brandy, wincing at the taste.

"But what I'm saying is that anybody could want to send a message," Ewan said. "What about that boyfriend of hers? He wasn't at the party tonight."

"Philip said that Mark was sick," I said.

"Well, that's an airtight alibi," Ewan replied, sarcasm heavy in his words.

"I hardly think Philip would lie about that—Marianne is his sister."

"He wouldn't have to know it was a lie," David pointed out. "Really, who's to say that it wasn't Mark?"

"I can't believe you're even entertaining that idea," I said. "Marianne and Mark love each other."

Jude looked thoughtful. "The majority of homicides are committed by someone known to the victim."

"Maybe they fought and in the heat of the moment, he killed her," Ewan said.

"And then brought her body to my house and painted my family crest around her?" I didn't know if it was the trembling in my voice or the logic of my argument that gave them pause.

Cara, meanwhile, had arranged herself on the spinning stool in front of the telescope and was idly turning knobs and dials. "Everyone liked Marianne," she said. "Even people who barely knew her. This person would have to have a really strong message if they were going to kill her. And they'd have to be a really mean, angry person. She was probably nice to them even while—" and here Cara broke off, refocusing her attention on the brass knobs of the antique telescope.

"I'm not trying to accuse the Rootless," I said. "I don't think they as a group would do anything like this. But an extreme individual within that group—"

Ewan threw his hands up in the air. "Like who? Like me? Like my little brother?"

"Like Smith."

There was silence as everyone digested this.

"Think about it. He was angry beforehand. He disappeared shortly before the lights went out. He was completely gone afterward. He could have done it."

"My father saw him in the library when it happened," Ewan said, his tone indicating that Jack's testimony sealed the matter for him.

"Did *you* see him in the library?" I asked softly.

"Are you saying that my father is lying?" Ewan's voice was dangerous.

Was I saying that? That the man that I had believed to be the most moral man in Kansas City was complicit in a murder? I didn't want it to be true, either, but something didn't add up. Jack's intensity this past month, his cagey behavior regarding the bloodstain on the patio . . .

My fingers tightened around the cup, but I refused to break my gaze with Ewan.

"Whoever did this hates the gentry. And they clearly want to stop any attempt at reconciliation between the two groups. Doesn't that sound like Smith to you? He has the motive, he had the opportunity."

David's pacing slowed. "Are you sure you're not targeting him because you don't like him? That you're not targeting him because he's a Rootless?"

I felt the implication of his words like a physical blow. "I would never accuse somebody merely because they were Rootless. I'm only trying to fit the puzzle pieces together as best as I can."

"Convenient that those puzzle pieces don't include Marianne's gentry boyfriend," Ewan muttered.

"I'm telling you, he wouldn't have done it. Not something that . . . gruesome."

"I seem to remember a similar thing happening last year," David said, "when your father and all of the gentry in this city were eager to believe the Rootless had attacked Cara, despite having no evidence. And the first time I met you, you told me that you were tired of people accusing the Rootless simply because they were there and an easy scapegoat. You were so

46

fired up, so ready to discover what really happened. What's changed?"

There was something in his face that I'd never seen before, not when he'd been looking at me.

Disappointment.

My chest hurt, but I couldn't unsay what I'd said. And I wouldn't. "Nothing's changed," I said softly. "Now, like then, I want to find out the truth. And I don't care how unpopular it is. I liked Marianne. She didn't deserve to die." I felt tears prickling at the back of my eyelids again and I took a deep breath, trying to steady myself. "And what happened tonight will derail all the negotiations and goodwill we've worked so hard to cultivate. Whoever did this has to be found and punished or things between the two groups will never heal."

Cara rolled her eyes. "She's getting into Crusade Mode again."

I set the cup down on a nearby table. The noise echoed off the glass walls and ceiling. "I'm not getting into any mode."

David crossed his arms. All the closeness we'd felt earlier, all the connection, it had vanished, bled away, and the separation between us felt like a gaping wound. But I knew I was right. I *knew* it. All the pieces fit, and I refused to lie about what I knew to be true. I crossed my arms, too, matching his stance, and said, "If Smith's innocent, then the constables will clear him. But until then, I am not revising what I said."

"Oh, yes, the constables," Ewan said. "The perfect paragons of justice."

I shot him a sharp look. "No one is saying the police are perfect—"

"They are paid by the gentry," Ewan interrupted. "Of course they aren't perfect. And I think once you've seen them beating your friends and tearing down your home, you would understand how 'not perfect' they are."

David angled himself toward Jude. "What do you think?"

"I think this is a very painful situation," Jude said carefully.

David sighed. "What do you really think?"

Jude put his hands behind his back. "I think Madeline is correct. This Smith man has the weight of evidence stacked against him."

"Circumstantial evidence," Ewan interrupted. "He was in the library—my father saw him."

"And that's enough for you?" Jude looked at Ewan, then at David. "One man's word."

David blinked. "He's Jack. He wouldn't lie about something like this. He has always told the truth."

"Except when he hid his identity for thirty years," I said.

Silence fell at that. David and I stared at each other for a long moment and in that moment, I saw how wide the breach was between our beliefs, between our theories and between our willingness to trust the man who had helped bring us together.

But I saw something else—tenderness, maybe. Respect. I let out a breath.

"It's been a long night," Jude said. "Maybe it would be best to retire."

Jude, sensible as always.

We dispersed, Cara and Ewan to their room, Jude and David downstairs to drive back to the Danas' penthouse, and me to my bedroom, but not before David caught me in a tight embrace in the hallway. I buried my face in his chest, finally allowing the horror of the night to catch up with me.

Though I knew the house was far from asleep, it was muffled and quiet in my corridor, save for the faint hum of the heater and the solid, steady beat of David's heart underneath his shirt.

He stroked my hair. "I know saying sorry isn't enough," he whispered. "But I'm sorry about Marianne."

I breathed into his tuxedo jacket, feeling my eyelashes brush against the silk lapel, closing my eyes against the fresh wave of tears.

"And I'm sorry we fought."

"Me too," I murmured.

"In fact, I'm more than sorry. I *hate* that we fought." He pulled back just enough to meet my eyes, lifting a finger under my chin when I tried to duck my gaze. "Let's never do that again, okay?"

I couldn't help the small laugh that bubbled out. David and I had spent a lot of time arguing before we became a couple. "If you don't want to fight, you are with the wrong girl," I said.

But his eyes were on my smile, and the corner of his mouth was hooking into a smile of its own. "No," he said, bending down. "I'm with exactly the right girl."

His mouth was warm and yielding, his kiss soft and chaste, but lingering. He smelled like spice and Scotch and expensive clothes, and I wanted to freeze him in time so that we were kissing in this hallway for the rest of eternity—no murder, no painted symbols, just us and our mouths growing hungrier and our hands growing more urgent.

He broke our kiss, moving his lips against my forehead and freeing me from the prison of his strong, tuxedo-clad arms. "You should get some sleep," he said.

He was right. But I didn't want sleep. I wanted him to drive away everything but us, everything but him.

"Stay," I asked. "Please."

His gaze slid past my face and to the door behind me, the door to my bedroom. His eyes darkened.

But he shook his head. "Not tonight. You need to rest." He brushed my cheeks with his fingertips and gave me a final kiss good-bye. And as soon as he left, the tears returned, and I didn't bother wiping them away.

"The funeral will be tomorrow," Jack said at the breakfast table. "The Wilders don't want to drag it out any longer than they have to."

The tears of yesterday had left me, and now I felt a peculiar emptiness, like a gray veil hung between me and the rest of the world. Mustering speech seemed a herculean task, and I had to concentrate for a moment to process Jack's words.

"Will you go?" I finally asked.

"I don't know how welcome I will be. Already, the tendrils of gentry outrage are reaching the news. They think I planned this all along, as a way to punish and humiliate them. They'll be calling for my head soon."

"I'm going," I said. "I can represent Landry Park."

"Yes. You still have some level of regard from both the Rootless and the gentry. Alas for the hope that those two worlds could ever be one." He gazed out of the window at the flurries dancing in the wind outside. I, in turn, gazed at him, trying to read the craggy lines of his face. Was he really sorry about last night? Or had it all played into a larger plan for him?

"This will sow new seeds of discord and mistrust, and it will prevent progress from ever being made," he continued. "The gentry believe the Rootless to be murderers, and the Rootless see the accusation as proof that the gentry are still oppressing them. Both groups are completely ready to believe the worst about each other. Not to mention that the Rootless seem willing to believe the worst about me. At least, some of them are. And that's enough to divide us, to weaken us."

He sighed after a moment. "And maybe they're right to doubt me. I've been here at Landry Park for a month, I've removed my brother from his place of authority, and still I've achieved nothing of concrete value."

Charlie's footsteps echoed in and out of the morning room; he must have escaped the new tutor Jack had hired to steer his studies. He had created an obstacle course out of embroidered cushions and stools and was currently timing himself to see how quickly he could get through it. He came in periodically to swipe triangles of thin buttered toast from the otherwise untouched food. Neither Jack nor I was hungry.

Inspector Hernandez had stopped by very early this morning to walk around the scene and to ask once again if there was anything else we remembered. There wasn't. But he did tell us that Marianne's beau, Mark Everly, had been completely cleared—several servants' statements and his estate's security showed that he'd fallen asleep in the afternoon and stayed in bed the entire night. The inspector also revealed that the police had discovered Marianne's tablet by the road in front of the estate and a bucket of frozen blood near the carriage house, blood they believed to be Marianne's.

It made me sick. "Why would anyone collect her blood like that?" I'd asked, horrified.

And then it had dawned on me. "The symbol."

"I think they meant to use her blood to paint the symbol. Perhaps in a fit of poetic reasoning, they thought it would be the most powerful way to send their message. But blood coagulates and thickens within a matter of moments, making it impossible to do anything of the sort if they weren't going to do it right away. They must have abandoned the blood and then forgotten about it."

I thought about this as I absentmindedly stirred my tea, the spoon clinking against the china. So they had left the blood and decided to use paint—where did they get the paint? Was it a spur-of-the-moment decision once they saw the frozen blood, or did they realize much earlier in the day that they needed to find another way?

I finally pushed away from the table. "I'm not feeling well," I announced. "I'm going up to my room."

Jack nodded, but his eyes were still far away. I got to the door and stopped, watching Charlie hop from cushion to cushion. "Uncle Jack?" I asked.

"Mm?"

"You would tell me if you knew who it was, right? The murderer?"

Jack turned to me and frowned. "What do you mean?"

"I mean, if the murderer were one of your people, you wouldn't try to hide him?"

"I'm not sure I like what you're implying, about me or my people," Jack said slowly.

I needed to become better at framing my thoughts. "Marianne was a good person. A kind person. So promise me that you're not protecting Smith. Please."

Something passed across his face—hesitation or reluctance

or maybe it was surprise. "I know you don't like Smith," he said finally. "Many people don't. He may be brash and young and angry, but he's *not* a killer."

"Okay," I said.

But all I could picture was Jack's face in the space between my question and his answer, where to me the truth had become plain. He was hiding something.

SIX

When I opened the door to my room, I saw David lounging on my bed, swiping idly through his tablet, his shoes dripping wet snow on my hand-embroidered bedspread. A scarf and coat were strewn over a nearby chair.

I managed to keep myself from noticing the long lines of his legs and the way his shirt stretched taut around his arms and chest. Well, I noticed. But I steered my thoughts in a less distracting direction.

"This is unexpected."

He tossed his tablet aside and stared up at me, his only reply a wide smile—a smile that was as confident as it was gentle. He'd come to see how I was doing, how I was faring after the brutality of last night.

I sat down on the edge of the bed. His eyes were so wide and so luminously blue, and his hair was tousled, and his shirt was unbuttoned at the very top, revealing the sharp curve of his collarbone.

I stood up again, swallowing. He'd been in my bedroom once before, at Victory Lodge, and he'd even carried me while I was in my nightgown, but something about being alone with him, both of us on the bed—it felt very intimate. Not that I didn't want *intimate*; I did, but I couldn't quite bring myself to sit back down, as if I were afraid that someone would open the door at any moment and catch us together.

And the memory of Marianne clouded everything.

His lips pressed together at my retreat, but he didn't try to coax me back on the bed. He sat up instead. "Is it always so easy to get inside your house?"

"What do you mean?"

"I mean, I was able to sneak in the back door without anyone seeing. It was unlocked and then no one challenged me when I strolled right in."

I studied him. He'd gone from insouciant to agitated in a matter of seconds. "They use that door for kitchen deliveries, which sometimes come very early in the morning. It's easier to keep it unlocked. Why?"

"I want you to make them lock it. And I want you to make sure this house is completely secured—windows and doors."

"David—"

He held up a hand. "I know. This is your house. You can take care of yourself and so forth. But if someone is killing gentry girls, I have to know that you'll be okay. I have to know that a murderer can't just waltz in and strangle you with piano wire."

I pulled him up and wrapped my arms around him. "I'll make sure. I promise."

He bent his face to mine, so that our noses touched. "Please be careful. I don't know what I'd do if something happened to you."

"You'd survive," I teased.

"I don't think so," he said, and then his mouth brushed against my mouth. But the kiss was brief; he moved away with a glance at the silver watch on his wrist. "I have to go meet my mother for brunch. But I'll come back later."

"Please do," I said, still feeling the ghost of his lips on mine.

The corners of his mouth turned up, and then he grabbed his coat and scarf and left. I sat on my bed, thinking for a minute. Then I went for my coat, too.

"Madeline! What an unexpected surprise." Jude's voice echoed through the sleek lobby of the Danas' penthouse.

"Can I come up?" I asked, skipping the pleasantries.

"David's not here—he went out with his mother."

"I know. I—I actually wanted to talk to you."

There was a pause. I traced the raised metal plate that spelled out David's last name as I waited. "Of course," Jude said, hesitation and happiness mixing together in his words. "Please come up."

Chiming, the elevator doors slid open and I went inside. The doors closed, and with a *whoosh*, it flew up thirty-eight stories, opening up into an airy room walled by floor-to-ceiling windows.

Jude greeted me immediately, bowing and kissing the back of my hand. I normally saw him in a tuxedo or in his military uniform, so it was a shock to see him in something as casual as slacks and a sweater. The soft cashmere clung to his shoulders and arms, highlighting the figure that had so many gentry girls swooning. When he raised his eyes to mine, I could see the winter sunlight refracted in his silver eyes.

I realized I hadn't spoken yet, and Jude let go of my hand, seeming uncomfortable. "Jude, I—"

He took a breath. "I want to say something before we talk about anything else. I want you to know that I don't begrudge you your choice. I can see how clearly you and David love each other. And he is my best friend—I want him to be happy. I want you to be happy, too."

"Thank you," I said, meaning it.

"I stand by what I said," he told me. "I would have made a good husband and a good partner."

"We're friends now," I said, trying to reassure him. "As long as I live, you'll have me and the Landry name to rely on."

Something in his face relaxed, and I wondered if that had been the true source of his worry—not our friendship, but if this botched experience had somehow limited his own ambitions. Jude saw himself leading America against the Empire and winning back the land lost centuries ago, and he saw Landry Park and its influence as central to achieving that goal.

"Of course, I don't know how much the Landry name is worth these days," I added, wanting to modulate his expectations. "Even the people who stand behind Jack would be happy to see the gentry estates and the Uprisen disappear altogether. Who knows what will happen?"

"No matter what happens, you will make sure that Landry Park survives, all while you choose to do the right thing." Jude's voice was firm and reassuring.

I hope so.

"I want to go to the Rootless ghetto," I said, switching abruptly to the reason for my visit. "I feel more certain than ever that Smith is behind this somehow, and I want to talk to him."

I expected Jude to ask why I was coming to him about this, or to insist that I should leave this kind of thing to the police, especially after I had been so vocal about trusting them last night, but instead, he put his hands behind his back and rocked back on his heels, like he did when he was thinking seriously about something.

"Do you think he'll be there?" he asked after a minute. "If he left the house last night, he may not have gone back home. Especially if he's guilty."

"Maybe there will be someone there who knows where he is," I said.

"It's worth looking into," he conceded. "I'll get my coat."

I put my hand on his arm, and he turned. "Thank you," I

said. "For coming with me and—" I didn't finish the thought, worried it would sound selfish or petty.

"And for agreeing with you?" he offered with a kind smile.

I nodded.

"I can be very loyal, even when it's unreasonable, which is why I make such a good soldier," he said with a smile. "But in this case, I'm agreeing with you because I think you're right."

I lifted my hand and he went to get his coat. While I waited, I wandered through the room, winding my way around low sofas and a large black piano. The penthouse was floored in wood so pale that it was almost white, and save for a hallway next to the elevator that presumably led to the bedrooms, the rest of the home was uninterrupted by walls or partitions. The vast expanse of windows revealed the rest of the glittering skyline, punctuated with bridges and slivers of blue sky, the river bluffs tall and sweeping in the background. The whole penthouse was sleek and expensive—just like the Danas themselves.

Jude reappeared in a peacoat and a large gray scarf cowled around his neck. He offered me his arm and I took it, feeling so at home with him by my side that I didn't let go the entire way down to the car.

The Rootless ghetto was on the eastern edge of town, a vast expanse of parkland that had been converted into a village of ramshackle buildings and underground sorting yards. My driver, a taciturn man called Reeve, pulled the car between the pillars of old stone and rusted iron that had once been a gate and then turned it off. There was an unspoken agreement between us not to drive the car into the ghetto; I didn't want to unnerve the Rootless by rolling through their village in the sleek vehicle, as if I were trying to parade my wealth. I also had the sense that the driver was—however unfairly—worried for the car's safety within the confines of the ghetto itself.

I paused a moment before alighting from the car. I didn't think that Jack would be thrilled by my errand, but this morning's interaction at the breakfast table had convinced me that he was hiding something. I had no doubt that the Rootless would tell Jack about my visit after the fact, and that he wouldn't be pleased.

It has to be done, I told myself. If Smith had really hurt Marianne—if he had really crouched next to her and drained the blood out of her body as the light faded from her eyes— then he had to be punished. He didn't get to live free while Marianne didn't get to live at all.

"Please wait for us," I told the driver. "We won't be long."

We started walking into the ghetto itself, tromping through the snow. I'd known that we'd be walking in the elements, and so I'd worn a warm dress with thick woolen tights underneath. Even so, the cold managed to seep into my feet and legs. I wrapped my short, holly-colored cape tighter around myself and bent my head into the wind, fighting against the sudden edginess that scraped at my nerves. Now that we were here, walking into the heart of the ghetto, I had a brief flicker of doubt. If Smith was really capable of murder, was it wise to confront him?

I reminded myself that I had Jude, and I had to hope that was deterrent enough for a man like Smith. Marianne's death had been cowardly, attacking a young woman while she was alone. I doubted he'd try anything violent in his own neighborhood, and certainly not with Jude around.

The small hamlet of corrugated metal and ripped plastic sheeting rose up around us, the harsh edges softened by the snow. Everywhere there were signs of improvement—piles of lumber and roofing materials, pallets of clean drinking water and rice. I knew Jack had been doing everything he could to alleviate as much suffering as possible until he came to a more permanent arrangement with the gentry, but actually seeing the results of the efforts was heartwarming. Even in the snow, people were building and repairing, mounting solar panels, and it looked like most of the shacks now had heat and light. Snatches of conversations and laughter floated on the wind. Something was kindling here. Hope.

The first time I had come here, I'd been with Cara, following David. People had stared, had sneered, and the reception I received from the men David had met with had been less than warm. But now, after Liberty Park, there were some who acknowledged me kindly, going so far as to wave and offer smiles, although there were more than a few who eyed me with a coldness that bordered on hatred. I smiled at them all, feeling uneasy as I did. I wanted them to like me and I wanted to help them, of course, but what would they think when they learned I thought one of their own was a killer?

"Let's try the tavern first," I said. I really didn't know any other place to start—I didn't know where Smith lived or if he was married or actually anything about him other than what he believed about the gentry.

By the time we reached the tavern, snow had gathered in my hair and on my eyelashes and Jude's cheeks were ruddy from the cold. With a trepidation that I refused to show, I pushed open the door and stepped inside the warm darkness of the Rootless watering hole.

There were only a few men inside, sitting at the battered tables, clutching cracked steins of beer. They didn't even bother looking at Jude and me when we came in, and I ignored them, too, instead making my way toward the bartender.

"Hello," I said as pleasantly as possible. "We're looking for someone."

The bartender looked at me—even covered in snow and with a dripping nose, my appearance was indisputably gentry—and then Jude, even more indisputably so. "Who for?" he asked.

"I only know his surname. Smith?"

There was a *thunk* as somebody set his mug on the table. I followed the bartender's gaze and turned to see a short man, covered in sores, broad-shouldered but rail-thin. Most Rootless men didn't live much longer than thirty-five or forty, and I could see from the lines of pain around his mouth and eyes that he was nearing the end of his life. My throat tightened. Pain radiated from this man like heat.

"I know where he is," the man said. His voice rasped over the words. "I'll take you to him."

He started walking, waving a hand for us to follow, and with a glance at each other, Jude and I did.

We wended our way through back alleys and narrow streets lined with shanties, and now as we walked, I thought about how little the extra lumber and roofing actually did. These people were sick. Dying. Somehow, while I was away, I'd conveniently managed to store that truth away. It was easy to remember that there was poverty and starvation only miles from Landry Park. But it was even easier to drain the color and experience from that knowledge, to unconsciously distance myself from it and the people it affected. It would take much more than a slightly improved shelter to mitigate the kind of hell these people had lived through.

I let guilt stitch small sutures in my suddenly tight throat, in my now rapidly blinking eyes. I held on to the guilt, letting it underpin my vow to do better in the future.

The man shuffled through the snow, each step costing

him visible effort, but the steps continued mechanically one after another, as if he'd been struggling through life so long that he'd forgotten how to stop. *This*, I reminded myself, *this is why the gentry and the Rootless have to figure things out.*

The man turned another corner and led us to a structure made partly of stone and partly of rusted sheets of metal. A new solar panel glinted on the roof and it had what appeared to be a brand-new door, but it did nothing to improve the feeling of cheerlessness about the place. Most of the other homes in the park were close together, their exteriors kept as tidy as possible, the noises of children and families crowding into the streets. But this house—this shack—was far away from any other building, surrounded by unidentifiable piles of scrap, all of it covered with snow.

The man who led us knocked once on the door and then pushed it open, beckoning us to come inside. We went, and it took a minute to adjust to the dim light. A small, new-looking heater sat in the corner, pulsing warmth into the room, but I could feel that heat being just as quickly sapped away by the cold dirt floor.

Smith sat in a chair by the heater, talking with two other men. He turned, his face folding into a frown upon seeing our guide. It wasn't a frown of anger, like I was used to seeing from him, but a frown of concern. There was something soft in his face, something kind.

"Russell, you shouldn't be out in this weather," he chided. "It's too cold."

Russell shrugged. "People from the other side of town looking for you. Thought I'd help."

Smith's eyes slid past Russell to where Jude and I stood.

"And what the hell are you two doing here?"

SEVEN

Jude stepped forward, offering a hand. "Captain Jude Mac-Avery. We're here to ask you about last night."

Smith spat on the floor. "I don't have to talk to you about anything."

"It's nothing formal," I said. "We're just trying to make sense of it all."

While we exchanged words, Russell made his way over to a chair, where he sat with an expression of relief. And seeing him and Smith in the same place, I realized how they knew each other. The same indeterminate hair color, the same water-green eyes, the same short frame that could have been called stocky had they not been so malnourished.

"You're brothers," I said.

Smith's eyes flashed at me. "That's none of your business."

"Peace, Robert," Russell said.

I was suddenly very aware that I hadn't even known Smith's first name, and I felt another small flush of guilt.

"I'm sorry," Russell said. "My brother can be very protective of me sometimes." He covered his mouth with his elbow and coughed, and even though I knew it was coming, I still winced when he pulled his arm away and flecks of blood were spattered on his sleeve. "Which is not the way it's supposed to be, you know. Older brothers are supposed to protect the younger ones."

"Well, you're the one who's about to die, so I guess it's up to me," Smith said. The despondency took the bite out of his voice. I felt a swift and unexpected tug of sympathy.

Jude politely cleared his throat. "Again, we're sorry to intrude—"

"I sense a *but* coming."

"A good friend of mine died last night," I said, leveling my gaze at Smith. "She was murdered and then her body was left inside my home."

Smith didn't react.

I continued. "Captain MacAvery and I couldn't help but notice that you had left before dinner. You weren't present when the charges were removed to shut off the power, and you also weren't there when Marianne's body was discovered."

"I was there," he said. "You can ask Jack."

"That's interesting because I don't remember seeing you. And I don't think anybody else does either."

"How quickly your allegiances change," Smith said. "One moment, you're all ready to play savior to the Rootless, and now you won't even listen to your own uncle."

"I listen to the facts," I said. "And I'm sorry, but your

behavior—and my uncle's—makes me think that you're hiding something."

"You think I killed her," Smith said. A knife edge of anger cut through his words. "You really think I killed that girl."

"It doesn't look good," Jude said. There was something so calmly authoritative about him that even Smith seemed to find it difficult to resist. "I understand that there's a lot of ill will you feel toward the gentry."

"*Ill will?*" Smith's voice grew dangerously close to breaking. "Ill will? That's what you call this? Look around you, army boy. While you're off playing soldier in the mountains, people are starving here. Freezing. Choking on their own blood or vomit, all while they have to stare at their friends and family doing the same. You have no idea what that feels like."

"And do you know what it feels like to have the blood drained out of you, drop by drop?" I asked, thinking of Marianne's bloodless body.

"I've watched it happen to my people my entire life."

"Just tell us, where did you go last night?" I asked. "Where were you when Marianne's body was being circled with paint?"

Smith leaned forward, enunciating his words very carefully. "I had nothing to do with it. Ask Jack."

"Where were you?"

Smith's eyes darted from me to Jude and then over to

Russell, whose heavily lidded eyes and slumped shoulders indicated he was having trouble staying awake. "I left after the power came back on," he said finally. "I didn't want to be around your type any longer."

"We were trying to make everybody feel welcome," I said.

"Does that make you feel better about yourself? One night in a warm house, a handful of nice clothes and plate of food so rich it will make us sick, and all the bad marks are stricken from the ledger?"

His words stung because they were true. Diplomacy had been an easy word to bandy about while I was in my marble-floored home, catered to by an army of servants, but these people needed change, *real* change. Immediately. And how fair of me was it to wait for that change in my ivy-scented bower, while they waited for it in the cold?

"And regardless of what you do or what your uncle does, it doesn't change the others. I wasn't about to stick around to be treated like dirt by Arthur Lawrence and his kind. So I left and came back here. I didn't even know that the girl had died until this morning when I heard people talking about it."

It bothered me the way he kept saying *the girl*, as if she were a placeholder for a person and not a person in her own right. "Her name was Marianne Imogen Wilder. She was eighteen and about to get engaged to Mark Everly. She was in my class at the Academy, and she was one of the sweetest people I have ever known."

"I don't care," Smith said. "She was just another gentry brat with too much money and too little sense. I didn't kill her, but," he deliberately slowed his speech, "I think she deserved what she got."

It took a minute for my mind to process what he'd just said. When I finally did process it, a flash of anger burned through me, anger so hot and so deep that the only other thing I could feel besides it was fear. Because a man who could say something like that about the recently dead was someone to be afraid of.

Jude took in a deep breath, his sense of honor insulted by this, but I spoke before he could react any further. "So you're saying that she deserved to die because of the class she was born into. But isn't that idea what you're fighting against? Aren't you saying that your people deserve to live free and happy no matter who their parents were?"

"That's different," Smith said. "That's justice. We have two centuries of sickness and early deaths to be recompensed for."

"Marianne's death is not going to change anything for your people."

"At least they'll have a small taste of what we feel day after day."

There was silence, interrupted only by the low hum of the heater and the steady but labored breathing of the dozing Russell. And my breathing, too—I could hear it, along with the pulse pounding in my ears. I bit down the wash of fear and concentrated on controlling my expression. I didn't want him to know I was afraid. I didn't want him to know I was angry. I'd learned from Father that inscrutability was a Landry's greatest weapon, and I could see now that it slightly unnerved Smith that I hadn't yet responded, that I hadn't looked away from him.

He finally stood. Though he was shorter than Jude, he was taller than me, and his stare bore down on me with a malevolent heat. "Did you come here looking for a confession?" he demanded. "You're not getting one. The constables will come regardless and beat and burn and threaten, just like they always do when there's a crime that can't be solved. It doesn't matter what I tell you or what I don't tell you. The end result will be the same."

"If you confess to what you did, you could spare the others," I pleaded. "You can stop the constables, and what's more, the gentry and the Rootless can start to trust each other again."

"Firstly, why don't *you* stop the constables, Miss Landry? If they're so loyal to the Uprisen, then they would listen to you, right?" His mocking tone left no room for mistaking his meaning; he was making a point, not a suggestion. "Secondly, why would you think that I would give myself up to the police if I killed that girl? So I can be imprisoned? Executed? For what? I don't *want* the gentry and the Rootless to work together. I don't want them to make peace. I want to see the gentry wiped off the face of the earth."

As he spoke, he had come closer and closer, until he was right in front of me. I didn't back down. Years of living with my father had steeled me for moments such as these; I kept my eyes on his and my back straight. "So you're not going to admit that you did it?" I asked. An icy well of calm had sprung up within me—another gift from my father.

"What difference could it possibly make?" And in his voice was an anger so bleak and desperate that I almost believed him.

Reeve dropped Jude off at the penthouse, and I rode back to Landry Park deep in thought. I had no real proof that Smith had killed Marianne, but the things he had said dug at me. His attitude about her murder was so cruel and callous, and the fact that he had only barely asserted his innocence—it had to mean something, right?

But it was Russell's tired eyes that truly weighed on my mind as the car was parked in the carriage house and as I walked to the front door. His eyes and the way he moved, as if every joint screamed, and the way the dirt floor bled the heat from the room, and the way I had forgotten in four short weeks everything I'd learned about the way the Rootless lived. Before I opened the front door, I stared at the still-stained stone where Smith had marked his rage last year.

We are rising.

I went inside, the smell of bread baking somewhere below filling the house, the warm air evaporating away the memory of the cold. The open doors to the ballroom caught my eye as I walked in. A maid was buffing the floor, which now appeared spotless. Although it wasn't truly clean. Like the gray stone on the front of the house, if I looked closely enough I would be able to see minuscule flecks of leftover red paint, infinitesimal reminders of the body that had lain there just hours before. I shed my cape and started for the stairs when I heard a low, appreciative whistle.

David stepped out of the morning room, eyes raking over my form, over the knit dress that softened my angles and clung to my curves. I blushed, not from embarrassment, but from a sudden heat that blossomed in my chest. I also felt shame worming in my gut; I knew he would not be happy to learn that I'd been chasing after Smith.

"I came back as soon as I could," he said, surrounding me with a tight embrace, his hands running down my back and along the sides of my hips.

"David," I said, but unlike this morning, my self-control faltered. I couldn't even pretend to want him to stop.

A hand pressed against the hollow of my back, just below my waist, supporting me as he leaned down. Instead of kissing me, he brushed his lips along my jaw and down to my collarbone and back up again. My coat tumbled to the floor.

"Where were you?" he asked, in between kisses. His breath

tickled my neck. "I came back and you were gone. I worried."

"I was out," I answered vaguely. The guilt wormed and crawled even more.

"Doing what?"

His mouth had moved to my earlobe, making it impossible to think clearly. "I—I went to the Rootless part of town."

The kisses stopped. David pulled back to look at me. "Why?" The huskiness in his voice had been replaced by wariness.

"I wanted to talk to Smith."

Even though his hand remained at the small of my back, I felt a distance between us. "And why would you want to talk to him? I thought we agreed that suspecting him of killing Marianne was unfounded."

I hated this—feeling as if I were trapped between my conscience and his. Between our different ideas of right and wrong. "You and Ewan agreed to that. Not me. And by the way, Mark was completely cleared."

"Did you ever think that maybe it was another gentry guest that killed Marianne? There were more of them at the dinner party than Rootless. Or maybe it was a constable? Maybe it was somebody paid by the Empire."

"Occam's razor, David," I said.

His eyes narrowed. "Did you go alone?" he asked, changing direction.

"No. I went with Jude."

He let go of me.

"You said you wanted us to be friends again."

He shook his head. "I didn't mean that I wanted you to go witch-hunting together."

"We wanted to talk. That's hardly a witch hunt."

"You are going to undo all the work you've done. Once they realize you're going after Smith for no reason—"

"I have plenty of reason."

"Jack said that he saw him there," David said. "Since when did Jack's word stop being good enough for you?"

"Since he started lying," I said, unable to control my voice any longer. "Because of this, the gentry will refuse to sit down with the Rootless. This *hurts* Jack's people, this *stops* any progress. And I'm sorry," I finished quietly, "but there's too much at stake."

"I guess we'll have to agree to disagree, then." There was a caustic lining to his words, a sting underneath the jocular tone.

"Don't you at least want to know what Smith said?" I asked.

He frowned. "Did he confess to the murder?"

"No, but he still said a lot of strange things, David. He said he wanted the gentry dead. He said he thought Marianne *deserved to die.*"

He rubbed at the bridge of his nose. "Madeline, thinking and saying horrible things may be reprehensible . . . but it doesn't make someone a killer."

"Only a psychopath could say the things he told us," I said.

David closed his eyes. To anyone else, it might have seemed only an expression of exasperation, but I could see the way his teeth worried at the inside of his lower lip, the oh-so-brief furrow of his brow. It looked to me like he was preparing his answer too carefully. David wouldn't hide anything from me, though. Not now, after we'd been through so much.

When he opened his eyes, the fire and irritation in his gaze had dimmed, only a bare ember now, and he held out his hands, palms up, as if in supplication. "I'm sorry," he said. "I don't want to fight about this. I just . . ." He trailed off, looking uncertain as to what to say next. A moment passed and then he met my gaze again.

I placed my hands in his. "Are we okay?"

"Always," he said with a smile, and the smile was wide and honest, and not a little mischievous. He went to kiss me again, but then his tablet rang, and he checked the screen, making a face. "It's Jude. We're supposed to have dinner with a visiting general. I should go get ready."

"A visiting general?"

"He's passing through on his way to the border. We've already sent all the reserve troops to the mountains as a show of power, but we might actually have to start fighting again. Enemy troops were spotted moving on a fort in the region."

The Empire.

They were the shadow behind the mountains, the unseen

force that shaped the rules of the globe. Would they capitalize on the national unrest caused by Marianne's murder? Would they lean on the Rootless to make good on their alliance?

"About the Empire," I started, but then stopped. I hadn't heard Jack speak about the Empire and Rootless alliance since that day at Liberty Park. Could the connection have disintegrated? Or at least diminished from what it was?

David gave a shrug that was anything but careless; he took the Empire and the threat they posed very seriously. "They've been slow to move after Liberty Park. Slower than Jack would have hoped. I think he's now seen the wisdom in distancing himself from them."

"So the Rootless have given up asking the Empire to help their revolution?"

He closed his eyes again, in that overly deliberate way, and something pinged at the back of my mind. Something like suspicion.

"Jack has decided to move in a different direction," David averred.

It didn't feel like a complete answer.

I thought about that as he went back into the morning room and got his coat, knotting his scarf around his neck as he came back out. He dropped a kiss on my forehead. "I'll be checking in with you. Don't go gallivanting around the city looking for trouble."

"I never gallivant."

"Madeline, please. There's a murderer out there."

"I promise to be careful."

He gave me a look as if he were parsing my words and had found them wanting, but I was given another kiss, all the same, before he turned to leave.

And then he was gone.

EIGHT
EIGHT

Wilder House was draped in black. Black cloths hung from the ceiling and black carpets lined the floors. Black-dyed flowers gathered in bunches along the walls, leading into the ballroom where the gentry families filled the rows of chairs with their own black-clad bodies.

Mr. and Mrs. Wilder greeted everyone numbly, quietly, with puffy eyes and slack faces that suggested long nights and cold tea and the kind of crying that made the muscles in your stomach jerk and seize. Philip wore his grief openly and tears glimmered at the rims of his eyes as he shook hands with the guests. After giving my condolences to Marianne's parents, I went up to him and offered a hug. He bent his head into my neck and breathed several difficult breaths before letting go. As I walked into the ballroom, I spotted Mark Everly kneeling by the glossy walnut casket, almost like he was praying. But his eyes were open and his fingers were wrapped around the edge of the casket, as if he could undo Marianne's death as long as he held on to her coffin.

The service was long, as gentry funerals tended to be, and I sat in the back for most of it, not wanting to see the ashy and still occupant, the shell of my friend. I also couldn't handle the stares of the other guests—not today. After Liberty Park, many of the gentry had started regarding me with a certain wariness—especially those closest to the Uprisen—and now that a gentry girl had been killed at my house, no matter how innocent I actually was, a miasma of suspicion seemed to follow me wherever I stepped.

About fifteen minutes into Philip's tearful eulogy, my cousin Jamie slipped inside the ballroom, edging his way past chairs and gentry feet encased in shining black shoes, and found his way over to me. "Sorry, I'm so late," he whispered. "Something came up."

"It's fine," I reassured him. I was more concerned with the fact that I hadn't seen David yet. I could even see the long lines of his mother's neck as she sat near the front row, right next to Jude, upright and chivalrous in his pressed military uniform, and near Cara, who wasn't sitting with her usual glamorous circle of friends. And when I saw the disgusted looks they cast in Cara's direction—looks far worse than any I had been given—I understood why. In choosing Ewan, she'd effectively closed herself off from her peers.

I turned my eyes back to Christine Dana and Jude. David had every chance to come and he had chosen not to. Even if he hadn't come for Marianne, he knew how upset I was at her death—he could have come for me. Jude barely knew Marianne and he was still here.

After Philip spoke and we sang songs that echoed off the parquet floors, the coffin was borne away to be buried, and we followed it to the city cemetery, where it was lowered into the earth in the slicing rain. I huddled with Jude, Christine, Cara, and Jamie, each with our own large black umbrellas, watching as the rain turned back into gloppy clumps of snow, the kind of snow that made noise as it fell.

It felt too surreal to be true, as if it were an empty box being lowered and a blank monument being erected. The idea that it was a girl my age in the coffin unnerved me. A girl who had once had her own thoughts and feelings, a girl I had danced with and eaten with . . . now she was nothing but a vessel. The thing that had animated her was gone, and we were burying nothing more than a collection of atoms that would eventually crumble into uncaring dust.

It was only after the coffin was in place and the crowd began to disperse that I saw David, leaning against a tree several plots away. He looked thoroughly soaked, as if he'd been there for the entire burial. Had he come for the service, too, and I'd just missed him?

Jude and I waved him over and he came to us, his coat open and gray silk scarf dripping water, shoes crunching through the sloppy, miserable snow.

"Madeline." He took my hand, his leather gloves wet and cold against my skin, and pressed it to his lips.

"You weren't at the funeral."

His face clouded as he let go of my hand. "I don't like funerals."

"No one does," I said.

He rubbed at the back of his head, then gestured vaguely to the crowd and to the open pit where Marianne lay dead in her casket. "This is so much like my father's funeral. The people in their black with their flowers and their handshakes . . ." He trailed off, watching the line of cars creep down the cemetery drive to the iron gates. "I don't like the ritualized grieving, the forced condolences. None of it's genuine, but then again, people don't really want the genuine feelings. The real anger. The real pain. They just want to hold their umbrellas and say sorry and go back to their lives."

My lips parted but I wasn't sure what to say. I'd forgotten about David's father and his death last year, even though it was the sole reason Christine and David had relocated to Kansas City. And I had never really asked David about it because he always seemed so collected, so confident—and it wasn't polite conversation. He was right. We gravitated toward what was easy, and nothing about death was easy.

As a group, we slowly drifted down the hill to the waiting cars. I pointed out monuments as we passed, Yorks and Osbournes, Lawrences and Landrys, all buried centuries ago. David nodded and asked questions as we walked, but I could tell from the distance in his voice that he was still uncomfortable, still wading in memories from the last funeral he'd attended.

The others splintered off, finding their respective vehicles, eager to be inside the dry, chauffeured warmth and on their way home. David made to open the door for me, but I stepped forward instead, boxing him in and pressing him against the car.

He stared down at me, surprised. "Why hello there," he said.

"I never asked you about your father," I said, brushing the snow from David's shoulders. "I should have."

"I would have talked about it if I wanted to."

"Do you want to now?"

He thought for a minute. "Talk?" He glanced down at us, at the way our legs tangled together, and then looked back up to me, his eyes dancing under long, wet eyelashes. "Not really. But I'd like to do something else."

We were in a cemetery and he was ridiculous and my face was streaked with tears and melted snow, but all those thoughts fell away as I wrapped my fingers around his tie and pulled his lips to mine.

That night, the Yorks hosted a large dinner and invited most of the gentry, who molted their mourning garments and changed into party clothes, like birds unable to forgo their bright plumage. A lively band played, and despite everything—despite Marianne's funeral and burial and the wet weather outside—the guests danced and drank and chatted as if nothing could ever disturb the serene bubble of their pampered lives.

I almost went home. I was still in my stiff black dress and my mind was still in the frozen cemetery—I didn't belong here.

"Madeline," Jamie said, approaching me from the side. He handed me a champagne flute, and I stopped my retreat. If there's anyone I would stay among the wolves for, it was my cousin.

"Do you mind if we talk?" Jamie asked, inclining his head toward a table. "Since I've managed to capture you alone for the moment? I know this is a difficult time, right after the service and all . . ."

"Actually, I would welcome the distraction. It's been a long day." As soon as I sat, a servant came over with a tray, and encouraged me to indicate a selection. I gestured at the seared bluefin tuna somewhat listlessly; the thought of eating so soon after the funeral tied my stomach in knots.

Jamie chose the fish, too, cutting the filet with precision as he began.

"Do you remember when your father came back from Liberty Park, after the Rootless had forced the gibbet food in his mouth?"

My lips parted, my brain trying and failing to switch from new pain to old pain. *How could I forget that day?* Father's jaw and his cheeks and his lips, raw and bloody and shredded; his back arching with pain; the way he squeezed my fingers, as if I were his lifeline to consciousness and he was afraid to let go.

85

I nodded.

"And you remember how I found something unusual in his DNA? The extraordinary way he seemed to be healing from his ordeal?"

I recalled Jamie's puzzled words at the time. *Repair at this speed and efficiency from a radiation injury so severe? I have never heard of anything like it.*

"You said that you were going to have it analyzed at the university's lab."

"I did. And I finally got the results today—that's why I was late to the funeral. I still don't understand a lot of it. At first, I thought it could be some sort of congenital disorder or simply a mutation that happened to be salubrious. We know that DNA mutates constantly, mostly unnoticeably and, very rarely, beneficially. But his DNA structure is an outlier from the normal scale of mutations. The efficacy and complexity with which his body is repairing itself—" He stopped talking, shaking his head. "I've never come across anything like it." He looked at me a bit hesitantly, as if he were worried about my reaction.

"Go on," I told him. "This is my blood, too. I want to know."

He nodded, staring at his tuna as he thought. I knew he wasn't seeing his food, but rather was seeing biological puzzle pieces in his mind—cells and mitochondria and biopolymers and nucleotides.

"So far, we've been able to isolate the abnormal DNA.

And—I'm glad you're already sitting down—it doesn't appear to be human."

I blinked at him for a moment, not sure if I heard correctly. I looked down at my hands, as if expecting feathers or scales to sprout out of my skin. "I didn't know that was even possible."

"Neither did I," he admitted, and he sounded a little defensive. But there was also an excitement in him, animating the long lines of his face. "This nonhuman DNA . . . it shares characteristics with something that's already catalogued. *Deinococcus radiodurans*—a type of bacteria they discovered in the 1950s. It has a phenomenal rate of DNA recovery—it can withstand intense levels of radiation. In fact, it's so efficient at repairing itself that people used to use it to clean radioactive waste, although that method required more work than ejecting the waste into space, as we do now."

"So part of my DNA is bacteria?" I asked, trying to shake off the feeling that something unnatural lurked in the most fundamental elements of my body.

He smiled in the way that a teacher might smile at a naive pupil, but it wasn't meant unkindly. "The bacteria has its own DNA, which was modified at some point. I suppose it's possible that somehow this happened naturally, spontaneously. Before the Last War, scientists were beginning to unearth things like this. Unusual mutations in individuals that gave them an advantage in fighting cancer or AIDS."

I peered into Jamie's face, noting the way his eyes traced the edge of his plate, around and around, as his long fingers made shapes and pictures on the tablecloth. "You sound doubtful."

He sighed. "I just don't know yet. The alternative is so strange . . ."

"And what's the alternative?"

He faced me. "That someone engineered the *radiodurans* so that it could be spliced into human DNA, which could only have been done by someone very clever and probably also very daring."

I thought about that for a moment. "So a person could have done this? But why?"

"The why is less perplexing to me than the how," he said.

I didn't mention that the *why* was infinitely more interesting to me. I watched Jamie's fingers swirling on the tablecloth, and I realized that he was absentmindedly tracing a double helix.

"Is there anything I can do to help you?" I offered, curiosity burning within me. "Maybe with finding books or papers in our library?"

His voice was hesitant when he said, "You can help me by giving me your blood."

"Ouch."

The needle slid under my skin, and, with a gush, blood began to fill the glass vial.

"Sorry," Jamie said, keeping his eyes on the collection tube. He deftly undid the tourniquet with one hand and pressed a square piece of gauze to my arm as he withdrew the needle. "Thank you again. Having a sample from you should help give me a starting point—what is natural for all Landrys and then what is specific to your father."

We were back at Landry Park, in a dark room hung with tapestries, rarely used because it caught the worst of the wind coming out of the northwest. Even the nuclear charges couldn't keep it warm. But it made a good place to take a quick blood sample—there was no chance of interruption.

"I'm happy to help." Although I was more scared than I wanted to admit about learning the results. There was no doubt in my mind that I had the same abnormality nestled under my skin. What if this mutation was a bad thing, something that would hurt me later on? I was already different enough, with bright red hair and skin the color of bisque. I didn't want my blood to make me different, too.

Jamie threw away the sterile wrappings and helped me stand. "I'm going to process this right away. Maybe by tomorrow we'll know more," Jamie said. "I'm going to ask the others for samples, too; Jude and David certainly, maybe Ewan as well. The wider the range of data, the clearer the picture." He gave me a quick, cousinly kiss on the forehead and strode to the door, excitement evident in his lanky frame.

He paused at the threshold. "Is everything okay?"

I wiped my hands on my stiff crepe dress, suddenly eager to get out of the mourning weeds and into something that didn't remind me of how everything had gone completely wrong in the last two days. "Of course."

I could tell he was reluctant to leave me, but also that he was eager to start investigating.

"Go," I urged. "Call when you find something."

He left. I wandered upstairs to change, finding Elinor changing the sheets on my bed. I went over and helped her, smoothing out the silky fine linens and straightening the counterpane until the bed was finished. Together, we stuffed the old sheets into a hamper to be taken down to the laundry.

Something occurred to me then, and hot on the heels of the realization was a flood of guilt that I had never thought of it before. "Elinor," I asked slowly, "what will happen to you if everything changes? If the Rootless aren't replacing the charges and the gentry aren't powerful anymore—if you didn't have to work at a house like this any longer?"

She stopped, bracing the hamper against her hip. A white cap was set onto her short dark curls and a black dress and pressed apron accentuated her shapely figure—she was beautiful. She could probably easily marry well, someone in the middle class even, although servants typically married within their own ranks, if they married at all. "I suppose I have wondered a bit about that," she said. "I guess I hope that somehow it will all work out. That I get to stay with you and the family. It's the only life I've ever known."

I sat on the bench. "But what if it doesn't work out?" I felt a responsibility for her and for all of the servants who had been like an extended family to me as I had grown up on the estate, a responsibility to make sure that the mitigation of gentry power didn't leave them without livelihoods, without homes.

"I don't know," she answered, shifting the hamper again. "But there are things I have wanted to do, in another life. . . ." She trailed off.

"Like what?" I was curious.

"Well, I think I'd like to go to school," she said. "I remember liking it when I was young, before my parents died. Maybe someday I could even go to the university."

And then she smiled her big smile, the one that was sweet and saucy at the same time. "But it's a total fantasy. I could never pay the tuition, and anyway, my place is by your side while you take on the estate."

"*If* I take on the estate."

NINE

I had just braided my hair and changed into a lace-trimmed nightgown when I saw the glimmer of a Cherenkov lantern outside my window. I was more than ready to throw myself on my bed and tumble into the dark reaches of sleep, but I still went to the window to see who was wandering the grounds this late at night.

Tall, broad-shouldered—my heart leaped as I wondered if it was David. Then the lantern swung and I saw that the person had bright red hair.

Ewan.

He walked up to the patio and stomped the snow off his boots, slowly, almost thoughtfully. The blue light gleamed on the platinum symbol, and I thought of the bloody snow. I thought of Marianne.

My body was moving before my mind could make a decision; I slung a robe over my shoulders and went downstairs to the ballroom.

Ewan was coming through the patio doors just as I entered the dim cavern of the empty room. He didn't seem surprised to see me.

"This is a big estate," he said, taking off his coat. "I just went for a walk and it took me over two hours to cover the perimeter."

I walked around the spot where Marianne's body had been found, my throat tight, averting my eyes, and joined him at the door, where he was looking out of the glass.

"I'd seen parts of the estate as a charge-changer, but I'd never been allowed to see all of the property before we moved here, and this last month I've been too busy to explore. I never realized there was so much—three gardens, an orchard, a maze . . ."

"And you decided to tour the grounds late at night? They really are to their best advantage when you can actually see them."

He kept his eyes on the lawn but jerked his head back toward the heart of the house. "I wanted to do it alone. Without my father or Charlie."

"Why?"

"Does there have to be a reason?" he snapped.

I held up my hands in surrender. "I'm sorry. And you know, if you wanted a tour, I would have been happy to give you one."

All of the heat went out of him and he rested his head against the glass. "I know. It's just—the estate is a lot to take in, and I wanted to be able to think about it by myself, process it on my own."

I sensed he was talking about more than the grounds.

"I never thought that I would live in a place like this. I never thought that there would be servants trying to dress me and bringing me food and following me around. And now here I am, not just living in an estate, but in Landry Park."

"Well, you *are* a Landry."

This was evidently the wrong thing to say, because his body tensed and he turned to go.

"Ewan, wait. I didn't mean it like that."

"Like what? The truth? Because it is true. I'm living here, dating my gentry girlfriend, and wearing gentry clothes. I don't even know who I am anymore."

This was my moment to say something profound, something comforting, but I came up blank. Instead, I touched his shoulder. "You're family, Ewan. And you'll see that Landry Park isn't all bad."

"Maybe," he said, doubt coloring his voice, and then he did walk away. I stayed for a moment, watching the moonlight pour through the glass and shine on the spot where we'd found Marianne. I wasn't foolish enough to believe that by being here I was any closer to her spirit—if there was such a thing. But there was a sort of peace associated with the spot, an anchor for my grief. Yes, it had all been real. My pain was real. The ballroom floor validated that; it held Marianne's death in its memory.

I felt suddenly very aware that I was alone, probably the

only one on the ground floor of the house. David's words came back to me . . . *there's a murderer of gentry girls out there.*

I forced myself to peer into the corners of the ballroom, tuned my ears for the slightest movement. A sharp noise—bright and sudden, like the sound of china cracking—sent me wheeling around to face the ballroom entrance. *It's probably just the cat. It's just the cat. Only the cat, jumping and pouncing and knocking things over.*

But there was nothing, not even the cat, only my breath and the slow churning of the furnace. I turned and that's when I saw it: a divot in the glass door right in front of my face, as if someone had hurled a stone right at my head.

I saw no one outside, no lights or shadows, no lurking figures. *You're being silly*, I told myself. The murder had put me on edge, dulled my logic with fear. It had probably just been something tossed in the air by the wind. But still, I left the ballroom with long, anxious strides, looking over my shoulder and clenching my hands into ready fists until I made it back to my room.

When I woke, I saw that I had a missed call on my tablet. My heart flipped over, hoping it was David, but it stilled as I swiped the screen and saw that it had been from Jamie. He'd sent a message asking me to meet him at his town house to talk about what he'd ascertained from my blood sample. I slid into a warm gray dress with three-quarter sleeves and a mid-length skirt, laced up a pair of ankle boots, and had Reeve drive me downtown.

Jamie's town house was narrow and old, but attractive in a tidy sort of way. I passed by the Public Hospital where he worked, the golden cupola glinting in the weak winter sun. Normally, Rootless and other impoverished citizens could be seen coming in and out, smoking cigarettes on the front steps or pacing the pitted paths of the anemic garden next door, but today the hospital seemed empty. Reeve drove a block farther north and west and parked in front of a row of terraced houses done up with redbrick and wrought-iron railings. I asked the driver to wait, and then went to the steps leading to the house, feeling a tremor of nerves as I stepped up to the bright blue door. What would I learn? And would I wish I could unlearn it?

I lifted the brass knocker, taking in the commanding view from Jamie's front stoop. The area around the hospital was high on a bluff, affording a generous view of the skyline to one side and of the river to the other. The day was cold but clear. I took a deep breath in, savoring the bracing air, and let the knocker drop.

Jamie answered at once, his already wild hair tousled and tufted, as if he'd been tugging on it in fits of energetic speculation. "Come up," he said by way of greeting.

Curious, I stepped inside. Normally, Jamie was assiduously polite. But there was something distant and distracted in his eyes, and I got the feeling that he had been working all through the night.

"I noticed the hospital seemed quiet," I said as he robotically took my coat and tailored leather gloves.

"It *is* quiet. The Rootless have mostly stopped coming since Marianne's death—whether out of fear or protest, I don't know. We've had a few visitors, but it seems like they are scattered somehow, and I think there's been some disagreement among them since Liberty Park." He raised his eyes to mine, the normally rich brown irises faded with exhaustion. "There is a rumor that I don't think the gentry have heard. . . ." He stopped. "Perhaps it's better not even to repeat. Who knows how much truth there is in it?"

"Jamie."

He sighed. "The word is that some of the Rootless want to refuse to change the charges altogether. Expired charges run for two weeks before they fail entirely, so it would be several days before anyone would notice, but if it's true, the gentry would be at some risk. Mild risk, mind you, so long as the exposure is short term. I think it's largely a scare tactic."

"But . . . everyone would know to blame the Rootless. That's why they've never done it before. And it would render the estates unusable, so what would be the point?"

"A small radiation leak would probably necessitate some cleanup, but as long as the house isn't, for example, sprayed with exploding nuclear material, it would be safe enough to inhabit after a few weeks." He looked me in the eye. "And how sure are you that the Rootless want to live in the estates? For the revolutionaries, the point might be making them completely useless."

I hadn't thought about that.

"It's a rumor," Jamie reassured me. "If I hear anything more, I'll go straight to the constables, but right now, it's just the word of a nurse who heard it from another nurse who heard it from a patient. And you're right. They'd never be foolish enough to do something so easily traced back to themselves."

I had my doubts. The thing about zealots like Smith was that their reasoning was impossible to suss out. There was no reasoning, really, no logic, no order.

"Anyway, you need to see what I have to show you. If I'm right . . ." He stopped again, but whether it was because he was doubtful or hopeful, I couldn't say. I filed away the information about the charges for later.

We went up the slightly dusty stairs to his office, a room of dark wooden paneling and overflowing bookshelves with a large desk set in a bay window. On one wall, the paneling was raised, revealing a screen that showed the same spiraling ribbon of DNA that I had seen the day Father was attacked. A large black box had been rolled into the room, and inside, I could see tubes of blood. More than one—he must have gotten the other samples he'd wanted yesterday.

Little screens under each vial showed numbers and letters that I didn't understand, and every so often, the machine would glow and chime, and then the wall screen would change. On the bottom of the screen, I saw a picture of a young man and a call record from just a few hours ago.

"Is that . . . ?" I didn't finish. Jamie was a very private person, and I probably shouldn't have even mentioned it. He walked over to the screen and deleted the call record.

"His name is Graham," he said quietly. "And things are . . . complicated right now."

"I'm sorry."

He shrugged. "It's not easy having an ocean between us." He brought the twisting ribbon of DNA back onto the screen.

"Whose is that one?" I asked, walking over to the screen.

"Your father's." Jamie picked up his tablet. "And here is yours."

A second corkscrew ribbon began turning next to Father's.

"And here is David's. And Jude's. And mine."

Three more ribbons appeared. Jamie pressed a button on the tablet, and the DNA models froze. He came beside me. "See this?" He pointed at the screen. "There is the sequence that is responsible for your father's healing. You can see how it's not present in David's or mine, despite the fact that I'm related to you. This suggests that it's not present in the Lawrence line—your mother's and my line."

"But it is present in my sample," I whispered, stepping

closer and touching the screen, as if touching it would make me understand. "So I can heal like my father? From radiation?"

"Perhaps."

"Is this hereditary?"

Jamie frowned at the screen. "I'm not entirely certain yet. Look at Jude's DNA. See how the structure of the sequence is there, but not quite intact?"

I nodded.

"So Jude seems to carry something similar to you and your father, but it's not an exact match. My first guess was that this was some mutation that occurred within the gentry early on in the gentry's formation, and because of the gentry tradition of marrying cousins, stayed strong in some lines, was absent from others, and was incomplete where the carriers married outside the families."

I didn't respond for a moment, allowing myself to digest all this.

"What about Jack?" I asked. "Is his blood the same as Father's and mine?"

"That's an interesting question—you three share so many other physical traits that I wouldn't doubt it."

I thought of Jack leaving his cane in the study, of the way he'd seemed so spry and energetic lately. Of the way the sores on his skin had faded to shiny pink welts. "I don't doubt it either. So Jude—he has something similar?"

"That's where it gets really interesting." He used his tablet to highlight Jude's DNA and bring it next to Father's. "So here you can see that these healing genes—they only match part of the way, as if they're only half there. Like the stem of the mutation is there, but it hasn't been activated yet or something.

"Like I mentioned earlier, my first guess was that this was a mutation that had filtered into the gentry, reinforced by the interfamilial marriage patterns. But then I started thinking about it—what are the odds that a mutation would have the exact same genetic copy as an existing species? It had to be intentional. And it makes sense, because what members of the gentry wouldn't have peace of mind knowing that they had extra immunity to radiation?

"And something else. Whoever did this also found a way to tie the DNA into your own so that it breaks down and ages at the same rate as everything else. So while it makes you resistant to radiation—and possibly most viruses and infections, I would think—it doesn't allow your body to repair itself indefinitely. As you would naturally age, the new DNA ages along with you, still protecting you from radiation, but allowing the genes controlling other functions like hair growth and organ function to progress normally.

"Simply said, you do not have an unnaturally long life, merely a very healthy one. Additionally, the DNA isn't magical—it won't prevent damage from being done. If you were constantly bombarded with radiation, you wouldn't be able to heal yourself completely. It would only be after the assault stopped that the DNA could get to work to undo all the damage."

Like Jack, I realized. That also explained why he was so much longer-lived than the other Rootless.

"So then I thought if your blood could heal you from radiation damage once the exposure had ended, could it do it for other people? Could it cure someone who was already sick?"

I sat up straighter as the implications of his questions sunk in. "You could use it to help the other Rootless."

"Yes."

My mind spun. I thought of Russell trudging through the snow, of Sarah collapsing in the park last year. If Jamie was right—and I recognized what a large *if* that was—but if he was, then the possibility for healing was endless. We could do more than change the class systems now; we could set things right permanently.

"But I'm not sure how to do it," he explained. "I feel like we could possibly modify the existing vaccines into an effective counteragent somehow, but I also think there is something important about the way the healing DNA is bound to your congenital DNA. They fit together, like a hand in a glove, and one can't work without the other. So unless a sick person had the same bond-ready DNA as you and your father, they wouldn't receive the same benefit."

"What if the nonhuman DNA was changed . . . adapted so that it could work for anyone?"

"That could work, but the problem is that I don't know how to separate the two and then alter the genes. And then there's the problem of production . . . how much blood of yours would I need to extract for one vaccine? For all I know, it could be a completely untenable number. I might need gallons of your blood."

"There are other Landrys."

Jamie gave me a look.

I stood to get closer to the wall screen, pressing my fingertips against the three-dimensional model, as if I could use it to touch the future. A better future, where no one—Rootless or gentry—had anything to fear from the specter of radiation.

"I'm going to work on it more," he said. "I'll call in some favors at the university. We have the right ingredients, it's just finding a way to stitch them together properly.

"And Madeline," Jamie added, the words hesitant and soft. "Maybe it would be best to keep quiet about this for now?"

"Why?"

Jamie ran a hand through his hair. "Nothing is certain yet. I'm working almost purely on speculation and—potential radiation counteragent aside—how do you think the Rootless would react to the knowledge that the Landrys are immune to radiation poisoning?"

I looked off to the side, the scenario rolling through my mind, envisioning the assumptions, the accusations, the fury.

"Yes, you're right," I said, pragmatism winning out over the guilty tangle that tightened in my stomach. "I won't breathe a word."

TEN

I should have gone home. I should have. But as the car drove past the hospital and down the treed slopes of Quality Hill, I saw the light flashing off the windows of David's penthouse, and I found myself asking Reeve to change direction before I could think better of it. I told him I'd message him once I was finished, and I stepped inside the chilly marble foyer, snow falling from my boots to the floor as I walked.

I pressed my finger against the buzzer and there was a pause before a smoky voice answered. "Hello?"

I looked into the camera above the speaker. "Hello, Mrs. Dana. I was wondering if David was home?"

"Of course, darling. Come right up."

And for the second time that week, I rode the elevator up into the Danas' spacious penthouse.

Christine greeted me with a kiss on each cheek while a maid took my things, and after I escaped them both, I found David at the piano, a glass of half-drunk whiskey sitting on the sleek black wood. He wasn't playing, but his hands rested on the keys as he stared out of the window.

I sensed he didn't feel much like talking, so instead I placed my fingers on the keys and began striking out the first deep and lively notes of Schubert's "Marche Militaire." I wasn't certain what would happen next, but then David swept his fingers down the length of the keys and joined in, his head down, blond hair framing his face.

We played the jaunty tune together, the notes filling the open space with an almost aggressive cheerfulness. It felt forced, the energy of the song, a song that couples danced to in wide lines, a song of swinging skirts and clasping hands and tapping feet on the floor. Not a song for days of murder and unrest. I had only chosen it because it was the first song that sprang to mind.

I was fairly accomplished at the piano—all gentry girls were expected to cultivate some level of skill with an instrument—but as I watched David's fingers move lightly across the keys, adding spontaneous flourishes and stylizations, I knew that David's abilities far surpassed mine. As we continued, the forced feeling of it eased, and I felt David moving next to me, becoming more and more wrapped up in the song. After it ended, we switched to Gershwin and then we ended with Tchaikovsky's "Waltz from Sleeping Beauty."

I closed my eyes as we played. We had danced to this song once, in Landry Park's ballroom, and even though I had been debuting with Jude at the time, I had been unable to think of anyone other than David.

The song ended and he reached over to touch my hand,

biting his lip, as if he were just as affected by the memory as I was. Then he withdrew, taking his glass and walking over to a window.

I followed him. For a moment we both stood there in silence, and I debated saying anything, but something felt strange between us, strange and watchful, like we were both waiting for the other to speak first. I remembered his face in the cemetery, pale and distant, and I wondered if he was still thinking about his father.

I slid an arm around his waist, running my fingers under his jacket. "You are pensive today."

He turned to me and rested his chin on the top of my head. "Just thinking is all." His hand found the cameo I wore at my neck, tracing its outline with a single fingertip. I could feel his touch burning through the thin wool of my dress.

When he spoke next, his voice was uncertain. Hesitant. "Do you . . . do you ever wonder about the future?"

"The future?"

He didn't meet my quizzical look. "You know." He swallowed, his usual charm and confidence gone. "Like *our* future."

My heart was pounding under the cameo necklace—I could feel it crashing against my ribs. "*Our future?* Like a future together? Like getting married?"

He nodded nervously.

A buzz of panic and elation swarmed in my chest and in my throat, and I practically hummed with the possibility. Did

I want to spend the rest of my life with this sharp-edged, mercurial captain? Could I imagine us still dancing together, still fighting together thirty or forty or fifty years from now?

Yes.

Yes, I could.

But our future didn't consist of only us. There was the Rootless and the Empire, and aside from all of that, I still wanted to go to the university, and we had only been truly together for a handful of weeks—

He sighed. "I knew you'd overthink it."

"I'm not," I said defensively. "I'm just . . . we haven't talked about it before."

His hands framed my face. "Well, I'm talking about it now. I love you, Madeline Landry. I want you. And only you. And it's going to be that way for the rest of my life."

"That's a big promise to make." I breathed. It was hard to think straight when he touched me like this—when his hands and eyes were full of prophecy and intimacy and fascination.

"But it's an easy promise to make. Because it's true."

"I don't trust liars. And you are the best one I know." But I was smiling when he kissed me.

"I'm not giving up on this," he whispered against my lips.

"I don't want you to."

Someone stepped in the room, heels clicking on the wood. Christine. David and I parted, although I was positive she had seen us and positive that my crimson cheeks probably revealed what we'd been up to even if she hadn't.

"Don't mind me," she said airily. "Just getting ready to go out for a bit." She swung a cape over her shoulders. "I'm going to have Jensen escort me to lunch. With the Rootless attacking members of the gentry, I don't feel safe on my own."

"Mother, please," David said, and I could hear the restraint in his voice. "There's no evidence to suggest that the Rootless are murdering the gentry. So far the police have no suspects."

She tugged her gloves on, checked her red lipstick in a compact, and then snapped it shut. "Jude told me that it's probably a Rootless person who killed Marianne Wilder. He and Madeline went to see him in the Rootless ghetto this week, and Jude said he was acting *very* suspicious."

"He said that, did he?"

David and I met eyes, then looked away again. Whatever enchantment we had woven together vanished, replaced by the same friction we'd felt the night of Marianne's death.

"Yes, so I plan to be careful until that man is arrested. You be careful, too." She pointed a gloved finger at both of us and then stepped into the elevator.

When she was gone, I faced David. Faced the sudden heat of his temper.

"Is something wrong? Are you still angry about me going to see Smith? I thought we were over this."

"I'm not *angry about it*," he said, "but I am upset, and about more than Smith. I'm upset that you won't listen to me. I'm upset that you've roped Jude into this—Jude, who is already on the fence about everything anyway." He turned toward me, and his expression was thoughtful and agitated all at once. "To be perfectly honest, you're acting how people would expect a Landry to act right now."

My anger at that surprised me, but I managed to tamp it down. "Please don't use my family against me. After all I've done to unravel the Landry legacy."

"But don't you see?" His eyes were pleading. "Accusing an innocent Rootless is exactly what your father would do."

How had we veered so suddenly off course? We had just been talking about marriage and a future together, and now we were fighting. I took a deep breath and tried to orient myself.

"I only believe what I do about Marianne's murder because I know I'm right. And my theory is not about prejudice—Smith has earned my suspicion all on his own. Even you have to admit that he doesn't look innocent."

"That's what the gentry thought about Cara's attacker and they were wrong."

"You can't claim that because something happened once a certain way it has to happen that way again."

"And you can't claim that just because a man is unlikable he's a murderer! He has an *alibi*, Madeline. What more do you want?"

And there it was again, that suspicion, the feeling that Jack and David weren't telling me all they knew, whether to protect Smith or to protect themselves.

Frustration welled inside me, but when I caught my reflection in the window, it was dispassionate and cold, as if the emotion were buried so deeply within that even I couldn't see it. Maybe I'd learned more from Father than I'd thought.

"If he were only unlikable, I would do nothing of the sort," I explained. "And how I feel about Smith has no bearing on how I feel about the Rootless. Nothing about what I believe and what I want to work for has changed. Can't you trust me? Can't you at least listen to what I've learned?"

"I listened the first time you told me; I know all the cruel things he said." He sighed, breaking away from our locked gaze. "And I do trust you . . . I . . ." His voice was no longer choleric but plaintive. "I love you more than anything. That's why I care so goddamned much."

I reached out, pressing my palm to his cheek, and he closed his eyes, relaxing into my touch.

"I'm sorry," he whispered.

"I'm sorry, too," I said, but I found the words difficult to say. I was sorry that we had fought, but I wasn't sorry about Smith. And I wouldn't be until the constables had declared him officially innocent.

He stepped closer, and I hadn't noticed the cold that crept in from the window until he pulled me into his arms and replaced it with his warmth. He bent his head down and touched his lips to mine, but the gesture felt fraught, not like the sweet embrace of earlier. Then my tablet chimed, interrupting the kiss. I dug it out of my pocket and saw that it was a call from Jack.

I disentangled myself from David and answered.

"Madeline," Jack said. His expression and voice were laden with urgency and something else I couldn't quite place. "You need to come back home, immediately."

"What happened?"

Jack glanced away from the wall screen from where he was making his call, and I noticed for the first time people moving in the hallway behind him. "There's been another death," he said finally. "A body found here at the estate."

My stomach squeezed. *Please don't be one of my friends, please don't be one of my friends. . . .*

"It's Mark Everly."

Mark. I let out a breath. Only a few days after his girlfriend's death.

"They think he was strangled. The constables are here now. You should come home."

"I will," I promised.

He nodded and glanced behind him again. The call ended and I hurriedly found my coat and gloves while David—who had heard the entire conversation—did the same. It wasn't until he and I were riding to Landry Park together that I realized what else had been in Jack's expression. Fear.

The blue lights of the constables' lanterns rivaled even the daylight as David and I walked through the front door. I spotted Inspector Hernandez almost right away, his face paler and more drawn than the last time I had seen him. He was speaking in low tones with a policewoman in the foyer, but he paused when he saw me.

"Make sure of it," he told the woman, who nodded and left. He came toward me and gave a short bow. "Miss Landry. I'm sorry to be here again under these circumstances."

Circumstances. Never had a single word been so far apart from its brutal, unbelievable meaning. "I am sorry, too," I said distantly. It all seemed so unreal, so unfair. I'd just seen Mark at Marianne's funeral, alive and walking and talking and—I took a deep breath, trying to stop the swelling feeling of shock and sadness.

What was I supposed to do? What was I supposed to say in this sort of situation? There was no etiquette protocol for finding dead friends on the grounds.

"Would you like something to drink?" I asked, grasping for anything approaching normalcy. My voice sounded peculiar but nobody seemed to notice.

"That wouldn't go unappreciated," the inspector admitted, and I rang for the drinks, my hand shaking as I picked up the silver bell.

"What exactly happened here?" David asked, getting straight to the point.

"One of the gardeners found Mr. Everly's body in the garden just an hour ago," Inspector Hernandez said. "It appears that he was attacked and strangled, although the drag marks suggest that he was killed elsewhere and then brought into the garden."

The double doors across the ballroom drew my eyes all the way from the foyer. They hung open, constables coming in and out, tramping snow on the ballroom floor, and I wondered where in the garden Mark had been found. Near the fountain? Near the rosebushes thickly glazed with ice?

"The security cameras . . . ?"

The drink tray arrived, and we all helped ourselves to coffee and tea. "Already checked," the inspector said in between sips. "There is only one camera that even vaguely captures the garden, and it only shows the entrance off the patio steps. Anyone could have come in through the three other entrances and would not have been seen. Which is possibly why the garden was chosen—it would have been a very discreet location to kill someone."

"And are you certain that it was the same person who killed Marianne?" David asked.

"Oh yes." Inspector Hernandez hesitated. "Mr. Everly's body has already been removed and the scene mapped. Would you like to see where he was found?"

"No," David said at the same time as I said, "Yes."

But David came along anyway.

A couple inches of snow had settled along the patio since last night, a sheet of treacherous ice lurking underneath. More than once, I found my boots inadequate for the walk, and David offered his arm while we slowly made our way down the steps. We passed constables carrying back cameras and opaque bags of samples and bright yellow surveying equipment, but when we entered the garden, we were all alone. There was a unique silence this garden had in winter, the absence of bubbling fountains and twittering birds. Only the creaking of the ice-laden branches interrupted the stillness, a stillness I had always considered peaceful but would now associate with death.

It was past the rosebushes, next to a statue of an angel with her face covered by her hands, that I saw it. The red atomic symbol with the slash through it. The snow around it was thoroughly disturbed, but I could still make out where the body had rested, right in the center where there was a gap in the red markings. Mark's tablet was marked by a numbered sign a few feet away.

David's hand tightened around my upper arm.

"It's paint once again—I think after his experience with

Miss Wilder, the killer must have given up altogether on the idea of using the blood for his artwork." Inspector Hernandez looked at me. "I have to ask you once again if you can think of anything, anything at all, that would pertain to Mr. Everly's and Miss Wilder's deaths. Two bodies on your estate in one week, both with the marred Landry family crest—I can't help but feel that the killer has you or your family in mind somehow. And there is another thing—something that didn't happen with Miss Wilder." He used his tablet to bring up a picture that I recognized instantly as Mark. The policeman enlarged the picture quickly so that I was spared a detailed examination of Mark's vacant eyes and slack features. He angled the screen to me. "Do these words seem familiar to you?"

The picture showed a note on Mark's chest, where black letters scrawled: *We are rising.*

I took a step back, my breath quickening. David saw the note, too, and he bit his lip. He knew what I was thinking—that it had been Smith who scrawled those words on my house last year, and that it must have been Smith who scrawled those same words to leave with Mark.

Inspector Hernandez tucked the tablet back into his pocket. "What's interesting is that we found this as well." He led us a few feet farther down the path, where clumps of snow mingled with frozen acrylic paint. "We think he tried to leave his note in the snow—again, it would have been a more dramatic touch—but either ran out of paint or perhaps spaced the letters poorly and realized he'd run out of room. So he decided on the quotidian but more reliable pen and paper. We'll be doing analysis to see if there's anything to be found from it, but the paper appears to be an old receipt of Mark's— a purchase of cuff links from last month. Not anything that would show us where the killer had been."

We were walking back to the house now, and the chill of those three words sank into me, weighing me down with a cold and leaden feeling of dread. *We are rising.* Why was Smith doing this?

What's more, did Jack know? Was he protecting the man who was killing people on the very land where he'd grown up?

ELEVEN

Jack greeted us as we walked back in, and even though my head was filled with red paint and ominous notes and the slightly blurry image of Mark's staring eyes, I noticed that he was walking without his cane again. I shot discreet glances at his face as we came closer. There were hardly any sores there now—only a couple pink spots marked where they once had been.

Jamie's theory had to be right. Had to be.

After a round of strained, but polite, farewells, the inspector excused himself, and David and I followed my uncle back to the library, where a fire had been lit.

Jack sat down on a sofa, resting his head against his fist, and David sat in a chair that faced the fire. After I perched on the arm of the chair, David reached over and took my hand. He hadn't worn his gloves outside and his hands were cold. I chafed them distractedly, thinking about what I had just seen in the garden. What I had just read.

We are rising.

"I'm losing the city," Jack said, rubbing at his cheek with his hand. A crop of white stubble had sprung up on his face, barely noticeable. It reminded me of how very much he wasn't Father, who had never been anything less than meticulously clean-shaven my entire life.

I wrangled my thoughts into some kind of order and forced myself to focus on Jack's words. "I don't think," I said carefully, "that you ever really had the city."

Jack looked pensive. "Perhaps we were foolish to think this could happen any other way."

I studied his face, the way his eyes narrowed and his lips set, as if he were steeling himself for a difficult decision. He had made many difficult decisions in his life, but when I thought of this last year, when he had allowed the violence against the Rootless to happen in order to build their rage against the gentry, I had to wonder at what kind of person was willing to make those kind of decisions. And I had to wonder at what kind of decision he was making now. David had seemed confident that Jack was done with the Empire, but that didn't mean he was done with fiercer tactics than diplomacy.

"Jamie heard something interesting," I said. "At the Public Hospital. It seems that some of the Rootless have decided to forgo changing the charges in the gentry houses. Do you know anything about this?"

Jack blinked, surprise washing over his face, but I couldn't discern if this was surprise that I'd heard of the plan or if it was genuinely the first he'd heard of it. "Madeline, I promise that won't happen, not on my watch." His voice was perfectly modulated to express earnestness and seriousness and just a trace of indignation.

I looked at David, who seemed to believe him. But I couldn't bring myself to take Jack at his word, not with everything that had happened this last week.

"Are you sure?" I said quietly. "Are you sure that some of your people wouldn't do it without your knowledge?"

"I'm not a god," Jack said. "It's possible that such a plan could be carried out without my knowing it, but that's the only way it would happen. If I knew of such a plan, I would stop it immediately—as much for our benefit as for the estate owners'. Leaving the charges in the houses—how long could we possibly expect to get away with a crime so easily traced back to us?"

"I agree," I said. And I let the matter rest, although a phantom of doubt still lingered.

Jack scratched at his jaw. "Another dead gentry heir—"

"Call Father home," I said, almost without meaning to. There was a moment between my suggestion and Jack's response where I considered taking it back.

But I didn't.

"Why," Jack asked calmly, "would I bring back the one person I intentionally removed from this city?"

David turned to look at me.

"Because, despite the fact that you are now the legal owner of Landry Park, he still wields the actual influence with the Uprisen. The gentry listen to the Uprisen; the Uprisen listen to him. Bring him back, make him see your side. Work together. With his support, you can tamp down the gentry suspicion and the possibility of violence."

"Work together?" Jack demanded. "What about our history would suggest that is even remotely possible?"

"What's the alternative? You risk letting your people be persecuted once again?"

A muscle around his eye twitched.

David's leg was bouncing now. I could feel it even as I sat on the arm of the chair. "Jack, she's right. What harm can come of trying?"

"Alexander will not be amenable to the idea. His pride is too great."

"Possibly. But can you claim that your own pride doesn't warrant a close examination as well?" I asked.

Jack glared at me. I stared back, unfazed. "Ask. The worst that can happen is that he says no. But if he says yes, you have a chance to defuse this situation before it explodes. *Please.*"

Jack was quiet for a moment. "I will think on it. I can't promise anything more than that for now."

I thought of Jamie's proposed radiation cure. If the Rootless had the real hope of healing and the end of their physical suffering, it would help, right? I opened my mouth, but something stopped me. Something about Jack, something about how fragile Jamie's idea still was, how yet unproven and possibly untenable. Would it do to raise everybody's hopes only to dash them once again if the much longed for cure turned out to be a failure? Jamie had asked for my silence for a reason.

I closed my mouth, and Jack stood and left.

After his footsteps faded away, David pulled me into his lap. It was unexpected and despite everything, despite Mark and the possible cure and the uneasiness that permeated the very atoms in the air, despite all that, I still could not stop myself from noticing how his eyes seemed to steal the color and life from everything around us.

"You're too clever sometimes," he said. "A clever girl stuck in a family of clever people. You'll all cut each other to pieces with your cleverness if you aren't careful."

"Do you think it's a good idea?" I asked. "About Father?"

He raised his eyebrows. "Are you actually asking for my approval?"

"Not in the slightest." And I meant it. "But I'm curious to know what you think."

He shrugged. "I think you're right—that it can't hurt to try. And I think that Jack will have to consider all his options if he has any hope of solving things without the Empire." At that last word, his face darkened. I knew he was thinking of the attack last November where he and Jude had beaten back the Easterners.

"I have to go back," he said abruptly.

My thoughts stuttered and scrambled, trying to follow the shift in conversation. "Go back where?"

"The army needs us—Jude and me. The Empire is moving again, Madeline. We have a job to do."

"Oh."

I had known that David had only been on a furlough, not home for good, but the reality of him returning to the mountains had seemed so distant and unreal. With him here, breathing and kissing and talking and touching, it seemed impossible that he could ever leave me.

"When?" I asked.

"We'll leave the last week of the month, the day after Lantern Day."

"The day after my birthday," I murmured. "I'll be eighteen."

He looked surprised as he tucked a stray lock of hair behind my ear. "I didn't realize."

I brought my hand to his, kissing the inside of his palm. "Now you know."

And please don't go, I wanted to add. But I didn't. I was stronger than that.

When Jack saw me at the dinner table that night, he made a study of his plate, focusing intently on the veal and the bacon-flecked spinach as if he'd never seen food before, and then excused himself quickly. I sensed he didn't want to talk about my father again, or at least not yet. But now that I had the idea in my mind, it was impossible to let go of it. Jack would never win the trust of the gentry—not even with me by his side. But perhaps he could win the trust of my father. Inside Alexander Landry was a man who had cared for his older brother with a deep and abiding love. Even politics could not stand in the way of that.

On my way up to my room, I ran into Cara coming out of the parlor, gin decanter in hand, wearing a loosely belted silk robe. I noticed her red eyes, her chafed nose, as if she'd been swiping at it with a handkerchief for hours. She'd been much closer to Mark and Marianne than I had, and I could tell Mark's death had been a horrible shock.

I opened my mouth to say something, anything, offer a word of comfort, but my tablet chimed, and Cara slipped past me as I fumbled with the screen, her fingers tight around the gin as she started up the stairs.

"Hello?" I answered, watching her as she retreated, wondering if I should go up to her later.

"Madeline." It was Philip Wilder, and his voice was low. "Some of us are meeting tomorrow. I want you to come."

"Who is *us*?"

"The children of the Uprisen. Tomorrow at Sai Thorpe's house. We've decided that we need to start taking action to protect ourselves."

I knew immediately what he was saying, where his mind was tending, but it still caught me by surprise. "Protect ourselves?" I asked, more to stall than to agree.

"Madeline. Haven't you noticed that all the victims are Uprisen heirs?"

"Of course, I've noticed," I murmured. I thought about his suggestion for a moment, weighing my response. Jack was currently not doing anything to reach out to the gentry, and somebody needed to keep the lines of communication with the Uprisen open. And if he wouldn't or couldn't, then it was left to me. I really didn't have a choice.

"I'll come," I said. "Of course I will."

"Good. Noon at Sai's."

I sat for a long moment after the call had ended, thinking about what Philip had said. I *had* realized that I could be in danger from the murderer: I had felt prickles of terror as I walked alone through the cavernous halls of my home, and I had panicked that night I found the chip in the ballroom window.

But Philip's call fanned the flames of fear even more. I thought of Smith as I left the room. Even now, he could be waiting and watching for me—or any other child of the Uprisen.

I climbed the stairs and went to the room that Cara and Ewan were sharing, a double-doored suite that used to belong to my grandmother. I rapped on the ivory wood until Cara opened it, smelling slightly of piney gin fumes.

"Ewan's not here," she said, and turned to go back inside the room. "He and his father went over to the east side of town."

"I wanted to talk to you," I said, coming in and closing the door. I saw her stuff a crumpled handkerchief in her pocket, as if she didn't want me to know that she'd been crying. I could respect that.

"Philip called," I said.

"What did that bore want?" she said, with forced lightness.

"He wants the Uprisen heirs to meet together at Sai Thorpe's house tomorrow. Everyone is afraid."

"So, what, we're all going to be afraid together in that decrepit Thorpe place? What's that going to help?"

"It's not about helping anything. It's about being together. And I think you should come."

"Why?"

"Because you also belong to the Uprisen. Because these people are our friends. And because two of our friends have already been killed."

Her throat caught.

"And whether or not you care about your inheritance, you are still legally the heir to Westoff Castle. You're in as much danger as the rest of us."

She sighed. "I'll think about it."

I stood. "We're leaving at eleven."

"I'll think about it."

TWELVE

Cara had called the Thorpe house decrepit and that wasn't quite right, but it was close. After the Last War, when homes and shops and schools were torn down so that the city could reorganize itself into a quilted patchwork of estates, the allies of Jacob Landry got to choose where they'd place their houses first as a kind of reward. The Glaizes built Glasshawke on a steep hill. The Osbournes chose a swath of treeless land laced with slender streams. And the Thorpes chose a dell near the fickle and frequently flooded Brush Creek.

The house Arjun Thorpe built seemed to welcome the shady dankness of the spot—a meandering concoction of stone towers and half-timbered halls, a fever dream of Gothic revival and Elizabethan England. According to all accounts, it started crumbling the moment it was finished and it had never stopped crumbling, meaning that more or less permanent scaffolding was always around the outside of the house, along with buckets of plaster and mortar and freshly cut stone. When Cara and I exited the car onto the cobbled drive, the amount of tangled ivy and overgrown bushes made it nearly impossible to find the front door.

The interior was not much better. Opulent furnishings and richly colored tapestries couldn't erase the gloomy stone walls and the pervasive smell of damp. A servant showed us into a long hall lined with antique weaponry, where a massive stone fireplace held a roaring fire and an iron chandelier did its valiant best to drive away the murk that clung to the corners of the room.

"This isn't a house, it's a theme park," Cara muttered. Part of me tended to agree, but then again, Westoff Castle wasn't the apex of restraint either.

Cara seemed better today, but a brittle fragility scratched at the edges of her words. I understood completely. Last night, I dreamed of Marianne's debut, of all the gentry heirs dancing and playing together while Jane and I had hovered on the periphery. Everyone had been alive, everyone fixed in their proper place in the glittering hierarchy of the gentry. When I'd woken and remembered, it had been like learning about their deaths all over again. I'd hugged my pillow and stared at the wall until the sun began peeking through the drapes and making diffuse lines across the floor.

Cara and I walked deeper into the hall. Several of the heirs were already at the table—Sai and Philip and Jane and—my muscles tensed—my horrible Lawrence cousins, Stuart, Tarleton, and Frank. A spread of meat and fish and wine had been laid on the table, and by my guess, the wine had been out a while, because the boys were gamesome and noisy, even Philip, who had sounded so serious on the phone. Although I couldn't help but notice the distance between Philip and the Lawrence boys. They'd always been close friends, but Philip kept his body angled toward Sai and Jane, and the brothers kept their conversation mostly among themselves.

Jane stood and gave my hand a gentle squeeze. "I'm pleased you're here. You too, Cara."

Cara, with incredible difficulty it seemed, managed a polite nod. I steered her to a chair before her veneer of etiquette cracked.

"Oh good!" Philip said. "I'm so glad you came. Hello, Cara."

"Philip," she said.

"I don't know if she should be here," Sai said.

We all turned to look at him.

He flushed. "It's just that—you know—she is dating a Rootless boy and all."

I could almost hear the wheels turning in Cara's brain as she processed this. She opened her mouth and I spoke first to head her off. "That Rootless boy is also my cousin, and you still invited me."

"Yeah, well, you can't help who your cousins are," Sai said.

Stuart smirked at me.

"But if you're choosing to be with the Rootless, then that means you're sympathetic in a different way." Seeing my expression, he hastened to add, "Not sympathetic *politically*, like you are, Madeline, but maybe sympathetic to all their methods, which we know you wouldn't be."

"Methods like murder," Philip added for clarification, although quietly. He didn't seem to have a problem with Cara being here.

"Stop dancing around it," Stuart said, shooting Philip a disgusted look. "We all know why we don't want Cara here."

"And why is that?" Cara said, emerald eyes sparking across the table. *Hard to believe these two were thick as thieves back at the Academy.*

"I think he's referring to, um, *intimacy*," Sai unhelpfully explained.

"Oh, so I'm unclean because I'm sleeping with Ewan?" Cara demanded, voice wavering with unspent emotion. "That is such bullshit. You can't catch radiation illness through physical contact, and even if you could, who cares, because it's us that gave them the sickness in the first place."

"I'm just glad I got to you first," Stuart said. "I wouldn't touch any slag who'd been with a diseased charge changer."

Cara stood so forcefully that she knocked the chair on the floor, and with some surprise, I realized that I'd gotten to my feet as well, cold anger pulsing slowly through me.

Cara's anger was all heat. "You know, sometimes I wondered if I would miss this. Miss you people. But you're worse than I remember."

"Cara," Sai said, "no one is trying to make you feel bad. But you have to see what consequences there are to loving that boy. . . ."

"That's exactly it. There shouldn't be consequences. I should be able to do what I want. I can't believe I came here thinking that we would actually talk about what happened to Marianne and Mark." She glowered at the gathered heirs. "You are afraid of all the wrong things. Which makes you weak. Worthless."

"Madeline, obviously I don't mean you," she said. I inclined my head in reply. "Or you, Jane," she added.

"Thank you," Jane replied serenely.

Cara gave the table a final look; scathing was nowhere near strong enough a word to describe the fire she bathed the fidgeting heirs in. She turned to leave. "I'll call for a car, Madeline, so no need to have Reeve drive me home." A glint of gold earrings, a swish of her fur coat, and she was gone.

Philip rubbed at his forehead. "Stuart, did you really have to say all that?"

"I'm only saying what we're all thinking," Stuart said.

"Enough," I said. "I don't care why you said it. It was wrong—wrong to think and wrong to say."

Jane was nodding next to me.

I heard my voice, heard how steady and reasoned it was despite the indignation that clawed at me inside. *Focus*, I reminded myself. *Save your anger for later*. For now, I would take this group in hand and do what we came to do—talk about the murders.

I sat. "So you think there's a pattern to the deaths?" I directed this at Philip, but it was Frank who answered.

"Of course there's a pattern," he snorted. "They were both Uprisen heirs, weren't they?"

"Not exactly," I said. "Marianne isn't—wasn't—the Wilder heir. Philip is."

People digested this.

"Except . . ." I mused out loud, "if Marianne was killed on the way to see Mark—Philip, weren't you originally going to go with her? Maybe the killer had planned to get you all along? And then made do with Marianne instead?"

"What does it matter?" Tarleton asked. "Heirs or second children, we're still being killed by the Rootless."

"It's not the Rootless who are doing this," I said. "It's *one person*. One deranged person."

"Maybe we should all avoid being near Landry Park," Philip said. "Since the two victims have been killed there."

"That's very true," I said. And then I didn't say any more for a moment, wandering through paint-splattered halls in my mind, halls filled with limp bodies, frozen bodies, bodies of people I knew.

"I think we all know what we need to do," Stuart said. "Have the police round up the Rootless. Force them to cooperate, beat the truth out of them. They know who the killer is."

"*No*," I said firmly, thinking of how David and Ewan had predicted that the police would do just that. I channeled every ounce of authority I could muster. "We're not letting that happen."

"But—"

"For now, we are going to do exactly as the constables advise: travel with other people, stay home if at all possible, and wait for them to do their job."

I had no idea how much power I actually held over these people—my father used to be the leader of the Uprisen, which meant that I would have inherited his role and at some point would have led the people in front of me. But that had always seemed very far away, after the deaths of our parents, far off in the future.

But my reasoning seemed to sway them. Everyone was murmuring assenting noises, except the Lawrence brothers.

"Don't cause any trouble," I warned them.

Stuart smiled. "And how exactly would you stop us, cousin dear?"

I passed the brick and stone police station on my way home, and I decided to stop in, thinking of my unproductive conversation with Smith. *Why don't you stop the constables?* he had demanded.

And those parting words from Stuart . . .

"Is Inspector Hernandez in?" I asked the navy-clad young man. He answered affirmatively and led me back to the warren of narrow offices. The man seemed familiar. I examined his face—I was good with faces, with details—but nothing came to mind. It was only when he raised his fist to rap on Hernandez's door that I saw the faded yellow bruises trailing from his jaw to his neck.

He had been at Liberty Park, I remembered with a flash. In the front, arms linked with other constables to keep the Rootless from overtaking the stage where my father had stood with the gibbet cage and the other Uprisen. I made a point to wait until he was completely gone until I spoke to the inspector.

"What can I help you with, Miss Landry?" There were bags under his eyes, and the room smelled of old coffee. He reminded me strongly of Jamie, surrounded by screens, nothing but his work and his exhaustion to keep him company.

"I just met with some of the other young gentry," I told him. "They are all very concerned that they will be targeted next by the killer."

"We are doing everything in our power—"

"I know you are," I assured him. "But I'm here to ask something different. I know you told my uncle and me that you would do everything you could to attempt to stop the police from attacking the Rootless at the gentry's behest."

Inspector Hernandez said slowly, "Yes."

"Then I would like your help in speaking to the chief of police."

It didn't take long to organize. Inspector Hernandez made

some calls, confirming that the chief was in and inquiring if he was available to see Madeline Landry of Landry Park. He was in and was available, and soon I found myself seated across from John Dewhurst. He was clearly as thoroughly gentry as I was, although not a firstborn child or he wouldn't have had to seek employment, however respectable and powerful.

"Miss Landry, how can I help you?" Chief Dewhurst asked pleasantly, although something edged underneath his polite charm. He was remembering Liberty Park and the role I played, no doubt, just as I was. He was remembering that my father was exiled, that an interloper was in charge of the estate.

"I'm here because I would like your word that nothing will happen to my uncle's people during this investigation." I tried to make my voice firm, authoritative as I had at Sai's house, but I felt so very aware of my lack of influence here.

He raised his bushy eyebrows. "Miss Landry, I can guarantee that the police will do everything in their power to keep this city and all of its inhabitants safe."

"I'm not certain that's true." I took him in—large waist, large mustache, heavy gold ring on his pinkie. I knew that men like my father and Arthur Lawrence kept Dewhurst flush in money in order to exert the maximum amount of influence, and I knew that as long as men like that were around, it would be difficult to persuade Dewhurst to act any differently.

But I had to try. I put on my best impression of Father and began, trying to channel the feeling of regality and conviction that he had always displayed so effectively. "Chief, Landry Park has always dictated the policy that the constables were to enforce. That hasn't changed. What has changed is that the estate is legally Stephen Landry's, and that the policy is no longer to use any sort of police presence or resources to harm or intimidate the Rootless."

"Is that so?" he asked, with a raise of his eyebrows.

I leaned forward, letting the truth burn away any pretense of subtlety. This was not a suggestion, this was a threat, and I wanted him to know it. "It *will* be so. Because this isn't only my uncle's wish, but mine as well, and you better believe that I will not rest until I see you removed from power if you at all stand in my way."

The chief's mouth opened and closed for a moment, as if he were at a loss for words.

Is this what being powerful feels like? No wonder my father enjoyed it so much. Then a wave of guilt surged through me. I shouldn't have this kind of power. No one should. A needle prick of a thought—or a fear—began to burrow in my mind. I ignored it.

"I trust that Landry Park will have your full cooperation," I said, gratified to hear how assertive I sounded, and gratified to see the chief nod.

And then I went home. Mark's funeral was that evening, and Cara was waiting for me to go.

THIRTEEN

THIRTEEN

Jack invited Father home. And Father accepted.

Two days later, a sleek black car rolled to the front of the drive, and I ran to the door to greet it. When my mother emerged, swathed in yellow wool and fox fur and her hair pinned up in chestnut swirls, I met her with a tight hug. It had only been a little over a week since I'd seen her last, but I'd missed her. I'd missed her complaining about my clothes and chattering about the latest gentry gossip. I'd missed her smell—ivy and sake and expensive makeup, although today the sake scent was absent. After smelling her addiction on her for so long, it was almost jarring not to. And when she let go of me to make sure that Father was able to get out of the car, I saw something different in her, something composed and suggesting substance and genuine kindness, as if throwing all of her energy into helping Father had transformed her.

She gazed at the entrance to Landry Park with shining eyes. "Home," she said. "Finally."

I went to help Father up the low stone steps, but he didn't need it, not really. He waved me away and used a cane to walk. When he stepped out of the crenellated shadows of the house, I caught a glimpse of his face, the thin tracework of scars now pale pink and white, visible but not horrifying. The improvement even in the last week was astounding; if I still had any doubts about Jamie's theories, they were laid to rest right then. Of course, if I could see it, then so would everybody else. The Landry invulnerability to radiation would not remain a secret for long.

I hugged him, too, and he hugged me back, just as tightly, dropping a light kiss on the top of my head.

"I'm glad you're back," I said, and heat pricked at my eyes.

"Me too," he said with warmth.

Jack was in the foyer when we came inside, along with a row of servants, who curtsied and bowed as my parents came in. There was a palpable air of relief at the arrival of my parents; many servants considered themselves well taken care of by the big houses, houses that represented security and steady wages. But shock flickered across all of their expressions at the sight of Father, of the face that barely resembled the raw and bloody visage they'd last seen. Jack showed no surprise at Father's appearance, however, his face impassive and his body language stiff and inscrutable. He had his cane with him, although it seemed more like a habit than a necessity since I never saw him lean on it anymore, and he nodded at Father's cane. "I suppose we match now."

"I suppose we do."

The cozy feeling of homecoming dissipated as quickly as

it had arrived, brushed aside as the two brothers faced each other for the first time since the riot that had left Father beaten and brutalized. A coldness blew between them, a coldness that snapped and cut, and they made no move to shake hands or step closer to each other.

"Perhaps we should get settled in," I suggested. "And then we can have an early dinner."

"Capital idea," Jack said, and spun on his heel to go back to his—and Father's—study.

"Well, he invited *us*, honestly," Mother said. "Why is he acting so put upon?"

"I imagine he was pressured into it by our daughter," Father said, glancing at me. "He is stubborn."

"So are you," I pointed out.

He made a noise.

"He's hoping that you can help him. Help us." I walked next to them as they crossed the foyer to the stairs. "I know the Uprisen will still listen to you."

Father gave me a sidelong glance. "And what exactly have you two scripted for me to say?"

I didn't take the bait. "The gentry are calling for Rootless blood. All we need is for you to call for peace and stability while the murder investigations are carried out. The Uprisen won't listen to Jack or me because we're too closely tied to the Rootless. But you—they will listen to you."

He gave me a nod to let me know that he'd taken in my

response, but it was not by any means a nod of compliance, and he kept walking. I let him, listening to the echoing tap of his cane on the marble and thinking that the conversation had not gone as badly as it could have. And that was something.

Dinner was as uncomfortable as could be imagined. Only my mother seemed to feel like talking, which she did in abundance while the brothers glared at each other over their glasses of wine. I realized that it had been longer than a month that she'd been exiled from her house—even before Liberty Park, she had suffered Christine Dana's constant presence, had shared a table with her husband's mistress. No wonder she seemed so happy now; she was home and, at least for a while, free from Christine.

I wondered how long that would last.

Eventually Cara and Ewan joined us. Cara was interested in all of the fashion and celebrity gossip that my mother wanted to talk about, and temporarily the dining room was filled with their meaningless chatter. I tried to join in every now and again, but it was difficult for me to feign interest in those sorts of things, and anyway, my mind was focused on how to get Father and Uncle Jack to work together.

"Madeline has been a great asset in advocating for the Rootless," Jack said pointedly. I chewed on the inside of my cheek. Rehashing my gentry defection over lamb with mint sauce was not going to endear Father into helping us.

Father's voice was chilly. "I see you have been very persuasive. I know that she insisted on leaving me and her mother in order to come back to you."

"It wasn't like that," I protested, flushing a little.

"Oh, wasn't it? You know, many people would be more than a little upset when their uncle maims their father. But perhaps I've been surpassed in your paternal admirations."

"Father," I said.

"Alexander, I've never known you to be jealous," Jack said.

"It's not about jealousy, Stephen." Father pronounced Jack's birth name with deliberate care, and Jack's jaw twitched. I noticed Father noticing that twitch, could see him marking that twitch away in his mental ledger. He'd gotten under Jack's skin.

The others at the table were now staring at their plates uncomfortably, all except for Ewan, who watched the sparring match as intently as I did.

"You're right," Jack remarked, recovering from his small reveal of emotion. "It's about possession. Admit it—you can't bear the idea that you no longer possess your offspring completely. She has listened to me and her thoughts and actions are no longer yours to claim."

I cleared my throat. I didn't particularly enjoy being talked about in the third person when I was *sitting right there*. "My thoughts are my own, actually."

"She will see through you eventually," Father said, ignoring me. "There's a reason this system has stood for two hundred years."

"And that reason is fear."

"Tell me," Father said, raising one eyebrow ever so slightly, "how much fear will the Empire bring? You've done your job in weakening our country, and now they are coming."

"I haven't spoken with them recently," Jack said, said like he was admitting something he didn't want to admit. "But they will not invade. They were only ever supporting us."

Father made a scoffing noise. "You always were so gullible."

"And you were always so arrogant."

"Am I truly the arrogant one? You sentenced me to torture—your own brother. You let them hold me down and feed me radioactive waste—"

"You were about to kill my son!" Jack exploded. "Did you really think I would let that go unpunished?"

"You gave up your right to dole out punishments long ago," Father said. "When you abandoned our family for those . . . *people*."

They stared at each other a moment, and then Jack threw his napkin down and left without another word.

"We should start planning the Lantern Day Ball," Mother announced at the breakfast table the next morning. There was a clinking as Jack set down his silver butter knife.

"Pardon?" His inquiry was polite, but the tension from last night still permeated the air, and I sat up straighter, poised to rescue my mother if necessary. Leave it to her to steer the conversation to planning a dance and inadvertently reignite a war.

Mother looked around the table. Sunlight dappled in prettily through the window, winking off the silver salvers and teapots. Cara looked barely awake, slumped in her chair, picking at a croissant drizzled with chocolate. Ewan and Charlie sat next to her, Charlie dispatching a quiche with startling voracity. As the silence went on, Ewan's and my eyes met. The corner of his mouth lifted at the same time as his shoulder, in a sort of *what can you do?* gesture.

It's funny, I thought. Our parents' contention would have driven Ewan and me further apart only a year ago. But now it seemed like we were both outside of it, as if the normal gentry and Rootless categories didn't quite fit us anymore.

Mother picked up her teacup. "Well, every year, Landry Park hosts the Lantern Day Ball. And it's coming up quickly— just a couple of weeks. We love hosting it because, of course, Lantern Day is also Madeline's birthday." Mother beamed at me.

"I'm afraid that's not going to be possible this year," Jack said.

"Why ever not?"

"Olivia," Jack said, in the tone one might use with a child. "Lantern Day celebrates the end of the Last War and the defeat of the Rootless. Do you really think my people would welcome seeing it celebrated again?"

Mother sputtered. "It's nothing *political*, it's only a chance for a party."

"That's how you see it," Ewan said. His voice was confident, definitive. Maybe he was closer to his father than I thought. "But that's not how we see it."

"And how will the gentry see it if the Rootless begin obliterating centuries of tradition?" Father asked. It was the first time he had spoken that morning, save for a few short words to the servants who moved in and out, bringing fresh food and bringing up the day's news on the wall screen. "In reality, Lantern Day is as far removed from its origin as any other holiday. It's a community gathering, an opportunity to be grateful to live in a time of peace."

"A peace that our ancestors won after starting a war to make money. A peace that was won with the blood of my people."

"How could they ever be your people?" Father asked. "Given where you came from, your lineage and education . . . how could you ever consider yourself part of them?"

"That's not something I would expect you to understand," Jack said frostily. "I never expected it. You are so set in your ways that you can't imagine any other life—all of the gentry are, but you most of all. Narrow-minded. Vindictive."

"And you are volatile and dangerous," Father returned, just as coldly. "Do not think that I'm alone in carrying our father's worst traits. There is just as much of him in you as there is in me."

I knew very little about my grandfather, except that he had a reputation for being exceptionally vicious to the Rootless and to my grandmother. But this insult seemed to lodge itself deeply in Jack, and instead of anger, an old, bitter pain flashed across his face. I took note of this, filing away this mutual pain between the brothers. It was a shared point—a very dark shared point, to be sure—but it was something.

Jack and Father said no more, and we drank our tea in silence.

That night, David and Jude invited Cara, Ewan, and me to the penthouse; they also invited Jamie, who declined, his voice ragged but determined. I decided to stop in to see him soon— perhaps tomorrow. Jude and I played chess while David picked at the piano and Cara tried to teach Ewan a gentry card game, which was immensely frustrating to him. Every now and again, I'd hear a loud, frustrated groan and several cards would go flying in the air, to Cara's great amusement.

David had refused to play chess with Jude because he was too good, but chess was a game I'd grown up playing with Father almost nightly, and so I welcomed the challenge.

"Not bad," Jude said as I captured his rook.

"Not bad yourself," I said, plucking the silver piece off the chessboard. I didn't want to let him know what a challenge he was to play, but he really was a formidable opponent, always thinking two or three steps ahead and covering every contingency. His only weakness was that he was unwilling to contemplate any loss. He wanted to save all of his pieces, and so he was extremely reluctant to sacrifice anything, no matter how strategically. I pretended I didn't notice this as I began building a trap for his queen, feeding him pawns and even a knight to lure him closer.

"Are you excited to be going back to the mountains?" I asked, hoping to distract him from my ploy.

Lonesome piano notes drifted across the room as Jude thought, his fingers caressing the silver queen. "I am excited to see my men again. I'm excited to focus once again on stopping the Empire, on one day reclaiming our land."

"Do you think that could ever really happen?"

"If we are strong enough, united enough. We need a leader—a real leader—not a president like we have now, content to do whatever the Uprisen tells him to do. We need someone strong. Like you."

"You're teasing me."

"I never tease." His voice was serious. "I know most Landrys are content to stay in the shadows, to advise rather than to lead. But can't you see yourself doing more?"

I could. As shy as I was sometimes, as introverted and quiet, sometimes I felt like if I could simply have control over things, just for a week, then I could set everything right. And who knew? If Jack and the Rootless had their way, universal suffrage would mean that once again it was the president who was really in control of the government, not the Uprisen. But could the people ever trust a Landry again? Could I ever trust myself with that kind of power?

"What about you?" I asked. He took my pawn, and I pretended to be frustrated at the number of glass pieces lining his side of the board. "You look the part, you're a national hero. You're ambitious. Why not?"

He smiled at me. "Why not indeed?"

I slid a bishop behind my screen of pawns. Jude narrowed his eyes but began angling himself toward the potential threat. "I am afraid I'm going to win this game," he said. He did almost seem sorry about it, too.

"Mm," I said. And then I pounced, using my second bishop to swipe his queen. Two more moves and I had his king surrounded.

Jude sighed. "I suppose I deserve that for anticipating my victory."

"No victory comes without sacrifice," I told him, reclaiming my captured pieces. "A soldier should know that."

"A soldier should. But not a captain. Each and every life is valuable. And if you don't believe that, you run the risk of killing men needlessly."

I held a pawn in my hand, rolling it back and forth, closing my fingers around it as that needle prick of a thought came back. A thought of sacrifice. "It's not always lives that have to be sacrificed. Sometimes it's a thing. Or a place."

"Perhaps. But what if you had sacrificed all those pieces and still hadn't won? What then? How would you justify that strategy to yourself? To someone else?"

Jude's thoughts were in the mountains, I knew. And instead of chess pieces, he saw his men. Brave boys, some enlisted from the middle class, some commissioned second or third sons of the gentry. But I was seeing a much bigger chessboard than the mountains—I was seeing the country, with the Rootless on one side and the gentry on another.

No, I thought. *That's exactly the wrong kind of thinking.* We weren't playing against each other at all. We were in this together.

Another burst of playing cards filled the air and Ewan loudly declared that he wasn't going to play any longer and switched on the wall screen. David had started playing Tchaikovsky, *Swan Lake* this time, but the music stuttered to a stop as we all saw what was on the wall screen.

"Holy hell," Cara whispered.

Hell indeed. The news showed a riot in the Rootless ghetto—constables dragging people out of their homes, Rootless children crying, masked men and women throwing stones and bottles at the police. The ragged haze of tear gas filtered in everywhere, and the orange of a small fire backlit the scene.

"Several arrests have been made," the reporter droned over the devastation. "The chief assures the press that the arrests are only temporary, to gather information about the murders of Marianne Wilder and Mark Everly earlier this week."

Of course, I thought. *Of course.* Dewhurst never had any intention of listening to me. He was cut from the same cloth as Arthur Lawrence and Harry Westoff and—it pained me to think—my father. Frustration and worse—humiliation—flooded through me. I had thought myself so influential, but in the end, I'd accomplished nothing.

Ewan was furious. "Those lying gentry bastards." Cara reached out to touch him, but he shook her off. "There will never be any change as long as the constables are controlled by the gentry. As long as there *are* gentry." He stood abruptly and walked to the door.

"Ewan," Cara said. "Stay."

"She's right," Jude said. He stood too and laid a gentle hand on Ewan's shoulder. "Take a moment to cool off before you do anything rash."

"And what would you know of it?" Ewan asked, shaking off Jude's touch.

"I've actually been in battle," Jude said. "I've seen people die in violence. People I was supposed to protect. I promise you: I understand."

"Then you'll understand that I have to go." And Ewan pushed by him and went to the elevator. We watched him go.

The tension in the room slowly dissipated after he left, cooling from a fever pitch to a dull thrum of anxiety.

"What will this mean?" Cara asked. "For Jack and your dad and the stuff they wanted to work on?"

We didn't answer her. Jude, David, and I stayed silent. Because we all knew it meant nothing good.

FOURTEEN

Instead of returning to Landry Park, I had my driver take me to the Rootless ghetto. I didn't know what I hoped to accomplish, I didn't know how I could help, but it seemed unthinkable to go straight home after seeing the flames and the brutality. Raids had never been uncommon and neither had unjustified arrests, but this—this burning and breaking and beating—this was a new breed of persecution entirely.

Reeve rolled close to the gates, but the entrance was blocked by fire engines and police cars. "Stop here," I told him, and climbed out, the wind twisting its icy fingers into my wool coat as soon as I was clear of the car.

"Miss," a constable approached me as I walked in between the police cars. "You can't be here."

The hell I can't, I wanted to tell him, but I kept my tone polite. "I saw the raid on the news. I wanted to see if anyone needed help."

The constable opened his mouth, but then I heard my name carried over the wind. I looked over to see Jack coming toward me in even, quick strides. The constables eyed him as he passed, unsure of what to make of this man who radiated authority, who carried the name they had been trained to respect and obey, but who was so diametrically opposed to gentry interests.

"Go home, Madeline," Jack said when he reached me. "The constables are insisting on interrogating every person here before they leave, but the immediate danger has passed for now."

"But I can help!"

"With what? Standing in line, waiting to be questioned?" He didn't give me a chance to reply. "I am here, I will make sure no further violent action is taken. Get some rest, because tomorrow we'll have much work to do."

"I won't leave," I insisted. "I can get blankets or warm drinks or maybe we could have Father come and talk to the constables—"

"Do you believe that he would?"

Did I truly believe that Alexander Landry would come to the Rootless ghetto in person and dissuade the police from doing the same thing he had ordered them to do a year ago?

I gave my head a small shake. I wished I could answer yes, but I couldn't. Not yet.

But I also refused to give up hope that I could change his mind.

Jack angled his body between the constable and me and dropped his voice. "Look, the situation here is tense. My people are barely willing to listen to me at the moment—they think that somehow I was involved with this raid. At the very least, they think since I'm not living among them any longer that I've forgotten them. I'm doing my best to convince them that I still care, but it is difficult. Do you see why having my thoroughly gentry, thoroughly Landry niece floating around would be problematic?"

"But if they see me helping—"

He sighed, face softening. "I know. But there are some who don't want gentry help, any gentry help at all. They would rather die than accept a cup of hot tea from a daughter of the Uprisen. Do you understand?"

Smith. I knew he must mean Smith. Somehow it always came back to him, his violence, his refusal to compromise. I couldn't believe that anyone was willing to listen to him. But people had been willing to listen to my father. Maybe people just clung to strength and obstinacy, no matter how outrageous it actually was.

Jack clapped a hand on my shoulder and then went back to the gates. I surveyed the scene one last time—the still-flickering flames, the Cherenkov lanterns glinting off the icy road, the crowds of Rootless huddled against the cold, some sobbing, some sullen, some yelling and shoving at the constables who tried to herd them back into line.

I got back in the car, my eyes stinging from the wind and the residual gas and the smoke, feeling helpless and alone. David messaged me in the car, asking if I was home yet—I hadn't told him about my spontaneous detour to the east side of town—and I didn't plan to now. I'd answer later, when I got home.

I normally didn't mind his concern for my safety—I understood it was well intentioned. But at the moment, it made me feel more powerless than protected. And there was already too much making me feel powerless tonight. But Jack had been right—my presence would have sunk his credibility just as he was trying to rebuild it. Tonight, he seemed so much more like the Jack I'd met last year—open and reasonable and frank. A born leader.

A man who could be trusted.

I couldn't sleep that night. I couldn't even manage to sink into a wakeful doze. I got up and paced and paced and paced until I could measure the exact dimensions of my room in footsteps, and then, when the sky darkened and blued, signaling dawn would be coming soon, I decided to go downstairs to the library and find something to read.

I stopped on the last step when I heard voices coming down the hall—Jack's deep voice and another one that wasn't immediately familiar. The police must have been finished with their interrogations if he was home again.

I debated going back upstairs or continuing on my way—I

wanted to hear about the rest of the night in the ghetto—but something about the conversation seemed private, not meant to be heard. I peeked my head around the corner and saw that Jack stood outside of his study, holding the door open. Glancing down the hallway as if to check if anyone were watching, a figure stepped inside. When he looked my way, the light of the Cherenkov lanterns fell on his face.

It was Smith.

Jack also looked up and down the hallway, and I leaned back, holding my breath for a second. It was dim and the hallway was lined with statues and busts that threw strange shadows along the walls, but I couldn't risk being seen. I had to know why Smith was here.

My uncle followed Smith inside and closed the door. I crept down the last stair and into the hallway and then pressed my ear against the study door, taking care to swaddle myself in shadow in case Jack consulted the estate's camera feeds. But even with my ear against it, the door was virtually soundproof. I tried along the seams and the door handle with little improvement. I could only hear the low susurrus of voices . . . none of the individual words.

A toe nudged my thigh. Cara stood behind me, her head tilted to the side. "What are you doing?" she asked.

"What are *you* doing?" I whispered. Cara was never up at this hour.

"Ewan is still out in the ghetto. I wasn't interested in sleeping." Her voice carried, unnaturally loud in the marble-and-wood-bounded corridor.

"*Shh,*" I mouthed.

"Why?" she said irritably.

Was it me or did it suddenly seem quieter? Like the barely discernible conversation had paused? I stood, grabbed Cara's hand, and pulled her into the morning room, only one door down from the study. I heard the study door open, as if someone were checking the hallway, and then I heard Jack say, "It was probably just a servant," as it clicked closed.

I thought for a minute. I desperately wanted to hear what Smith was saying to Jack. I wanted to know about tonight, about the divisions within the Rootless, what he was planning, and just as importantly, if Jack knew, like I did, that Smith was the killer. If Jack was covering for him.

Cara was pulling on my nightgown. I brushed her off. "Stop. I'm trying to think," I whispered. The door was a failure, but maybe the window outside? *Too cold.* And rustling through the frozen bushes would surely draw attention.

Cara pinched my arm. I barely managed to stifle a yelp. "Ouch!" I hissed. "What?"

She pointed up to the grate. "Does this room share a duct with the study?"

I stared at her for a minute, then glanced up at the vent, placed high on the wall. I mentally accessed a floor plan of

Landry Park—there was nothing between the two rooms that I knew of—no hidden staircases or cupboards.

"Yes," I said, not bothering to hide my excitement. "You're a genius."

"Obviously," she said.

We carried a leather bench over to the wall and stood there together—me on my tiptoes—listening for snatches of the conversation as they drifted through the duct.

"... too dangerous," Jack was saying. "I won't let you risk it."

"It's for *us*," Smith said passionately. "For *our people*. The reward outweighs the risk, wouldn't you agree?"

A pause. "I can't justify calling such an end a *reward*. This plan has always left a rancid taste in my mouth. That's why I can't agree to it. I appreciate you coming to me, asking for my help. But in the end, it will only hurt the cause more than it will help. It could hurt our people, Robert."

"Our people," Smith spat. "They're starting to see you for what you are, you know. They know where your true sympathies lie."

"Thankfully there are some who are still willing to listen to reason." Jack's voice was unreadable.

I heard footsteps, as if someone was pacing agitatedly. "Reason? How about justice? How about equality? How can you not see that this is the best way to bring down the gentry, to make them hurt?"

I sucked in a breath. Was he really talking about what I thought he was?

"It's not enough that Alexander Landry is a hundred miles from here; his entire way of life needs to be torn apart and burned," he continued, and I waited for that moment when Jack would reveal that Father wasn't a hundred miles away, but only a hundred yards away, here at Landry Park.

But he didn't. I didn't know if it was to shield Father or to shield his own reputation, but he didn't respond at all, which clearly goaded Smith.

"You're getting weak," Smith accused, footsteps still echoing through the grate. "You never wavered until you moved back into this . . . this . . . palace." He could barely get the word out, it was so filled with hate. "All this fine living—heaps of food and silk sheets—it's making you soft. Turning you into a gentry again."

"Don't question my loyalty," Jack said, and for a moment, he sounded every bit a Landry—emotionless and ruthless and certain.

"Then don't give me reason to," Smith replied. "Stay the course. We are so close." Here his voice dropped lower. I couldn't make out anything he said.

"It *would* be an opportunity," Jack admitted, his voice also quieter but still audible.

"So let us take it," Smith hissed. "You won't have to get your precious hands dirty if you don't want to. Leave it to me."

There was a long silence. "I will think on it."

I could practically hear Smith roll his eyes. "Stop thinking and decide. Back in the ghetto, we don't have the luxury of time."

"The gentry don't have it, either, if you plan to leave the charges in their estates without changing them."

"The charges should begin to expire in about two weeks," Smith said, pride in his voice.

So the rumors Jamie had heard were true. The gentry were living in houses that were possibly no longer safe, or at least wouldn't be safe for long. And Jack had lied to me—he did know about this plan. A quick burst of fury rolled through me, boiling, refusing to die down to a simmer. Chief Dewhurst lying was one thing. But my own uncle . . .

"I told you that was a dangerous plan," Jack said, sounding angry now. "The risk it would incur—"

And then the furnace kicked on, sending a waft of hot air through the grate, masking the words from the study and making it impossible to hear any more of their conversation. Cara and I looked at each other.

"I can't believe it," Cara said incredulously. She hopped off the bench, landing easily on her bare feet. I could see her bright pink toenails even in the near darkness.

"I know." But in a way, I was relieved.

I had been right.

Cara left me without saying good-bye and I trailed after her, making sure to stay in the shadows as I walked back to the stairs and up to my room, not wanting to risk being seen by Jack or Smith or the security feeds that Jack checked every morning.

I settled myself in bed, chewing on my lip as I stared at the lightening sky outside.

Jamie's rumor was correct. The Rootless were ceasing to change the charges, without telling the gentry.

I was torn. I didn't want them to change the charges any longer, but stopping without telling anybody was unbelievably cruel. People would get hurt.

It depends on how long they're left, I reassured myself. The charges would stop working after two weeks, and then the gentry would know for sure that they were living with expired charges. And short-term exposure could be easily mitigated with medical treatment—it had nowhere near the impact of long-term radiation poisoning.

But still, the thought of the gentry slowly sickening, of the houses full of statues and tapestries and gowns filling with poison, it gave me chills.

No. I would not let that happen.

Inspector Hernandez saved me the trouble of going to the station. As Mother and I sat drinking tea the next day, Crawford announced that he'd come by for a visit. I offered him tea and he shared a cup with us, and then Mother excused herself to check on Father. I decided to use the opportunity to detail last night's reconnaissance to the detective. I explained what I had heard about Smith's plans to make the gentry suffer, but when I got to the part about the charges, I faltered, thinking of yesterday's violence. I did trust the inspector, but he'd have to alert his superiors, who would alert the Uprisen. And the Uprisen's response would be all too predictable.

I took a sip of tea, now lukewarm, as I weighed it in my mind—poisoned gentry versus abused Rootless. The gentry had two weeks left. The Rootless would be persecuted almost instantly. If I could convince the Rootless to listen to me or even just let them know that their plan was no longer secret, I could stop it without anyone being hurt.

I swallowed my tea and smiled. "That's all," I concluded. "That's all I heard."

The inspector nodded as he looked over the notes he'd been taking on his tablet. "I can't say that I haven't suspected something like this. We'll be keeping a close eye on Smith and any of his known associates from here on out."

"That's all?" I said, unable to keep the disappointment from my voice.

"Without hard evidence, it's difficult to do more," he said kindly. "So far, we've been unable to extract any conclusive forensic information from the scenes. We did find the source of the paint, however. York House two streets over was having its south-facing doors repainted, and the workers reported a can of paint missing to the estate's butler the day after Marianne's death. The paint's a match."

"So the paint was stolen, not bought," I said, thinking of Smith.

"Correct. But the surveillance videos from the estate—which are admittedly limited in their scope—don't show anyone approaching from the back or the sides of the grounds, as you might imagine a thief would. The only way they could have gotten to the work site would have been through the house itself, and the house was filled with guests for a luncheon that day, so it wouldn't have been easy."

I felt a flicker of agreement at that; no gentry house would be impervious to a stranger, and a Rootless stranger at that, simply strolling through it, not with servants running to and fro and gentry guests drinking and chatting. It was hard to imagine Smith going unnoticed.

But the Rootless did know all of the side doors and cellar entrances and basement tunnels of the gentry houses, all the necessary paths for slipping into the charge stations and then exiting without being seen, without bothering the gentry with the reminder of their existence. If anyone could sneak through a gentry house unnoticed, it probably would be a Rootless.

Inspector Hernandez moved on, still looking at his tablet screen. "We are assuming that the killer is male, given that the bodies were handled and moved without being dragged. And we know that he's fairly new to the business of killing—the two nonlethal head wounds to Mr. Everly seem to show that the killer attempted to bludgeon him before resorting to strangulation.

"But other than that, we really don't know much. Since you didn't actually hear Smith confess explicitly to any of the murders, your testimony would be helpful to shore up an otherwise strong case, but unless circumstances change drastically, I don't feel comfortable making an arrest based on that alone. For now, all we can do is wait and watch, and hope something new comes into the fore."

I closed my eyes a moment, digesting this information.

"I understand," I said. "I admire your dedication to following the letter of the law." And I meant it, despite my disappointment that nothing would be done about Smith at the moment.

"The city would be a better place if all of the constables felt the same way," he said.

I agreed and offered him more tea, which he refused, and then he left, asking me to give my regards to my uncle and father. I tried to think of what to do next. If the real killer was arrested, if the tension between the two factions eased, then the problem of the charges could be dealt with—the houses converted to wind or solar power or a payment schedule or *something*.

I could do that in two weeks. Right?

FIFTEEN

"You have to talk to the Uprisen," I said. "Today."

"I have to do no such thing," Father said, looking up from the book he was reading. The morning light made the library a patchwork of shadow and sunshine, but he didn't squint or flinch as he looked up at me. He closed his book with a sigh after it became clear that I wasn't going to leave. And I wasn't. I had come straight to Father after Inspector Hernandez left the house, determined to find a way to set things right.

I started again. "Last night was—"

"Last night was not so aberrant if you consider the circumstances," he said coolly. "I don't see the need to condemn the natural response to two wholly unnatural crimes."

I sat in the chair next to him. We could continue like this—arguing without any intention of revising our preconceptions, him interrupting me, me being resentful of being interrupted, getting nowhere.

But I didn't want to. I had spent last night awake and worried, I had spent this morning feeling the futility of my scanty testimony about Smith, and I had no desire to fight. Instead, I reached out to take his hand, wrapping my fingers around his pinkie like I used to do when I was a little girl.

"I understand why you're angry at the Rootless. I understand why the gentry are afraid, and I understand that the constables are afraid, too. This is the only way they've ever known how to act, the only way they've ever even thought of acting. And their fear has a very real basis now—two gentry heirs are dead." I paused, collecting my thoughts for a moment, trying to decide how I wanted to phrase what I was going to say next. "But I also understand why the Rootless are afraid. Why they're angry. Their rations, their homes, their freedom are constantly subject to the gentry's whims, and it doesn't matter how unfair it is, how unethical it is—they have no recourse. None at all. And even if they manage to escape all of those other horrors—unlikely as that is—they will still die young and in agony. Can't you understand why they would feel nothing but resentment and hatred? We *made* them feel that way."

Father regarded me with unreadable eyes. "This is the set order of our world. These people came from those who fought against our ancestors, Madeline. People who would rather carry signs and chant than find proper employment." His voice echoed throughout the library. "The Rootless are where they are because they came from a band of shiftless degenerates."

"If people carry the sins of their fathers, what about you? What about your father? What sins are you responsible for?"

There was a chink in that steely gaze, a flicker of pain and then one of doubt. I let go of his finger, and he let me, his gaze sliding off my face and onto the floor.

"Think about it," I urged, and then I left the library.

Hours later, as the light was fading into the watered-down gray of late afternoon, he found me in the parlor—reading while Charlie steadily maddened his tutor with his inability to sit still. Father said nothing, simply stood in the doorway, but he was in a coat, scarf, and gloves, and I knew that he was going out.

"Are you coming?" he asked.

He didn't need to explain any further. I was already standing and gathering my things, and I was bundled in soft wool and silk and ready to leave in a matter of moments. Father directed Reeve to drive us to Westoff Castle, where some of the Uprisen were dining together tonight.

Father remained silent during the drive, and I knew that this trip was a concession born out of extreme reluctance and doubt, a concession wrenched from him by the painful memory of his own father. I also recognized that he felt somewhat manipulated by me, and that there was a new element of grudging respect between us, evident in the aloof but not hostile way he glanced at me.

Our arrival was unexpected, but the butler showed us into the mauve and gold parlor anyway, where my uncle Lawrence, Mr. Glaize, and Elizabeth Osbourne—Jane Osbourne's mother—sat with Harry Westoff.

"Alexander!" Mr. Westoff leaped to his feet and came over to shake Father's hand. "Good Lord, man, I had no idea you were back in Kansas City. Please, have a seat. Let me ring for a drink and maybe a cigar? No? A drink, at least, then."

A vague look of distaste flitted across Mr. Westoff's features when he saw me, but he didn't remark upon my presence. I found a place to sit next to Mrs. Osbourne, whom I'd always liked and respected.

"I can't stay long," Father said, easing himself into a chair with a stiffness that betrayed his lingering pain. He and my uncle Lawrence exchanged a nod. "But last night's events compelled me to come here. Thank you." This last was to a servant, a young footman who presented Father with a drink on a gleaming tray. The servant bowed and made to leave, but not before his eyes swept the room in a way that made me uncomfortable. Like he was cataloging everything and everyone in it.

"Tell us," Uncle Lawrence said, "how you came to be back at Landry Park. Did you find a way to push your brother out? Is he no longer a threat to us?"

Ah. They don't know that Jack brought Father here to help him. And Father didn't seem eager to disabuse them of that notion. "No, gentlemen," he said. "My brother and I are staying at the estate together."

Uncle Lawrence's mouth pulled down at the corners. "I'm sorry to hear that. That must be miserable for you."

"You have no idea," Father replied.

"I think it's nice," Mrs. Osbourne said from next to me. "If you two can put aside your differences and live together, then surely there is hope for the rest of the city."

There was a moment where the others looked studiously away, not meeting her eyes, save for Uncle Lawrence, who fixed her with a cold stare. But she didn't seem bothered by this; a resolve settled in her features. "And you will recall how I feel about the two factions living together. You know I also warned you against your actions at Liberty Park, Mr. Landry, though you didn't listen then."

Father's face remained calm and implacable, but I could see that he didn't like to be reminded of his mistakes. "You were—and are—correct, Mrs. Osbourne," he said, inclining his head toward her. "This is actually what has prompted my visit, this re-evaluation of our methods with the Rootless. Last night's raid at the ghetto seemed unnecessarily provoking. With a killer on the loose, don't you feel that was unwise?"

"Not if such a tactic catches the killer," Mr. Wilder said viciously. "He's here, in this city, still living while my daughter is dead. And you—and *you*"—he indicated Elizabeth Osbourne with a jab of the finger—"better believe I will do anything to find him and punish him."

"Even if innocent people get hurt?" I asked softly. "Is that what Marianne would have wanted?"

"She can't want anything now. She's dead, and some Rootless bastard took her from me." Tears shone in his eyes. "And I don't care how many arrests it takes or how many shanties are destroyed. *I will find him.*"

"It's not pragmatic to inculcate a cycle of violence at this point," Father asserted. "I sympathize with your pain, Mr. Wilder, I do. But I also worry about the ripples these arrests and beatings will create. Do you think if you haven't caught the killer yet that he will be dissuaded from his agenda by all this? Do you think that he's sufficiently frightened of the gentry now? That he will cease from killing more teenagers?"

He answered his own question, "Of course not. The murders themselves are proof enough that he doesn't fear us, that he hates us, and actions like last night's will only fuel him further."

The servant returned with a tea tray. The group ignored him, but refrained from speaking until the parlor door had closed behind him.

"Alexander," Harry Westoff said after the pause, "it's not like you to be so . . . conciliatory."

"Or passive," Mr. Wilder added bitterly. "Inert."

"They mean to say that you're acting *weak*, Alexander," Uncle Lawrence said, baring his teeth in something that passed for a smile.

Father smiled back at my uncle. I could feel the unseen sparks flashing between them as they stared at each other. "There's nothing weak about steering the gentry to survival, Arthur. Or perhaps you'd rather the rage-driven Rootless murder us all?"

"They must be taught a lesson!" Uncle Lawrence growled, thumping his walking stick on the thick rug for emphasis. "They have forgotten the natural order—no thanks to your incompetence and your shameful brother—and order must be restored! At any cost!"

Father was never one to waste time arguing or talking when he felt it wasn't in his best interest. He stood. I did as well.

"Let it be known that I counseled reason," he told them. "Let it be recorded that I tried to sway you all away from further death. And it's not because I've gone soft on the Rootless," he said, forestalling what had surely been on the tip of Uncle Lawrence's tongue. "But because I have no wish to see gentry heirs being murdered. Let's go, Madeline."

And go we did, the cloud of Uprisen anger following us as we went. I only looked back once, to give a nod to Mrs. Osbourne, who waved back at me with long and elegant fingers. Her, at least, we could count as an ally.

The rest of the evening at home passed without a single comment from Father about what had transpired at Westoff Castle.

I watched him carefully for signs of irritation or frustration or even confusion—it couldn't have been easy to argue with his peers, the closest people he had to friends, after all. But his face and body language betrayed nothing, nothing except for the same impassivity that he always wore.

I myself felt discouraged by the encounter, by how quickly and decisively the Uprisen there had dismissed any leniency or change in direction. They were as obstinate as ever, perhaps even more so, with outrage and grief fueling them.

At least Elizabeth Osbourne seemed amenable to peace, I told myself, and that was a small comfort.

Going up to my room to prepare for bed, I was met on the stairs by Ewan, who spoke quietly to keep his voice from carrying. "Did your father go to meet the Uprisen today?"

"Some of them, yes," I responded. "Like Jack and I had planned. He went to convince them to stop the violence against the Rootless."

Ewan ran a hand over his mouth—a thick ginger beard was filling in the contours of his face, making him look wilder than normal. "There's a Rootless informant at Westoff Castle. A footman. He saw you two at the Castle and alerted the Rootless."

I knew there had been something unsettling about that servant. "Did he tell them what Father said to the other Uprisen? That he wanted the raids and arrests to stop?"

Ewan shook his head. "I don't think he heard that much.

But he told the Rootless that Alexander Landry was back in town and once again conspiring with the Uprisen. Word has already spread among the community. Smith and some others—they're calling for your father's blood once again."

I let out a breath. "And Smith will have figured out that Jack concealed Father's return. This isn't good."

"Just be careful, okay?" Ewan advised. "Your father, too. At least for a couple of days. Smith's anger may burn itself out with all the other things going on, but I wouldn't count on it."

Neither would I.

The sound of shattering glass jarred the household awake late that night, sending Morgana tearing from my bed and adrenaline flooding through me. I rushed into the hallway, not bothering to find slippers or a robe, wincing at the flood of blue light as Ewan appeared with a Cherenkov lantern.

There was a muffled *boom*, low and contained, and then a scream. It came from Father's room.

Ewan ran down the hallway and I followed him, and we pushed open the door, releasing a wave of choking smoke. I brought my nightgown up over my face and went inside the room, futilely trying to wave away the smoke. The light from the Cherenkov lantern was swallowed up immediately, but I could hear coughing and followed the noise to my parents' bed, where I found Father trying to help Mother up. I wrapped my arm around her waist and together we managed to steer her out of the room and into the hallway.

Ewan reemerged from the smoke with the lantern, and in the blue light, I could see a thin trickle of blood tracing its way down my mother's forehead. My heart flipped over for a minute, until my mind caught up and I could see that she was alert and steady, that the wound appeared very small.

"What happened?" I asked.

"Later," Father said. "We need to get your mother some help. We'll go downstairs and call a doctor before we do anything else." He guided Mother to the staircase.

Ewan looked grim as he watched them go. "It looks like a homemade bomb." He rubbed at his forehead. "Like the kind I used to make when I ran with Smith's crowd. Not a lot of shrapnel— they're more about making noise than hurting someone."

"Hurting someone? Well, we can't have that," I said bitterly.

"I had no idea Smith would act so quickly," Ewan said, almost sounding defensive. "But the news that your father was once again meeting with the Uprisen must have been too much, especially after the raid." I could tell from his voice that a part of him empathized with Smith's anger, even if he didn't entirely condone its expression.

"My mother was in there," I told him, not caring that a shaking passion was creeping into my words. "And what if they'd gotten the wrong window? Or what if Jack had been sleeping in my father's old rooms?"

Ewan started back toward his room, then stopped and looked at me. "You still don't get it. Anyone living in this house, anyone with the last name Landry is the enemy to my people."

"And does that include you?"

The wisping smoke and blue light made it impossible to tell if his face was troubled or resigned. "Maybe."

Dinner was even more tense than it had been two nights ago. Even David, who'd been a constant at Landry Park, more watchful than a guard dog, had begged off before the meal, not eager to sit down between my father and my uncle after the bombing.

"Maybe we should lock the two of them in here and the rest of us can eat somewhere else," Ewan had suggested as we walked into the dining room. "I'm tired of our fathers having the same fight over and over again. I'm ready for action."

It sounded like something Smith would say. "Action like throwing a bomb through a window?"

Ewan glanced over at me. "I may be a Landry now," he said. "But I'm not Landry enough that I'm ready to hurt people on purpose."

I ignored the dig.

Someone had the idea of playing music on the wall screen while we ate, and so graceful violin strings floated through the room, covering over the awkward silences. We all seemed to be ignoring one another, even my mother, who was normally very talkative. A small white bandage peeked out of her hair, a reminder of last night's fireworks. The constables had come, yet again, and questioned my parents, had taken the twisted smoking remains of the bomb, but all the components were easily sourced and the construction was amateurish. The bomb could have been made by literally anyone, although even Jack had to admit that it looked like a Rootless response to my father's return. We now had constant police patrols roaming the perimeter of the grounds, which at the very least alleviated David's fears for my safety.

Father had been quietly livid all day, livid in a way that only people who really knew him could discern. To anyone else, he must have looked very collected, equable even. But I knew what I was looking at, and I could see the way his fingers tightened around his wine goblet, the way his eyes raked Jack with blistering anger. It was frightening even to look at him, but I couldn't blame him for being upset. If that bomb had been any more powerful, he and Mother could be dead right now. And Jack seemed almost blasé about the whole thing. He'd known about the charges . . . had he known about the bomb, too?

But no, I reminded myself. He'd kept Father's presence from Smith, knew that Father had visited the Uprisen on a peaceful errand. He wouldn't do something like that.

I hoped.

While Father focused his attention on Jack, Charlie drew at the table, his feet idly kicking the legs of his chair, his eyes flicking from his paper to my father frequently. There was a certain jumpiness about him that tore at my heart. I knew the gibbet cage was never far from his thoughts—or his nightmares—and my father was probably as terrifying as ever to him, with his scarred face and his impenetrable, rage-radiating silence. Charlie sat as far away from Father as humanly possible.

My scalp crawled at the memory of Charlie's dirty, thin face under the gibbet cage as it swung in the wind, at the memory of my father's voice, so assured, so powerful, shouting Charlie's death sentence into the frosty January air.

I occupied myself with slipping my spoon into my bisque as cleanly as possible, trying to reach the bottom of the bowl without making the surface of the soup ripple or move. I was getting very good at it, and also the practice of watching people without letting them know I was doing it. I especially watched Jack, my trust in him now filament-thin.

"I've been thinking, Olivia . . . ," Jack said, after the silence had gone on too long and I had achieved close to three hundred successful spoon-dunkings. "Perhaps a Lantern Day Ball isn't such a bad idea after all."

My mother perked up. "Really?"

"It *is* our Madeline's big day," he continued, "and I wouldn't want to cheat her out of her deserved festivities, not on her eighteenth birthday."

Father was staring hard at Jack. So was I, mentally looping and reanalyzing his conversation with Smith. There was an ulterior motive to this. There had to be.

"Of course, I must insist that my people are invited and included. Another attempt to bring them together, eh Madeline?"

The smile on my face was so painfully forced, I knew he had to see it. But he beamed back at me anyway. "I think this ball might be a wonderful opportunity. For both of our peoples," he said.

An opportunity for what? Had he finally agreed to whatever Smith had been asking him to do? Or was I just being paranoid?

"Can you vouch for our safety at such an event?" Father asked. "Clearly, your people have no trouble bombing and murdering—"

"You are venturing into speculation now, little brother," Jack said. "And as long as the gentry behave, then my people shall, too."

Father's jaw twitched. When he was in control of Landry Park, he would have unleashed hell on the city after being attacked like he was last night. But now he was completely powerless, and he knew it.

Mother, however, seemed to feel back in her element. "We'll

need to make sure the gardens are cleared and heated—it will be crowded—and we'll have to order in lanterns, like we did last year." She brought out her tablet and started tapping in notes to herself. "The food—and you'll need a dress, Madeline—and invitations should have been sent out two weeks ago, but I could probably manage them in a couple of days. It's short notice given that Lantern Day is really only a week away, but it's such a tradition, I think we could get away with it this once. Jack, did you know that two years ago, the president himself came? He toasted our Madeline at her sweet sixteen. How perfect is that? I'll invite him again. . . ."

"I'll leave it in your capable hands, Olivia," Jack said, bowing his head.

"I'll invite some of the Uprisen wives in tomorrow to help me," she said, more to herself now than the family. "We can do a brunch in the ballroom while we plan. Excuse me, I should really go speak to Crawford about it now."

She left the table, and then Jack went, followed by Ewan and Cara, until it was Father, Charlie, and me. Charlie made to scoot out after Ewan, pushing his chair back and walking quickly toward the door in the way that someone might try to quietly but quickly skirt a sleeping panther. But he tripped over the rug near Father's chair, crayons and papers spilling onto the floor.

Charlie's fear was palpable even from here. He slowly knelt to pick up his things, his face down, his shoulders hunched.

Father leaned down and helped gather some of the wayward crayons, and when Charlie looked up instinctively, I saw my father blanch. He took Charlie's chin between his fingers and tilted his small face toward his.

I sat forward in my chair. There was nothing dangerous Father could do here—nothing that I could think of, at least—but I didn't want him putting Charlie through any more hell than he'd already been through.

I won't let him hurt you again, I wanted to say.

"You look like him," Father said. "Like your father. And your grandfather."

"People always tell me I look like my mother."

"People are wrong," Father said. Not harshly, not cruelly, but matter-of-factly.

Charlie lifted his chin a little. Defiance or pride or something else that said *I'll believe what I want to believe.*

"More than anything," Father continued, "you look like my Madeline did when she was a girl."

Charlie said nothing.

Father sighed and ran his fingers along his jawbone, as if feeling his scars—a new gesture he'd acquired since Liberty Park. "Charles, I want to apologize."

I almost dropped my dessert spoon.

"I take family very seriously. Very, very seriously. And if I had known that you had one drop of Landry blood in your veins, I would have never have had you arrested or brought to the cage. That was wrong of me," he added slowly, as if he could only drag the words outside of himself with the greatest effort.

"It was," Charlie said, with unexpected vehemence. "It was *mean.*"

Father nodded.

"Does this mean you don't want to hurt me anymore?"

Father looked down. "No." His words wavered. "I—I don't want to hurt you. You don't need to be afraid of me." He let go of Charlie's chin.

Charlie stood and extended his hand. Surprised, my father took it. "We can be friends," Charlie said solemnly.

"Good," Father said, the phantom of a smile pulling at his scarred mouth.

Charlie left the room, arms full of artwork, and Father leaned back, staring at the wine in his glass.

"That was kind of you. Especially given what happened last night."

Father frowned at the mention of last night, but he only said, "Family is family, no matter what the circumstances." He took a drink. "If you'll excuse me."

As he left me alone in the dining room, I had a thought. Just the other day I had been wondering how to bring Father and Jack together. I had noticed their shared pain. But now, I also saw something else that was shared. Not joy or love necessarily, but something that held both pain and joy together. Family.

My tablet chimed; it was a message from David.

Turn on the news.

I found the nearest wall screen and located the news in time to see the fire-bombed constabulary swathed in black smoke, flames licking the sky.

Rootless activists bomb police station in retribution for earlier raid read the dispassionate caption. My first thoughts were of Inspector Hernandez. I hoped he had been safely away from the station.

My second thought was that this was the first time the Rootless had ever struck back on this scale . . . but not the first time this week they'd used a bomb. There was no way Jack hadn't known about the police station. But did that mean he'd also known about the attack on my parents?

I leaned my head against the wall, the patterned wallpaper cool and textured against my skin. Every tendril of hope, every scrap of progress—was it all extinguished and destroyed before it could ever amount to anything more? The Rootless had every reason to fight, I knew, but they were also blind to the fact that fighting would only heap more pain, more suffering upon them.

I sent a quick message to Inspector Hernandez, and I got an equally quick response. He'd been away from the station at the time of the attack, as had most of the constables given the late hour. No officers had died, although several had been injured.

I turned off the wall screen, trying to think of what to do. Last year, I would have gone to Father or to Jack, passing on my worries like they were a physical burden I could lay at their feet. Maybe even yesterday, I would have done that.

But not tonight. Tonight I endured my worries alone.

Mother dragged me out to the greenhouse the next afternoon, ostensibly to gather fresh flowers, but actually so she could complain.

"And then she said that she wouldn't on any account come to any ball, not here, and then I said, you're acting as if you wouldn't be caught dead at Landry Park and she said, that's exactly it, I don't want to be caught dead there or killed there or *bombed*—Madeline, are you listening?"

Not really. I'd been thinking about how the police station had been attacked last night, about how a bomb had been thrown through my parents' window the night before that, about how two of my friends were dead and I didn't know who was next.

I handed Mother a particularly full bloom. "Sorry. What were you saying?"

She took the rose and laid it carefully in the basket dangling from her arm. "I was telling you that it's a week out from the Lantern Day party and the Uprisen are now refusing to come, knowing that Jack and his people will be here. They're all afraid of getting murdered."

"Maybe it's okay if they don't come," I said. "With Jack's people, it will be a very full party already...." I didn't mention that I was reluctant myself to welcome the Rootless after what had happened the last two days.

Mother narrowed her eyes—not at me, but at the phantom of the ball looming in the distance. "No," she said. "Don't you feel that we've earned this party? After all we've been through? The attack and your father's injury and exile and—"

"Four weeks away from home was hardly exile."

She ignored me, her gaze still fixed on some snowy point outside the window. "If only I could simply convince them to come. They have to. It's unthinkable to turn down an invitation to Landry Park."

"Aren't you a little worried about hosting such a large event? With the killer and the bombing?"

"Well ... yes." She stepped to the plant next to me, her delicate face furrowing. In the full light of day, it was so easy to see how much healthier she looked compared to last year—eyes clear and skin dewy. "But we will have the constables here. And," she lifted up her chin, "aside from the fact that it's one of the most important days of the year, nothing should stop us from having a party on your birthday."

I wasn't so sure. The bombings seemed a very compelling reason not to, but then again, hadn't I been the one just a week ago preaching about moving forward in the face of adversity? About how bringing the Rootless and the gentry together was the best thing we could do?

But aside from the class-driven violence, there were the murders. It was hard for me to feel any enthusiasm for a party after what happened to Marianne at the last one, and so soon after Mark's death, but it was important to keep trying, to show the murderer and the gentry alike that this new dynamic was not going to shift or hide itself away. Things had changed and would continue to change until there was room for everyone to have a normal life.

I moved on to another rose, searching for the right point to place my shears. "I suppose Father could try talking to them again? Maybe if he urged them, they would reconsider their attendance?" Though after his chilly reception at Westoff Castle, I wasn't at all confident about his chances of success.

She looked at me, excitement repooling in her dark brown eyes. "Yes! That's a brilliant idea!" She handed me the basket. "He'll see how important this is." A quick kiss on my cheek and she was gone.

After she left, I sighed and moved to the next row, where the white roses bloomed. I started shearing them off, and for a few quiet moments, the metallic snip and the occasional gust of wind were my only company. I found myself absorbed with the roses, the way their creamy hearts unfurled into silken petals, thinking of a conversation I'd had with Father last year where he'd told me that Jacob Landry had bred black roses, pure black, and that they no longer grew on the estate. It was a strange story, I realized now; Jacob Landry didn't seem the sort of man to have casual hobbies.

The door to the greenhouse swung open and I turned, expecting David or even Jude, but it was my cousin, red-cheeked and tired-looking, with a scarf covering the lower half of his face.

"Jamie!" I hurried over to him to give him a hug, nearly stabbing him with the shears in the process, and he patted my shoulder and unwound the scarf from his face.

He was smiling. "I'm close. I'm so close to puzzling out what makes the mutation tick."

It took me a moment to remember, I'd been so preoccupied with everything else going on.

The cure. My heart stuttered with possibility.

"Tell me."

"I needed a live subject to work on. I went to the ghetto two days ago, asked around. Apparently, most animals stay far enough away from the sorting yards to avoid any radiation that might possibly leak out. Except, a few years ago, some sadistic soul tried to start a dogfighting ring in one of the unused underground sheds. It never came to anything—the dogs were too sick to fight—but at any rate, several of those dogs are still limping around the ghetto, sick and passing on their illness to their pups."

My stomach turned at the grisly story.

"I brought a few back to the town house with me to start testing, which is, of course, extremely illegal and very unethical." He looked troubled. "I was reasonably certain that the prototype I'd made would have no ill effects—and really, what did these animals have to lose? But there was no way I could be entirely sure. Normally, these kinds of things are developed over the course of months or years, with rigorous trials before they even begin to think about testing them on living creatures. But I needed to be sure that I was working in the right direction—" he scratched his head. "I hoped that it would be okay."

"And it was?"

"I was able to re-create something similar to your mutation, combining some elements of canine DNA and the *radiodurans* DNA. I injected the dogs the day I got them— two days ago. Yesterday, I documented increased appetite and significant healing in the skin lesions. This morning, only one dog still has a limp—and that has improved from what it was—and all of them have exhibited a decrease in lethargy. I don't know what the effects are internally yet, but they must be extensive. Overall, there is no doubt in my mind that the principle of the idea is sound."

"Could you use it on people?" I asked, trying to modulate

my eagerness, trying to think logically about what avenue to pursue next. But this was the first good thing to happen in a week, and I couldn't help it.

Jamie's excitement faltered. "I don't know. I had hoped to modify the existing reproductive vaccines, but they are so specific to their purpose that it may be impossible. And I don't know if I could create a human formula completely from scratch."

I tried to order my thoughts, catalog the possibilities and next steps. I felt a tug of reluctance at my next words, a small drop of doubt about Jack and the way that he'd obscured knowledge about the charges, the way that he might know about the bombings and the murders.

But he was still the leader of the Rootless and this counter-agent was for them. Maybe this would further convince him to stay away from the radicals in his faction.

"We have to tell Jack and Father," I said. "And maybe they'll know someone who can help you—a scientist or contact in the government or someone, anyone at all. We have to find a way to make this happen—this could change everything."

SIXTEEN

Jamie returned that night with his tablet and papers and, as Crawford led him into the parlor, I went in search of my father and uncle. I had thought it best to wait to tell them about Jamie's discovery until he could show them the proof. I also wanted them to see this together, and I knew getting the two of them in the same room after the bombing wouldn't be easy.

So when I asked Father, and then a few minutes later, Jack, to join me in the parlor, they had no idea that they would see each other or witness the solution to the suffering of the Rootless. In particular, I needed Jack to hear this. Whatever he was planning with Smith, whatever he had planned—or at least known about—it had to be stopped. And if there was a real answer to the Rootless's suffering, then there would be no need for violence. At least, that's what I hoped. I'd read enough history books to know that wasn't always the case; even after the overthrow of the French monarchy, the revolutionaries had still slaughtered tens of thousands.

Father raised his eyebrows when he walked inside the room and saw Jamie shuffling through papers in his favorite high-backed armchair. Jack came in a few minutes later, a hardness creeping into his face when he noticed Father, but thankfully he made no remark about it. Instead, he greeted Jamie and me warmly and offered to get Jamie a drink, which he declined.

"Father, Uncle Jack, Jamie has been working on something. And we think you should see it."

Jamie cleared his throat and began to explain what had led to it all, starting with his discovery about Father right after the attack and ending with the dogs back at his house. He showed them his notes and some of the models from his lab. I watched their faces carefully as they listened, trying to gauge their reactions. Like good Landrys, they remained emotionless, their thoughts inaccessible. But I was a Landry, too, and I could see the twitch underneath Jack's eye and the slight pucker in my father's cheek, as if he were consciously holding back a response.

Jamie finished. "I think we have a real chance to adapt this into something that could benefit the Rootless, but this is somewhat outside of my scope. I'd like to bring in other scientists—maybe from abroad since the field is so weak here—to collaborate on my work. With some effort, we could have an immediate future free of radiation sickness."

Jack and Father glanced at each other. For once, it wasn't hostile or questioning, but a look of shared knowledge, of *are you going to say it or am I?*

My uncle cleared his throat. "That was most elucidative,

Mr. Campbell-Smith. I had never before considered that the Landry DNA could be put to such a use—I assumed the complications involved would preclude the process of converting it into something for public use."

His words ran through my mind again. And again. And I realized what he was not saying, what was hidden by omission in his words. "You knew . . ." I said slowly. "You knew the DNA was different."

There was a moment before he nodded. "Yes."

I paused a moment. This I had not accounted for.

I looked at Father. "You too?"

"Yes," he said evenly.

I pushed down the indignation that swelled in my chest. I should not have felt betrayed by this. I should not have felt slighted, transgressed, just because Father had known something I had not. But it was there all the same—a gash of angry hurt. Father had known my entire life that we were different, and he had never told me. Never once had he thought to mention that we were protected from radiation, that we carried in our very cells something alien and unnatural.

I turned back to my uncle. When I spoke, my voice was entirely steady. "So when you let Father be taken by the Rootless, you knew that he would be okay."

"I had a reasonable assumption, yes." That explained why he hadn't been surprised at Father's healed face when he'd returned home.

"If you knew," Jamie started, "then perhaps you know how this particular mutation arose? Why?"

Father looked past me to the portrait hanging on the wall. It was an old portrait—one I barely looked at—of Jacob Landry posing near his laboratory equipment, his right hand outstretched, as if welcoming the viewer to step into the painting and touch the electron microscopes and beam tubes for themselves. At his feet, a sleek gray cat sat next to a basket of black roses, one paw outstretched, as if the painter had caught the cat ready to pounce on the petals.

"Of course," I said, more to myself than to him. "The roses."

"Jacob Landry always had a talent for the biological sciences," Father said. "And he had amazing foresight. I think it's only natural that he wanted to bequeath a form of protection to his descendants."

"Protection from *his* creation," I said.

"Yes."

"So how does it work?" Jamie asked.

Jack leaned back. "It's quite simple. Any child sired from a Landry is born with the base of the protection. But Jacob Landry didn't want immortality, and pairing the full strength of his creation with a rapidly growing child proved difficult. So he found a way to pass on the foundation of the mutation, and then created a serum that would activate the protection after the child's rate of growth began to slow, usually a year or so after the onset of puberty."

"I didn't get any serum," I said, thinking back. I was certain that Father had never mentioned anything of the sort while I was growing up.

"Oh, but didn't you?" Jack asked. "You don't remember being violently ill? Being injected over and over again with needles? Writhing in pain? For a year perhaps?"

My mouth parted but no words came out.

"Three injections a day for nine months," Jack continued. He rolled up his sleeve. "And those scars don't heal quite the same. They actually linger." The inside of his elbow was white and bumpy, riddled with pits and holes. "It hurts, rewriting your DNA. It hurts a lot."

I know. If I rolled up my sleeve, I would see the same kinds of scars.

"You," I said to Father. He didn't look at me at first, keeping his eyes on the fire. But when I didn't speak again right away, he raised his eyes to mine. "I thought those were syringes of medicine," I said. "I thought you were trying to help me."

"I was helping you," he said. "I was giving you a gift that would protect you your entire life."

"You were hurting me," I whispered. *"On purpose."*

Those needles, always brought on silver trays, as if they were delicacies or desserts straight from the kitchen. Needles that pricked and then scorched, sending flames rippling on the inside of my skin, sending knives of pain deep into my bones and organs.

And Father had been the one to wield those syringes.

"We all had to do it, Madeline," he said. "Every single one of us. Every Landry child born in this house."

I looked at Jack. He nodded.

"What does this mean for Ewan and Charlie?" Jamie asked. He was typing furiously on his tablet, taking notes on everything we said. "Are they fully immune?"

"They are not," Jack said. There was a slight bent in his words, a specific cadence that suggested a snarl within Jack's meticulously cultivated morality. Living outside of the estate, he wouldn't have had access to the serum even if he wanted it, but for a resourceful man like Jack, I doubted that would have been an insurmountable obstruction.

"You wanted them to be immune," I said. It wasn't a question. "But you also couldn't justify giving them protection when the other Rootless wouldn't have it. You were willing to sacrifice the health of your children for your principles." I didn't say it accusingly; I understood completely his decision and I also understood completely why it would still eat away at him.

I wondered if Ewan knew that he had missed the chance to be protected—how he would feel if he did know. But if Jamie succeeded, I realized, he wouldn't have missed his chance. He could be as protected as the rest of us.

"You know," Father said to Jack, "you're here now. Home now. In a few years Charlie will be ready. We could give the serum to him, make sure that he's safe."

That was so Alexander Landry. Blood before everything else, before even the enormous divide between him and his brother. It gave me a particle of faith that these two could work together.

"How can I in good conscience do that when there are other children I know and dearly care about who will not be safe?"

"How can you in good conscience deny the gift to even one child, much less your own?" Father countered.

"In a few years, it won't matter," I said. "Because the Rootless will no longer be changing the charges. They will be voting and living freely, and we will be using some other source of energy—and if not that, then we will hire paid workers with more than adequate protection to change the charges."

Father steepled his fingers, his expression making his thoughts on the matter plain.

And then Jamie cut in. "Begging your pardon, but it also won't matter if we can get this serum working correctly. Because then *everybody* can have access to Jacob Landry's achievement." He turned to my father. "So the Landrys already have access to a formula for a vaccine?"

Father nodded. "Yes. When a child is ready to receive the serum, the formula is given to a private laboratory, which produces the material."

"So there are people with experience in doing this sort of work." Jamie looked immensely relieved. "Would you be willing to lend me this formula then? With the help of the laboratory, I think we could accomplish this."

"Of course, we'll lend you everything you need," Jack said. "I will warn you in advance that I'm not sure how the serum will work on adults. It's made to be used on children. I don't think it will work any other way. And the pain and suffering involved with absorbing the serum—the process can take up to a year. It would be impossible to expect that kind of recovery of the Rootless; with as weakened as many of them are, I don't know that they would survive the process."

Jamie wrote all of this down. "There's a chance that I can adapt the mechanism and modulate it so it acts more like the fertility vaccines," he said, stylus still moving on his tablet screen. "It may not provide as extensive protection as the Landrys have, and it may not be possible to engineer it to be passed down from generation to generation, but surely there's a way we can reimagine it so that it will work on adults and with less severe side effects."

"If you do, I am confident that you will find a number of volunteers who would be eager to take the chance," Jack continued. And he smiled—a genuinely happy smile. "And if this works, then you may have just saved us all."

When Jamie left a few minutes later, I jumped to my feet to follow. Jack would probably not elect to stay in the room with Father, and I certainly didn't want to be alone with him, either—not until I sorted out how I felt about the serum.

About the missing year of my life, spent coughing and hacking and sinking into violent and terrifying fever dreams.

I held Jamie's notes while he shrugged on his coat. "I think that went well," he said.

"I do, too." My answer was robotic. Jamie noticed.

"I think your father was doing what he thought best," he said gently. "He wanted to protect you."

"But he didn't give me a choice! Or even a reason. If I had known *why* I was suffering . . . but instead, I knew nothing. He didn't even tell me afterward. In all these years, he never thought to tell me. When would he have ever told me if you hadn't started designing this remedy?"

"I imagine he would have told you before you had your own children," he said. "You would have had to learn sometime."

The thought of doing that to my child—inflicting that kind of pain—made me physically ill. Had my mother known? As she watched me suffer, had she known it was my father behind it all?

He put a comforting hand on my shoulder. "I am sorry. But there is a bright side. We are closer than ever to helping the Rootless. And that's what you've wanted all along, right?"

"Yes."

"Good." He took his notes and tablet and tucked them under his arm. "You know, I've been thinking about Ewan and Charlie, and how they are Landry children who haven't been exposed to the serum . . . I wonder if they would let me take samples as well?"

"Probably." I found it difficult to care in that moment. Jamie gave me a swift kiss on the cheek and then left, and I went up to bed, rubbing the insides of my elbows, willing myself not to dream of pain and syringes.

SEVENTEEN
SEVENTEEN

During the night, another raid happened. And this time, there were no arrests, no canisters of tear gas, no rubber bullets. This time, the constables set every single Rootless home alight and burned the entire ghetto to the ground.

I woke up to several messages on my tablet—from David and from Jamie mostly—and a wall screen rife with images of crying, soot-covered children, and firefighters grimly hosing down the smoldering remains of the homes.

And in my own house, I could hear the yelling all the way from upstairs.

Elinor had been in to bring up a carafe of coffee, but had already left, so I pinned up my hair in a simple twist, pulled on a dress of flowing silk jersey, and then hurried downstairs.

"You can't tell me that the Uprisen had nothing to do with this," Jack's voice boomed up the stairs.

I heard Father's voice retort, "I am not denying it. I'm only pointing out that I personally had nothing to do with it."

"Olivia told me you spoke with them yesterday on the wall screen."

"Yes, to invite them to the blasted ball! Not to advise them on handling the Rootless."

I followed their voices down the first floor hall. They were in the morning room, but either everyone else had elected to take breakfast in their rooms or else they'd come down and then cleared out as soon as Father and Jack started fighting, because they were the only two people in there. The day was extraordinarily sunny and unseasonably warm; clumps of snow were sliding wetly from the roof and the icicles dripped in merry drops in front of the many windows.

"You have to admit that if they had not bombed the station— and our house—this would not have happened."

"It should not have happened anyway! Where is justice? Where is due course? Where—" Jack saw me in the doorway and paused, his chest heaving.

"Good morning," I said, although I couldn't look Father in the eyes. Last night had been a parade of nightmares from my stolen year, my year of sickness. *My year of the serum.* I couldn't shake the feeling of being lied to, of being purposefully hurt.

"Good morning, Madeline," Father and Jack said together, and then shot each other resentful looks, as if one had robbed the other of the chance to greet me. Or perhaps resentment at the reminder that inside, they were so much the same, down to the very timing and inflection of their words.

I pushed my anger down, tried to focus on today, on only today. "Are you talking about the fire last night?"

Father leveled his gaze at me. "You know full well we are."

I poured myself a small glass of pomegranate juice and took a croissant from a tray. Neither of them said a word as I took my seat.

"Will the Rootless come to stay here?" I inquired.

"Many of them," Jack said. His voice was still stained with anger, but there was something else in there, a ragged unhappiness, and I remembered how tenuous his control of the Rootless had become, how so few of them trusted him after learning that he was a Landry.

"Some of them don't want to come," I said. It wasn't a question.

Jack turned his gaze to the melting world outside the window. He had lost more control than I'd thought—maybe he *had* been ignorant of the bombings before they happened.

I wondered if Father was going to tell Jack that there was no earthly way that the Rootless could stay here, even just a few of them, not at Landry Park of all places, but then he said, in a short, matter-of-fact voice, "I suppose it's not an impossibility to host them here."

Jack looked as shocked as I felt.

Father seemed impatient with our surprise. "It would only take a week to rebuild most of those shacks. I'm sure they can endure close quarters for that long."

More silence.

"What?" Father demanded. "We have more than fifty acres here—"

"It's not that," Jack said. "It's only that I cannot tell whether this comes from a place of unfeeling practicality or a place of nascent sympathy. I would have thought after the bombing that you would be entirely adverse to the idea."

"Perhaps this is an opportunity," I spoke up, buoyed by Father's unexpected acquiescence. "The Rootless are displaced as it is—why not rebuild with actual homes? Why not shut down the sorting yards for good and move the estates to some other source of power? Why not now?"

"You are suggesting that the gentry restructure their entire way of life in a matter of weeks," Father said. "I can't imagine any of them will warm to that scheme." His mouth grew tight. "Though apparently I can't speak for them any longer, since they refuse to listen to me. I can only surmise."

"Alexander surmises correctly," Jack said. "The gentry would never go for it. It would be a beautiful plan, but it will never happen."

"I have to ask," Father said, "is there some other plan in mind? Does it involve the Empire, by any chance?"

Jack gave Father a hard look. "No. I have learned from that mistake. But you better believe that I will do what's necessary for my people. No matter the cost."

Father's answer was swift and cold. "Then so will the Uprisen."

EIGHTEEN

"Madeline?"

It was Ewan.

"Are you busy?"

I shook my head no. Busy implied productivity, industry. And there was nothing industrious about spinning out a thousand black scenarios, all ending with a ruined city and a fractured family.

"My people are starting to arrive," Ewan said. "Your father and mine have ordered in tents and supplies, but we could use another set of hands."

"Of course," I said quickly, eager to help and even more eager to get away from my thoughts. "I'll only be a moment."

After I'd changed into pants and boots, I went down to the ballroom, which was teeming with Rootless, all dripping snow, all clutching bundles of desperately salvaged items, all afraid and lost looking. I couldn't begin to count them, but from what I remembered of the mob in Liberty Park, this would only be about half of the Rootless, possibly a little less.

I wondered about the others, the ones who refused to come. Where would they stay? What would they do to keep warm and fed?

And the ones who did come, I couldn't keep myself from searching their faces. Had any of them been the one to throw the bomb through Father's window? Were we inviting danger by inviting the Rootless to Landry Park?

I took a deep breath. I was having a knee-jerk reaction. It was illogical and unfounded and I would stop right now.

I found Uncle Jack near the front of the room, conversing seriously with the servants, and I was surprised to see Father next to him, adding in information about where to find such and such resource and where to procure barrels for the drinking water. His expression wasn't pleasant or helpful exactly, but it wasn't openly bellicose, and there seemed to be something neutral in his resignation, something benign. I decided to take this as a good sign.

I also decided to ignore the thorny prickling of anger at my throat as I approached him, to ignore the vivid memories of my illness and the knowledge that he had been the one to cause it. I knew somewhere in my mind that he thought he had done the best thing for me. But it was too soon for me to let go of everything else: being injected, being sick, being kept in the dark and denied knowledge. I could only ignore it for the moment and hope that I had time to process it later.

"How can I help?" I asked.

Father wasted no time. "The tents need to be laid out in ordered wide rows along the lawn, but first the snow needs to be melted. I've called for more solar heaters from our neighbors, and they should be arriving shortly. Organize the melting and the arranging of the tents. If possible, we should have a solar heater per tent—if not, then find a way to connect the electric ones to the house. Either way, warmth is the first priority, so make sure that each family has their own heater. I saw Cara down here somewhere, ostensibly to help, so find her and press her into doing something useful."

Orders given, he nodded at me like a general might nod at a trusted subordinate. I didn't trust my face or voice not to reveal the confusing mix of feelings inside, so I left him and Jack without a word, and immersed myself in the task at hand.

The day was filled with work, and no able body was spared, including Cara's, whom I charged with distributing tents. I helped roll the heaters around the lawn, which very quickly turned the field of snow into a swamp, and then I organized the rations and sleeping bags. All told, over five hundred people took shelter at Landry Park that night, as many indoors as we could fit, filling every room and every available space. Women, children, and the sickest got priority, and the others made do on the driest parts of the grounds.

Dusk found me rolling a solar heater down to the end of the lawn with the help of a Rootless man named Paul. He was tall and thin, and his family had come in later than most, as if they'd hesitated before coming to the estate. I felt his eyes on me as we walked; he wasn't staring but glancing, as if trying to make up his mind about something.

I should say something, make conversation, ease the strained divide between us, the Landry and the Rootless, but my disquieted mind came up empty. I'd never been good at that sort of thing, quietly gracious like Jane Osbourne or vibrantly talkative like Cara. So we walked in relative silence a few more minutes. It was slow going, pushing the heavy thing through the cold, wet grass, the wheels sinking into the soggy ground.

"At least the snow is melting," I attempted.

Paul didn't answer.

"We're ordering more heaters in, so hopefully it will be fairly comfortable out here. The heaters are very strong—great for keeping the cold at bay. We use them for outdoor parties—" I stopped, feeling suddenly awkward.

He looked over at me, and I didn't need to see it to know that it was the look of a man who was not impressed.

We reached the spot, a section of the lawn where the snow still lay like a thick blanket, and I flicked the heater on, watching the solar panels unfold themselves. Lights flickered along the sleek front panel and warm air began wafting away from the machine. Within an hour or so, the air around it would be mild and the snow would be gone.

I turned to go back to the house.

Paul cleared his throat. "Is it true what they're saying about you?"

I kept my eyes on the ground, not wanting to give anything away. "What exactly are they saying?"

"That radiation can't hurt you. That all of the Landrys are immune to radiation poisoning." His voice was flat, affectless.

I looked up at him, startled. "How did you hear about that?"

"It's a rumor that's been going around today. Someone heard it from Jack late last night, and it started to spread before . . . before *they* came." The pain in his voice was the iciest and also the emptiest bitterness I had ever heard. The bitterness of someone who'd even begun to give up on anger.

"Paul—"

"So this whole time," Paul said, "none of you have ever had anything to fear from the charges. Not even Jack."

"It's not that simple—"

"And the Landrys were just content to sit back and watch everyone else suffer, knowing they'd never be at risk of getting sick." Paul's indignation pulsed through his words and I found myself taking a step back, feeling a rush of defensiveness . . . or maybe shame.

"It's not like that," I said. "Well, not *entirely* like that. We can still be affected, we can still be hurt if we're exposed. My father was gravely injured at Liberty Park last month; it's just that then he was able to heal from it. And we want to find a way to use the genetic mutation to help people—to help you."

"Like the vaccines they give the pregnant women?"

I studied him in the fading daylight. He looked as if he were possibly in his late twenties, and probably a packer—the most dangerous job of all. Skin lesions crept up his neck and the whites of his eyes were a sickly yellow. If he had bitterness that smothered anger, then no doubt it also smothered hope. "Like those, except this would be for men and women, children and adults. And it would last forever. If we are able to do this, you would be the last generation ever to know what it's like to be sick with radiation poisoning."

He didn't reply for a moment, turning his face to the sunset. "I suppose that's something to think about." And he offered the horizon the barest hint of a smile, although it was laced with suspicion and laced with doubt, and I knew that Paul would not be the only Rootless person who greeted the news of our mutation with resentment.

And who could blame him, really?

I fell into my makeshift bed after two in the morning, the sky a dim purple underlit by the hundreds of Cherenkov lanterns that had been set outside in neat rows, marking where the tents would go when the lawn dried out. The hum of the solar heaters could be heard even in the house. I'd given my room—and my bed—to some of the sickest members of the Rootless, and had made do with a throw pillow and a thin blanket that was normally strewn in an artfully rumpled manner across a bench in my mother's room. I found a quiet corner of the library and tucked myself in among the leather-bound volumes and manuscripts, and fell right away into a deep, dreamless doze.

The next morning was no less busy, and made even more so by the struggle to get supplies. Almost half of the gentry were unwilling to contribute supplies or funds to help the refugees or the rebuilding efforts, and it became clear that no help was coming from the government, even to those Rootless who had chosen to stay in the ghetto.

Most of those who stayed were young men and women. But the old and the infirm and those with young children continued to trickle into Landry Park, the promise of warmth and better shelter enough to stave off the bitter sting of pride. Jack sent what he could over to the ghetto, though there wasn't much to spare, along with a promise that he would fight for the gentry to give them proper homes—real homes, permanent and secure.

As I worked, I tried to look for David, checking my tablet obsessively. This was the kind of thing he would normally help with, so where was he? It was like Marianne's funeral all over again.

I also kept an eye out for Smith, worried that he would be staying here, where he had possibly killed two people, and then worried when I didn't see him at all. Like a spider on the ceiling, his presence would make me anxious, but even more worrisome was his absence—where had he gone? What was he waiting for?

Cara and I were handing out foil packets of cold food when Father emerged from his study, obviously irritated, his jaw working. A man, busy herding his children out to the tents where they were staying, ran right into him. Father's eyes flashed, and my hand froze, the foil packet hovering in mid-air. Then Father raised an arm to steady the man and asked him if he was okay. The man nodded, relieved, and they went on their separate ways.

I couldn't imagine any situation before Liberty Park that would have induced Father to touch a Rootless—the taboo was too strong. But it was almost impossible to avoid with the house as crowded as it was—maybe it didn't mean as much as I wanted it to.

Jude arrived halfway through the day to help unload boxes of supplies, and something about his presence seemed to enliven everyone in the house. Even the Rootless knew who he was, and since only a handful of them knew about their own secret alliance to the Empire, they all treated him like a hero, like a celebrity, for his valorous defeat of the East. After an hour, I could barely see Jude for the swarm of people that crowded around him.

He finally made his way over to me, stopping multiple times to shake hands and accept heartfelt *thank you*s for coming to help them in their time of need.

"You are very popular," I remarked with a smile.

"They're only reacting to the fact that I've been on the news," he said with a dismissive shrug.

"They're reacting that way because you've come to help. Because you are a gentry man, in the military no less, and you are talking with them and touching them. *That's* what they appreciate."

"I'm not doing anything you wouldn't do. Or David."

"David's not here," I said.

He looked surprised. "He's been outside all morning. I thought you knew. Did he not come in to say hello?"

I pressed my lips together.

That was all the answer Jude needed. "He was probably too busy to come in and greet you," he said. "You know how he likes to throw himself into things."

"I would like to throw him into some things right now."

Jude let out a laugh at that. Several admiring glances came from the females in the room. Jude didn't seem to notice. Instead, he put a comforting hand on my back.

"I just wish he would have said hello," I said. I couldn't explain exactly why that bothered me, but it was out of character for him. For us. It felt too close to fighting

Jude looked into my eyes. "He cares about you beyond

what you can even conceive—believe me. I live with him. I can attest to that. But you know how he can be. . . ."

That wasn't a satisfactory response and Jude seemed to know it, because he added, changing the subject, "Would you like to go to a party with me tonight?"

"What?"

He saw the look on my face and hurriedly added, "As friends, of course. I mean, David will be going, too, so it's not like, you know, *that*."

Jude was so rarely flustered that it was almost adorable. But I couldn't enjoy it; I was too busy wondering why David hadn't invited me to this party if he planned on going himself, and if that was connected to him avoiding me today.

I glanced down at the boxes of foil packets that the kitchen staff had spent all night preparing, and at the tide of humanity that teemed all around the house and grounds. "I can't go to a party right now. I have to help."

"It will only be for a few hours," he cajoled. "And I always enjoy them more when you're there."

"I hardly ever enjoy them at all, so . . ."

"Everyone will be there. Philip and even Jamie, and Jane Osbourne . . ." He continued listing my friends and members of the Uprisen, and I remembered with a sinking heart that it had been my goal to keep friendly lines open with the gentry and that it was more important now than ever.

"Fine," I said, cutting him off. "But I'm not staying late."

He gave me one of those smiles that looked so good on the wall screens—white teeth and a square jaw and the hint of a cleft chin. "Wonderful! I'll be back around seven to pick you up?"

"Will David be with you?" I asked hopefully.

"Christine is one of the organizers, so she and David are going early to help prepare." He saw the look on my face. "Madeline—"

"Seven is fine," I said. I realized that I had been searching for a glimpse of David as we talked, that I was only partly aware of Jude still standing next to me, still talking to me. *So he's not picking you up,* I told myself. *You'll see him at the party. You're worrying about nothing.*

At some point, Jude bowed and left, and I think I mumbled something in the way of a good-bye. The whole afternoon, I never saw David once, and despite how much I ached to leave my table with its boxes of food to go find him, I didn't. Half out of duty—I was needed where I was—and half out of pride.

By the time seven rolled around, I'd managed to round up Elinor to do my hair and find a dress, although she clucked in disapproval when she spotted the simple navy gown I'd chosen.

"Is Captain Dana going to be there?" she'd asked. I'd stopped wondering a long time ago how Elinor seemed to know everything in my life. The servant gossip network was faster than any tablet broadcast.

"Yes, he'll be there."

Immediately, she went into the closet and materialized with something figure-hugging and glittery, something Mother had bought me last year and I'd steadfastly refused to wear ever since.

"Elinor, no."

She'd raised an eyebrow at me, in that way that said *don't I always know best?*

"It's too tight," I complained, turning away. "I can't wear that."

"If you and Captain Dana are fighting, then this is exactly the kind of dress you need to wear. Get his attention. He's used to looking at you like an heiress. Make him look at you like a woman."

Finally, I relented, and she zipped me into the silver dress. It had long sleeves, a scooped neck, and a narrow skirt that clung to my hips and thighs. Elinor styled my hair and rustled up some very tall heels.

"I look like Cara."

"You look like you're going to knock every boy at the party off his feet. Which means you'll remind him of how hard he needs to work to keep you."

I didn't remark that he already had me—had me too much—and that was part of the problem. That he could wound me so easily with his casual silences, his thoughtless exclusions.

And so I waited uncomfortably in the foyer at seven, trying to stand so that the—admittedly modest—slit in the skirt stayed closed, and hoping Jude wouldn't think I looked like a tart. I shouldn't have worried—he barely seemed to notice what I was wearing. He simply gave me a gracious bow, thanked me for taking time out of my night, and took my elbow to steer me out to his car.

The party was actually a gala event at the art museum, an institution that had been standing in Kansas City since before the Last War. The gentry nibbled and quaffed among pilfered Egyptian sarcophagi and blank-eyed Greek gods. Music echoed in the main hall. Jude was almost instantly set upon by the partygoers, and with an apologetic look, he let himself be led off to a cluster of men and women standing by the huge black pillars. David was nowhere in sight, though I could see the glossy black head of Christine Dana bobbing as she circulated throughout the room.

I needed a moment to regroup before I was forced to mingle; I found a flute of champagne and wandered upstairs. I slipped inside a desolate corner that housed the pre-Empire Asian exhibits, and drank my champagne while my eyes wandered over the deep reds and the pale jades, ink and paper drawings of mountains, and bronze vessels wrought in the shape of dragons and men.

I stopped in front of a colorful wooden statue of Guan Yin, seated in an almost casual manner, a hint of a smile around his full lips. For a moment, I felt at peace, just me and the bodhisattva and the delicate sounds of strings wafting in from downstairs.

My reverie ended as I heard the unmistakable sound of footsteps—male footsteps, I discerned, since there was no telltale *click click* of heels. I turned, and there was David silhouetted in the doorway of the exhibit. Only yesterday, I would have hurried to him. I would have felt no shyness, no fear.

How much can change in a day.

He came toward me, and when he reached me, he took in my dress, slender and sparkling, and his eyes burned.

"You look very nice," he said with a voice that bordered on hoarseness.

A stupid part of my brain wanted to revel in this, but it was quickly pushed to the side. "Why didn't you see me today?" I demanded. My words echoed off the parquet floors and lacquered pillars. "I know you were at the estate. Why couldn't you have taken just a moment to say hello?"

He rubbed at his forehead. "I don't know."

"What?"

"*I don't know.*"

I didn't know what to say to that. How could I demand an answer from someone who didn't even know his own thoughts?

He lifted the flute from my hand and set it on a glass display case. "Look at me," he said.

I did.

"I'm sorry," he said. "It's easier for me to pretend away something than to deal with it. I know we disagree about Smith, and it kills me to have anything between us, no matter what it is."

"I'm not wrong."

"Neither am I."

How could it be that the thing that had brought us together would be the thing that drove us apart? David's moral compass, his perseverance to find a life without guilt, was the thing that had drawn me to him, that had fascinated me. It mirrored my own aspirations. We were both searching for our grail, knights on an impossible quest, because this grail didn't exist. There was no shining castle at the end of the road. There was no amount of compassion or aid or wealth that I could bestow that would erase my own beginnings in a place of privilege while others had been born in a place of suffering at the margins of society. So what did that mean?

He reached out and touched my face. "What is my Madeline thinking?"

"I'm thinking of us. I'm thinking of Galahad."

He smiled ruefully at this.

"Are you really angry with me about today?"

"A little."

And then my lips were on his. He stumbled backward, but steadied me in his arms, running his hands down my bare back to the swell of my hips. He parted my lips with his, putting a hand behind my neck, and I slid my hands inside his tuxedo jacket, feeling the flat lines of his torso and back underneath my palms. There was pressure in the kiss, almost like we were challenging each other, fighting with each other, and his eternally restless hands skated the lines of propriety. He pressed me even closer and I pulled at his jacket lapels, and there was just as much fury as there was desire, as if we could conquer each other morally if we conquered each other physically. Then there was the sound of someone uncomfortably clearing their throat, and we broke apart to see Jude staring at us.

NINETEEN

His face was unreadable. "I didn't mean to interrupt you," he said, and there was a strained cast to his words.

"Jude," David said, but whatever he was about to say next was cut off by Jamie's entrance.

"Oh good," he said. "I've been looking for you, Jude. And Madeline, too. Hello, David." He seemed utterly oblivious to the tension between the three of us.

David sighed, his eyes rolling up to the ceiling. "Hello, Jamie."

"Jude, I need to speak with you, and I thought it would be best if Madeline was with us. Do you have a minute?"

"I have all the time in the world," Jude said.

"And am I allowed to be party to this conversation or do you all wish me to be gone?" David asked.

"Nobody wishes you to be gone, David." And now there was more than a hint of irritation in Jude's voice.

"Um, we can talk at a different time if you would like," Jamie suggested. There was a little bit of color in his cheeks, and I could tell that he was uncomfortable.

"Now is fine," Jude said firmly. To emphasize his point, he

sat down on a bench in front of the bodhisattva, a glass of something golden cradled in his hands.

I sat down, too, smoothing my skirt as I did and crossing my legs. David gave me a look. Something told me that his eyes were measuring the exact distance between Jude and me.

"Right," Jamie said, eyes flicking over the three of us. "Apologies to Madeline, who's heard all this before. So, I've been finding a way to turn Alexander Landry's blood into a workable formula to be used on the Rootless. And, as you know, I took samples of your blood as controls, to try to assess if this DNA belonged to the gentry as a whole or to the Landry family in particular."

David leaned closer to Jude and made a *give it to me* gesture, and Jude automatically handed him his glass of whiskey. Neither took their eyes off Jamie.

"Alexander and Stephen Landry have given me the formula that they have been using within the family, and that, plus the help I'm now getting from my contacts at the university, means we're making good progress on transforming the serum into a cure, like a vaccine, but something that can be used on all the Rootless. But when I was organizing my research to give to the scientists at the university, I noticed something strange. . . ." He cleared his throat again, meeting our stares. "See, there's one other person who shares the Landry DNA, though only partially. Jude."

Jude remained very still.

219

"You're saying there's something unusual about my sample?"

I recognized the concern in his words and remembered the feeling of being told that you weren't normal. I put a hand over his hand, a gesture that David didn't miss and also a gesture that Jude shook off.

"There is something unusual, yes, and that thing is the same thing that is unusual about Madeline's blood. And every Landry's blood."

Jude said nothing. No one else did either.

Jamie continued. "Landry children are born with the foundation of this anomaly, which is then added to by serums administered around the onset of puberty. It was only after discussing the implications of this for Ewan and Charlie that I realized that you were connected. Jude, you were clearly never given the serum, and so you are not immune to radiation in the same way that the serum-infused Landrys are." Jamie shifted his weight. "But you have the foundation, just like Madeline and her cousins do. The only situation in which this makes sense is one where you are directly descended from a Landry."

Silence in the gallery as theories assembled and disassembled and reassembled themselves in my mind. Jude was related to me. He had to be—how else would he have gotten the mutation? I turned so I could fully study him. In profile, it was apparent—the high brow, the strong nose, the gray eyes. Only the red hair was missing.

The first time I'd met Jude, I had felt certain that we'd known each other somehow. Like we'd met in another life, like we were friends and our friendship had been half buried by a lifetime of memories and acquaintances.

And now I knew why: Jude was family. I had recognized in him a fellow Landry: the same ambition, the same reserved pride.

"I ran your DNA and Alexander Landry's through the machine, this time not to search for the *radiodurans* DNA, but to see if there was a paternity match."

I felt a hollow fear.

"Was there?" Jude asked in despair.

"No."

I let out a breath I didn't know I'd been holding. So did he—a heavy breath. No one seemed to want to peer at the idea too closely—that I'd shared a kiss with a man that could have been my brother. That I could have married him.

"But the results indicate that you are a very close relative of Alexander's. If I had to guess, I would say his nephew."

"So you're saying that I'm adopted?" Jude's voice was choked now. "That my parents aren't really my parents?"

Jamie gave Jude a reassuring sort of smile, but underneath it was the look of someone who had rehearsed a conversation in a lab and had expected it to go just as well in real life.

Jude stood. He looked at Jamie, then at David, and then at me, and I knew he was doing the same thing I had just done, tracing my face for familiar features, staring into my eyes, which were the exact same shade of silver as his.

He turned on his heel and left the room with long strides. I stood to go after him, but David put a hand on my shoulder and shook his head. I understood. David was his best friend—and right now, I was a reminder of everything that was upsetting him.

David's dress shoes drummed on the floor as he hurried after Jude.

It was only Jamie and me now. I rescued my champagne flute from the top of the exhibit case and drained it in a hearty swallow.

Jamie looked regretful. "I didn't mean to upset him."

I set the empty glass down. "Does this mean Jack is his father?"

"I don't know. We'd need a sample of Jack's blood, which I still haven't gotten."

"We need to talk to him."

"I agree."

I stared at the statue, so content and comfortable, as still and peaceful as my thoughts were wild and racing. Jude was related to me—possibly a cousin—possibly a first cousin. Jude could be Ewan and Charlie's *brother*.

"How are you holding up?" Jamie asked. "I know this is news for you, too."

"I feel . . ." I searched myself. There was the surprise, and the lingering confusion over the whole situation, and the sense of having been betrayed by my father when it came to the DNA and my illness. But about Jude . . . "I feel almost *happy*."

"Happy?" Jamie said. He blinked. "That is . . . surprising."

"I don't know, I just—I always felt like Jude and I were connected somehow."

"Not like this, surely."

"No, I didn't ever imagine this. But look at all he's done—it makes sense, doesn't it?"

"That a national hero would be a Landry?" Jamie smiled and offered me an arm, and I took it, knowing it was time for us to go back downstairs.

"At least there is a place for Jude in my life now."

"Wasn't there always?"

"With the failed engagement behind us? Always knowing that I'd chosen David instead? What man would want to maintain a friendship in those circumstances?"

"I think you're underestimating his capacity for polite martyrdom," Jamie remarked, but we were back into the fray of the gala before I could respond.

Jamie and I mingled, and I made sure to talk smilingly to the Uprisen men present, who all smiled back, except for my uncle Lawrence, who asked tetchily if my father was still allowing "that Rootless scum" to live at Landry Park. When I answered affirmatively, he made a scoffing noise and walked off without another word, cane clicking on the floor.

I talked to Philip and Jane, whom I noticed were standing very close together, and I made a point of avoiding my Lawrence cousins, who were busy drinking all of the champagne and heckling the stone-faced waiters.

Around midnight, I started looking for Jude to go home. I called both him and David on my tablet and got no answer. Just when I was about to give up and ask if I could share a cab with Jamie, I turned a corner into a large room and found Jude staring at a Caravaggio.

"Where's David?" I asked.

"I told him to go away."

"You did?" I asked.

"I wanted to be alone with my thoughts for a moment. I asked nicely, though."

I wasn't sure exactly what to say, worried that everything that came to mind would sound false or patronizing. So I did something I hardly ever did, and I slid my arms around his waist and gave him a hug. He must have been surprised, because it took a moment for him to reciprocate the gesture, and he was careful to keep his hands near the center of my back. I pressed my cheek into the smooth satin of his lapel. "I am so happy that you're my family."

"Really?" His voice was rough again, uncertain.

"Really." I tightened my embrace.

He rested his chin on the top of my head. "I'm proud to be

related to you, Madeline. But what am I supposed to do now? My parents are dead, I can't get answers from them—"

"We'll ask Jack," I said. "Right now, if you'd like. We can wake him up and demand the truth."

"It's late. . . ."

"It's your life, Jude. Don't you want to know?"

He stepped away from me and glanced up at the painting. Saint John the Baptist, eyes cast down, draped in red. "Let's go."

Landry Park was mostly asleep when we got there, filled with the whispers and stirrings of the people sleeping in the ballroom and the quiet coming and goings of the people from the dry and blue-lit tents outside, but devoid of bright lights and chatter.

"Okay," Jude said, taking a breath. "Let's find your uncle."

TWENTY

We walked to the study, which was empty, and I had just resolved to go upstairs to Jack's room when I noticed firelight flickering from the library.

Father and Jack were inside, sitting across from each other, talking in low voices, voices that were only lightly laced with acrimony. Jude and I came in, and they paused.

"Isn't it a little late to just now be getting home?" Jack said.

"Parties generally last later than your bedtime, Stephen," Father said. "Good evening, Madeline, Captain MacAvery. Did you have a good time at the gala?"

It was so strange, being greeted like it was simply another evening out, another normal gentry evening—not like there were half a thousand Rootless camped on our lawn or that Jude had just learned that he'd been lied to his whole life and that he was directly related to someone in this room.

"Can we talk?" I asked. "The four of us?"

Father looked at the space between Jude and me—a space too wide for the talk to be about anything matrimonial—and nodded slowly. "Of course."

Jude and I sat, Jude crossing and uncrossing his ankles as if he couldn't get comfortable.

"Two days ago, Jamie talked to you about what he'd discovered about our DNA," I started, after Jude said nothing. "When he was first trying to figure everything out, he took samples. He sampled Jude."

There was no change in expression from either Jack or Father. I went on, unsure. "Jamie found that Jude has part of the same mutation. He's one of us."

Jude raised his head slightly, gazing at Father and Jack with a calm patience. Jack said nothing, but I noticed he was almost unnaturally still, his hands resting on his knees, his breaths coming in precisely measured inhalations and exhalations.

And then Father's head swiveled to stare at Jack, his eyebrow arched, his eyes lit with burning interest. "Stephen?"

Jack didn't answer, but he leaned forward, narrowing his eyes at Jude—not in suspicion but in scrutiny. Jude said nothing, meeting Jack's stare with an even expression. Jude was good—even I couldn't discern what he was feeling, and I'd seen him agitated and confused not fifteen minutes ago.

I wanted to break the silence, force the answers out into the open, but I waited instead, knowing that people with secrets were uncomfortable with silence, uncomfortable with the dynamic of power that silence created. It was one of Father's tricks, one that nearly always worked, although Jack was a

Landry, too, and just as skilled at manipulating a conversation.

But maybe he wanted to share, because he spoke first. "I suppose there is a possibility that this is true." A thickness underscored his words, and he turned his head away from us, keeping his eyes on the fire.

Father braced his elbows on his knees and put his head on his hands, looking keenly interested, and even a little amused.

Jack took a heavy breath. "You have to understand that when I decamped to the Rootless, I didn't really think about the implications of my Landry heritage, of the mutation that I had never asked for. I knew I might be healthier than some of the others, might live a little bit longer, but I didn't realize how much longer." He closed his eyes for a moment. "I married not long after I ran away. The Rootless marry young, for obvious reasons. And she died when I was thirty-two. Any other Rootless man would be staring into his own grave at that age. But I was just beginning to realize that I had a whole life ahead of me still. I would take another wife and watch her die and then maybe another, and I couldn't stand the thought of being in an endless spiral of loving and grieving, loving again and grieving again."

He opened his eyes. "This was before we'd come anywhere near negotiating with the Empire. Things looked hopeless for the Rootless. And I felt like maybe I had made a mistake in leaving home. I thought maybe it was time for me to return,

to make my apologies to Father and beg to be restored to the family. I made it as far as the gates."

"What stopped you?"

"Emilia Thorpe."

Sai Thorpe's mother, who'd been dead for several years.

"We'd dated before I disappeared," Jack explained, eyes still on the flames. "As a young man, I had planned on marrying her before I decided to run away. And then, of course, she married Mikul."

"What happened?" Father asked.

"It was before I'd had Sarah or Ewan or Charlie, before she'd had Sai. She was unhappy with Mikul—they'd never cared for each other, not the way she and I had when we were young. I was desperate to anchor myself to my past. She was desperate to feel love again."

Father made a derisive noise, like he was watching a poorly written melodrama on the wall screen.

"You are hardly one to judge, little brother. Faithfulness is not exactly one of your strong suits. And in any case, it was only once. Being with her, being in the Thorpe mansion while her husband was away—it reminded me of everything I'd hated about the gentry. I returned to the ghetto right afterward. I knew she had gone by herself to visit family in Europe shortly after . . . I never imagined it was to hide a pregnancy."

There was a silence. Jude was staring at the hand-knotted rug between the sofas, looking lost.

"Jude . . . ?" I asked.

He looked up. "*You* are my father?" His voice sounded like it was stretched too thin. As if it would snap at any moment.

"You have to understand," Jack pleaded, finally turning his face to Jude's. "I never heard from Emilia after that time, and I never imagined I would have any reason to." His voice grew a little desperate. "If I had known there was a child—family is paramount to me—I would have been in your life."

Jude was barely listening. "How did I end up with my adoptive parents? Why did they never tell me? Why did she never try to contact me?"

Jack cleared his throat, as if trying to regain mastery of his emotions. "Emilia's uncle was in the military. I can only assume that's how they knew your parents."

"But my parents—" Jude broke off, gray eyes glassy.

"They are still your parents," Father interjected firmly. Everyone seemed a little surprised; comforting someone in emotional distress was a rare thing for Father. "They are the people who raised you, who cared for you. They are the ones who made you who you are. Not Stephen or Emilia."

Jude nodded robotically. "Of course." He stood. "Thank you for your time. I should go now."

"Are you sure?" Jack asked, making to stand as well.

Jude held up a hand. "I just need some time to think, that's all."

Jack looked like he wanted to press the matter, but Father

shook his head at his brother and said, "We will talk later, Jude. Our door is always unlocked for you."

"I'll walk you out," I offered. We left the library together, and I shivered in the cool air of the hallway.

"How are you feeling?" I asked.

"Strange," he admitted. "I just realized Sai is my brother. I barely know him and we're related."

"Half brother," I corrected.

"And Ewan and Charlie, too—" He paused at that. "Ewan and I are very different, aren't we? For being brothers?"

They were: one all fire and passion and the other all coolness and discipline. But I could see the similarities now that I knew to link them together—the drive, the pride, the fierce beliefs in right and wrong.

"And don't forget that you are my cousin."

"What a tangled web we are," he said with a brave attempt at a smile.

"It's the gentry," I said seriously. "I think you'd be hard-pressed to find any family in the city less interrelated."

"I suppose that's true. I just never imagined that I would ever have brothers, and that the girl I . . . the girl I had once hoped to marry would be my cousin."

We stopped in front of the door. "Will you go back to the penthouse?"

"No. Yes. Possibly." He rubbed at his jaw. The shadow of stubble had begun to form, giving his face an uncharacteristic

desperation. "I may drive around the city for a while. Try to regain order of my thoughts."

I squeezed his hand. "Just remember how happy I am to call you family."

He squeezed my hand back and let go.

"You're a Landry now, Jude. There's no escaping it."

I said it with a smile and he returned it with one of his own, but as he walked through the door, the words hung in the air with an ominous weight.

TWENTY-ONE

The next morning, I woke on the floor of the observatory, blinking at yet another unseasonably warm and bright day. Sunlight glinted off the brass. My back and neck ached from a second night of sleeping on the floor. I stood and stretched, adding my soft bed to the growing list of comforts that I'd taken for granted. That I'd never even contemplated being a thing to take for granted.

Elinor came up the stairs, still managing to look fresh and pretty and neatly pressed even though the house laundry and washrooms were overrun. "Your mother is looking for you. She's out in the greenhouse now—said she needed flowers for a luncheon."

"Thanks, Elinor." I raised my arms high over my head, hearing my back erupt in a series of pops. I relaxed them, still stiff, but feeling a little better. "How are you doing with all the people in the house?"

She shrugged. "Not that much different than a large house party, really. Same sort of logistics, just on a larger scale. And it's nice to help those poor people. They are so wretched. You

can hear them coughing all night long. That project of Mr. Jamie's can't be finished soon enough."

She saw my look of surprise—Paul was the last person outside of my circle that I had told about the serum—and smiled. "Your uncle has been talking to the Rootless about it. Word's been getting around."

I wanted to feel like this was a good thing—it was, I knew it was; the cure would bring hope and would also attract more Rootless to the bargaining table, even if some were still resentful about the Landry immunity. But part of me fretted about the fragility of it all. If the serum didn't work, would the crushing disappointment just make everything worse?

After I changed, making sure to put on boots and a cape, I went out to the greenhouse. I hardly needed the boots—thanks to the solar warmers, the faded grass was as dry as it would be on a summer's afternoon. The warmers made the air around the tents mild, almost pleasant, but a sharp wind from the north told me that the warm spell of late was almost at an end. With wind like this, we'd be expecting another snowstorm soon.

As I walked, I noticed that the lawn was less swarmed than it had been yesterday—several tents that had been erected the day before were now folded into neat piles of canvas and aluminum rods, and the solar heaters had been rolled back up to the house. I frowned. Had they found more room in the house for the refugees? Or had another gentry family offered

to take them in? Surely I hadn't been mistaken in my estimation of the numbers yesterday.

Mother stood alone in the greenhouse. She wasn't cutting roses; she didn't even have her basket and shears. She simply stood and stared. In her fawn dress of gathered silk, and with her warm brown skin and brown hair, she looked like a sepia photo from hundreds of years ago. Perfectly lovely, perfectly still.

She didn't seem to hear my footsteps as I approached, and she gave a little start when I came up beside her. "Madeline!"

"Sorry."

She shook her head. "You'll give me fright lines if you do things like that."

"Elinor said you were looking for me?"

She turned, and I could see that she'd been crying. "Did you know *that woman* came over last night?"

"That woman?"

"Christine Dana."

Oh. Oh dear. Now was not the time for her to rekindle her romance with my father. "Did she . . . come to see Father?"

"No. She came to see me."

I had not anticipated that. "What did she want to talk about?"

Mother threw up her hands. "How am I supposed to know? I immediately demanded she leave. Does she think that she can have my affections along with Alexander's?" Her voice turned hard. "No. That's the one thing she will not steal."

We were quiet for a moment, the glass walls of the green-house straining and rattling in the wind.

"We were best friends once," she said. "But it was so long ago, and I was so stupid then. I couldn't see how conniving she was. We were closer than sisters. Until . . ."

She didn't need to say it. We both looked back at the house.

"He was the bachelor every girl dreamed of marrying. Handsome and charming and a Landry. Christine and I were only fifteen when we came to our first ball here, and he was twenty-one. He seemed so much older than us, so worldly. And that first time, he chose Christine to dance. They seemed so perfect together. She could say all the right things, laugh just the right way. He chose her to dance again and again that night, and when we went back home, I thought Christine would float away, she was so happy."

Mother tucked a rare stray tendril of hair behind her ear. "But the next night, at Westoff Castle, your father asked me to dance. I can still remember the look on Christine's face, how hurt she was." Mother closed her eyes. "I can still remember the way he held me. It was like magic. Of course, that was before I knew that his father was making him choose me for my family's money."

I bit my lip. This was Mother's story, but the places and players seemed so easily my own. I remembered watching David and Cara dance, feeling my heart twist, and then danc-ing with David and feeling it leap.

Mother must have sensed what I was thinking, because she turned to me. "I knew it was hard for you to watch Cara debut with David, but at least it all worked out in the end. You got David, and you and Cara are friends again."

I didn't bother to tell her that Cara and I weren't friends before that, but in a way, Mother was right. Not only had David and I ended up together, but Cara and I had become, maybe not quite friends, but something close to it. The three of us were so much less tangled and tormented than my parents and Christine Dana.

I wrapped my arms around my mother. "Father loves you," I said to comfort her, even if I didn't know if it was true. "He hasn't seen Christine since he's come back."

She brightened at this. "Maybe they've finished with each other. Although it is hard to tell. Your father is so secretive."

Secretive. I almost didn't want to ask her about our other family secret, to ask if she knew what poisoned salvation swirled inside those syringes. I didn't know if I would like the answer.

But I asked anyway. "Mother . . . when I was sick a few years ago, did you know why?"

She pulled back to look at my face. "It was a fever—the same kind your father had as a boy. Why do you ask?"

"You never knew that someone was making me ill?"

She looked aghast. "No, darling, no one was making you ill. It was a fever. Everyone said so. The doctors even made you a special medicine to help fight it."

"You never thought that it was the medicine itself that caused the fever?"

"Of course not! Why are you talking like this? Who would want to hurt you?"

"Never mind," I said, giving her a quick kiss on the cheek. "It doesn't matter now." Although it did matter a little— knowing that she'd been as ignorant as I was gave me a small kind of comfort. At least one parent hadn't intentionally hurt me.

I should tell her, I thought. I should tell her about the Landry DNA and its far-reaching implications and how confused I felt about it all. But I didn't. I didn't want to relive my own initial sense of betrayal by watching hers, and I couldn't endure the inevitable verbal unpacking of it all, where she would curse my father or bless him, fuss over me even though I was perfectly healthy now, grouse about how she'd been denied this special protection.

She'll find out soon enough, I rationalized. With the way the rumors were spreading, it wouldn't be long.

I handed her the shears and a basket, knowing that she'd feel happier doing something, happier with her mind off Christine Dana. As I walked out, I could hear the low *snip, snip* of the blades cutting the stems, the sound rising above the roses and the vines and troughs of soil, and then I closed the door behind me, and every noise was stolen by the wind outside.

*   *   *   *   *

When I went back in the house, I passed by Jane Osbourne helping a child tie her shoes. Jane's face seemed flushed, her eyes bright, as if she'd been exerting herself. But she had a cheerful expression and she hummed as she cinched the girl's laces into a knot.

After she was finished, I approached her. "I didn't know you had come to help."

"My whole family did," she said, and when I cast my gaze about the room, I could discern several Osbourne children, ranging in age from fifteen to five, all with bouncing corkscrew curls and all helping, even the youngest, who trailed behind one of the servants, carrying a pillow.

I touched my chest above my heart, suddenly intensely grateful for my kind friends. She and Jude and David and Cara, stepping into help. "That's very good of you," I said, trying to put some of the emotion I felt into my voice. "Thank you so much."

She gave the crowd around us a small smile. "It's the least I can do. After my mother told me that the Uprisen were dragging their feet on rebuilding the ghetto, despite her best efforts—and your father's, I might add—I felt that we needed to come. Try to make a difference, however we can."

"Why are they dragging their feet?" I asked. "Surely they don't want the Rootless living on an estate near them much longer."

Jane nodded. "There is that, but I think it's because they've just learned that the Rootless aren't changing the charges, at one house, at least."

My heart stopped, coming back to life with a thudding that I thought might bruise my ribs. This was my fault, I realized. I had known about this, and if I had been brave enough to tell the police about it, it would have never gotten this far. But I hadn't, wanting to protect the Rootless, and now they would suffer from the gentry's wrath anyway.

"The story is that a servant heard a soft beeping in the charge room at Glasshawke and went in to investigate, and discovered that the charges were about to expire and hadn't yet been changed—normally charges are changed weeks before they'll expire," Jane said. "The Glaizes immediately alerted the other gentry in the city to inspect their own charges. They are furious—Mother says they are contemplating horrible things. . . ."

"And if the Rootless haven't changed the charges? What then? They can't arrest them all—then no charges would be changed."

Jane looked at me, brown eyes bleak. "But see, it's not just the charges. The Uprisen think they are murdering their heirs as well; they want to make an example of them. And then truck in Rootless from another city. To *replace* them."

"To replace them?"

And then I understood, and the understanding made my stomach twist. "They wouldn't kill off an entire city's Rootless population. They couldn't. They might talk about it, but they would never actually do it." But as soon as I spoke the words, I realized I had no confidence in them.

Jane seemed to struggle to regain her normal placid optimism. "Of course. You're right—they wouldn't. Even the Uprisen aren't that inhumane."

Jane's little brother, all wide smiles and crooked teeth, sidled up to Jane and slipped his hand in hers. "Can you help me find the bathroom?" he asked, in that slightly dancing way that meant he was mere moments from disaster. She gave me a rueful smile, and tugged him across the ballroom and through the butler's door.

Immediately, I turned away from the ballroom to find Jack. He had to know that the Uprisen now knew about the unchanged charges. More than that—he needed to be persuaded to have the almost-expired charges changed out. If any gentry felt as much as a headache from the radiation, then they would use it as an excuse to hurt the Rootless. Being in Landry Park wouldn't protect them, not if all the constables in the city came with their guns and their batons.

I finally located him outside, talking heatedly with a couple that had their scant belongings in bags near their feet. Whatever the conversation they were having, Jack seemed to be losing ground, as his voice grew more and more intense and they finally picked up their bags and left, going not to the tents on the lawn, but around the house to the front, as if they were leaving. I waited at a respectful distance until he had watched

241

them go and then approached him. It was so bright that I had to squint when I looked up at his face.

"Can we talk?"

"Certainly," Jack said, eyes still on the side of the house where the couple had left.

"Is everything okay?"

He put his hands behind his back and examined his feet. "Some of the Rootless are leaving."

"Leaving? To go where?"

"Back home," he said softly. "Back to the ghetto."

"But there's nothing there—everything was burned!"

He shrugged. "They'll make do somehow. The others are, though barely."

"But why?"

"Can you really not guess?"

I remembered Paul and our conversation on the lawn. "Is this about the mutation?"

"It appears so. Just another example of how I've become untrustworthy in their eyes, hiding something like that for so long. And the more untrustworthy I become, the more attractive Smith's ideas are."

"Ideas like what?" I whispered, thinking of Marianne and Mark.

Jack gave me a look, as if he could guess exactly where my mind tended. "Not murder. But other extremes, like calling in the Empire."

"Or not changing the charges?"

That gave him pause. "That was not something I agreed to," he said after a moment. "I've always felt it was too foolish a plan; it would only arouse the gentry's fury, and we know they're not above punishing us all if they can't identify the real culprit. If Smith and his associates have done this, it wasn't with my consent."

He's lost control of the Rootless, I realized.

"However it happened, the gentry know. Or at least they suspect."

"Which house was it?"

"Glasshawke."

I watched his face. There was almost nothing readable there—no guilt, no glee, nothing. But something about the way he cast his eyes west, toward Glasshawke's windowed edifice glittering in the sun, made me think that this whole business weighed heavily on him. "Please send someone to change the charges," I said. "I know this was Smith's doing, but you can undo it so easily, and maybe, just maybe, the gentry will be able to overlook it."

Jack raised his chin ever so slightly, eyes still on the Glaizes' estate. "Smith's original plan was to have the gentry forced out of their homes in a matter of weeks. He wants the estates gone altogether—torn to the ground, the earth salted where they stood."

My instinctive reaction was horror, even though I saw

the twisted logic in it all. "But how could he use radiation as leverage when that's what the gentry have done to him?"

"My dear niece, that is precisely why he feels he can—and should—do it. He wants to start fresh as a nation, he says, start fresh with new power sources and new social structures. And as long as people listen to him, then he will have more momentum than me."

"Not if we convince the people otherwise," I said. "Convince them that it will be better to wait. Convince them that it would be worse to bring the Empire here."

"Would it really be worse?" he said, more to himself than to me, and I caught a glimpse of the same man who intentionally let his people suffer for his cause.

"Please," I said, trying to drive his thoughts away from whatever calculations he was making, trying to appeal to his sense of reason. "Send someone with protection to change them, at least at Glasshawke. They can do it quickly and safely, and before anybody gets hurt. You can smooth over any damage." *And give me time to stop Smith from doing anything else.*

He didn't respond.

"Jane Osbourne's mother thinks that the other Uprisen would make an example out of this city's Rootless," I said. I'd been reluctant to add this element into the conversation—it would only enrage Jack. But maybe it would make him see the value in staying his chosen course, in avoiding the Empire.

"The Uprisen would kill or arrest you all and then bring in Rootless from another city."

"A bluff," Jack said dismissively.

"After all you've seen—after what happened with Charlie— are you willing to bet that it is? Are you willing to take that risk?"

He licked his lips, looking away. "If only your father could have done more to sway them. I worry his presence here is doing more harm than good."

My throat tightened at the thought of Father and Mother being sent away from home, no matter how hurt I still was over the truths he'd hidden from me. I had missed them while they were gone, I wanted them near me. And besides that, I still felt that Father could be useful. I *knew* it. Maybe the Uprisen hadn't listened to him initially, but he had been their unchallenged leader once. That had to work in our favor somehow.

"I think he should stay," I said. "At least until this present situation is played out."

Jack said nothing, but after a minute, he gave the slightest of nods. I exhaled in relief, and got back to the subject at hand.

"Just consider changing the charges. We have enough gear for it to be safe for one person. The charges don't even have to be sent on the trains—just lock them in a lead bin in the yards."

He rocked up on his heels and back down, still thinking. "I'll think about it," he finally said, and left.

I gave Glasshawke a final look of my own and then followed him into the house.

For the next few hours, I found employment wherever I could, ending with a turn at the table we were using to hand out lunch. Several of the Rootless—men and women—had volunteered to help take over the cooking and subsequent distribution of meals, in order to take the pressure off of Martha and the rest of the staff, but I was still helping. It was strange; all my life I'd watched other people doing things for me—drawing my bath, pouring my tea, laundering my clothes. And within the space of a couple days, it had become distinctly uncomfortable. With the Rootless here and with so many things to do, there didn't seem to be a place to stand by and observe—every available set of hands was needed. I'd jumped in, and now that the dust had settled and the Rootless—and the estate—had fallen into the routine of housing and feeding such a group, I found I wasn't ready to jump out. There was something comforting about helping in such a tangible way, meal by meal, tent by tent.

"Madeline."

I turned to see Father, and I apparently wasn't able to keep my emotions from flashing across my face, because he looked distinctly uncomfortable.

"About the serum."

I let out a breath. So we were finally going to talk about it. I kept my face down, not wanting him to see how unbalanced the whole thing made me feel.

"You seem to feel ambivalent about it. Am I correct?"

"You are."

"I want you to know that I'm, ah, I am sorry."

I looked up at him. He was apologizing? To me? This made two apologies in the space of a week—surely a record for him.

"I should have told you," he said. "My father told me before he did it. I'd seen Stephen go through it, and I knew—I knew what to expect. The thing was, when my father explained to me what was happening, it didn't make it easier. It made it harder. I dreaded the shots, knowing the pain they'd bring. I already hated my father, but he made my mother inject me, and I began to hate her, too. The whole ordeal made me long for ignorance, made me wish that I had simply suffered thinking I was ill with a normal malady, not a manufactured one. It was harder having an illness that *could* be stopped, but *wouldn't* be stopped."

"So you lied to me."

"I thought it would be easier. And . . . I confess, I didn't want you to hate me. I didn't want you to feel the way I felt about my mother, the one person dearest in the world to me besides my brother. I had hoped to spare you."

"I see."

"But that was wrong of me. I should have told you, given you all the information. I should have trusted you."

Before I could comment on this uncharacteristic expression of regret, I saw my cat dart in between people's legs, a blur of gray. Charlie followed with a group of his friends, whooping and laughing. One of them had a leash and I had the sense that they were trying to force Morgana into taking a walk, an endeavor which I surmised would end in someone getting scratched.

"He looks so much like you did as a child," Father said. "Whenever I look at him, I see you." He shook his head at some private thought. "I've barely grown accustomed to having two nephews. And now I have three."

My mind clicked over from four years ago to last night.

"Does it—Jude's parentage—mean anything for the estate?"

"Mean anything?" He studied me. "What are you really asking?"

"Does it mean that I will still inherit Landry Park?" My cheeks warmed at admitting to having such a selfish thought when there was so much else going on, so much else to worry and think about. When there was a possibility that there wouldn't be a Landry Park to inherit.

"Yes."

I closed my eyes a moment, unable to stop the wave of relief that crashed through me and the wave of guilt immediately following that.

"Gentry law only recognizes heirs born into a marriage

between two members of the gentry, unless the will is amended to make a special dispensation. It's my understanding that Ewan has not expressed interest in becoming the inheritor of the estate and additionally, your uncle gives me his assurances that he has no interest in denying you the estate. His sole purpose in assuming control was to unseat me." Father's voice was not angry or bitter, but calm—phlegmatic even. "I can't see Captain MacAvery suing for a dispensation, and I also cannot see it getting granted if he did."

"Good," I said, and then I hated myself a little. "I mean, I hope it works out so that everyone is happy."

"At any rate," Father said, moving past the discussion of the estate, "we've been invited to Glasshawke tonight for a party. Apparently, the Glaizes are determined to show the Rootless that they plan to continue living exactly as they have before. And don't worry about the rumors—I'm assured that the estate is quite safe for another two weeks."

I'd had more than enough Glasshawke for one day. "I'm not worried about it at all. But do I have to go?"

He raised his eyes to the ceiling, shaking his head. "Some things never change."

"But—"

He met my eyes. "If we want some form of negotiation to move forward—negotiation that does not involve my brother bringing the Empire down on our heads—then we need to curry goodwill with them."

"If you could lead them again, then it wouldn't matter if we curried goodwill or not."

Father looked down at his cane. "I don't know if it's that easy. They are all used to the idea of me making the decisions, but yet they had the police call in the attack on the Rootless without my knowledge or my consent. Yesterday, when I tried to speak to them about the potential cure, about a possible restructuring of the jobs of the Rootless and about rebuilding Rootless homes, they showed no interest. I'm no longer to be trusted, it seems. A king without a kingdom."

He and Jack both.

I sighed. "I don't want to go to the party."

"You never do."

TWENTY-TWO

Jack sent the changers. He gave me a look when they set off across the lawn to reach the estate by the back way, a look that said *on your head be it*. But the changers were allowed in, allowed to replace the charges and leave with the expired ones. They wore gear, and Jack arranged for a gardening truck to drive them back to the yards.

"That didn't seem so bad," I offered later. He didn't respond.

I went up to get ready for the party with a weary mind, guiltily wishing that I had never met Jack, that the Rootless had chosen a different time to rise up, that my biggest problem was still convincing Father to let me go to the university. I swatted the selfish thoughts away, finished dressing, and met my parents downstairs to go to the Glaizes'.

Glasshawke was lit up, completely and decadently luminous. Even separated by our wide lawn and the maze at the end of our property, I could see from our darkened ballroom that every window of their estate shone with light. Their vast pleasure gardens and patio, both littered with the ice sculptures that they commissioned for every winter party, twinkled with hundreds of tiny lights. Of course, even though our estates adjoined, we didn't walk, we drove, and when we arrived, the line of cars outside suggested that every gentry family in the city was in attendance.

The Glaizes had been industrialists once upon a time, making their money from contracts with the military, manufacturing the critically strong glass that made up helicopter and plane windows. After the war, they remade themselves as gentleman farmers, but the legacy of their glass fortune lived on in their massive house, with its hundreds of windows, large and small. The house fairly blazed, streaming light out onto the snow-covered lawn and crushed gravel drive.

Father, Mother, and I were helped out of the car by a pair of black-and-white-clad footmen, and then escorted to the front doors, which were also made almost entirely of glass.

Inside was a true ball. Women danced in sumptuous dresses, the golden light from the chandeliers catching on the jewels in their ears and around their necks, and the men accompanied them in crisp tuxedos and shoes that shone as brightly as the jewelry. Smartly dressed footman circulated throughout, one arm tucked behind each back as they held aloft gleaming silver trays of champagne and cigars. An eight-piece band played on the strings and piano, and everywhere was the smell of delicious food.

When I looked at the guests as they danced and flirted, I saw nothing in their faces to suggest worry or anxiety, even though they danced in a ballroom that would have been rendered dangerous in a matter of days if Jack had not acted. It was as if nothing had changed, as if nothing were ever going to change, as if the idea of there not being parties and luncheons and extravagant dinners that lasted until the moon itself went to bed was simply unimaginable.

It disheartened me to realize it, but there was a part of me that wanted to stop and drink this in, engrave every second and every detail of the dancing and the eating and the drinking into my memory. There were parts of this life that were cruel and ridiculous, but there was beauty, too, elegance and a mastery of pleasure and contentment. And I would miss it. Even as I knew this all had to change, I would miss it.

"Madeline!" someone called across the floor. Father nodded at me to go, and I followed the voice to a corner where Philip, Jane, and the Lawrence boys were standing.

"I didn't know you were coming tonight," Philip said.

"I didn't know either until just a while ago." I smiled at Jane. "Thank you again for all your help today."

Philip looked at me curiously and I explained, "Jane and her family came to the estate to help us with all the displaced Rootless. It was very kind of her."

"Hardly a great kindness given the situation, but I was happy to help and would love to help in the future," Jane said in her quietly gracious way. Philip wrapped an arm around her waist and brought her close, looking ready to either canonize her or kiss her. He seemed to realize that we were all looking at them, and he quickly dropped his arm. Jane pressed a hand to her cheek, as if it burned.

"Speaking of great kindnesses," Tarleton said, clearly bored by the fledgling romance, "I hear that the Landrys are actually superheroes. Have you heard that, Frank?"

Frank nodded, taking a drink. I turned away from them both, suppressing an eye roll. It was enough to deal with the backlash of legitimate anger from the Rootless, but to hear the Lawrences carping about the mutation was too much.

"And now they're going to give their superpowers to the Rootless," he went on. "Of course, they're not bothering to give them to the gentry because they're a bunch of—"

"Do you have something you'd like to say to me?" I asked Tarleton.

"I'm only saying that secrets don't make friends. And now that we know about your little secret . . . well, you can expect that our parents will not be keen to help the Landrys anytime soon."

Stuart interrupted in a singsong voice, "Oh look! Here come your boyfriends."

Despite myself, I glanced over my shoulder to see Jude and David entering the ballroom together, both in sharply pressed tuxedos, their steps perfectly in sync.

"Excuse me," I said, ignoring Stuart's snide laugh, and moved off toward the two men I wanted most to see, all too ready to leave the discussion of the mutation behind me.

Jude smiled politely at me as I approached, but David's

shoulders were tense, his face sharp, and so when I reached them, I greeted Jude first, not wanting to cut myself on whatever bad mood had taken hold of David.

Jude kissed my hand—a dry and quick gesture—and straightened. There was no trace of the hollow confusion he'd felt last night. He seemed like he always did—certain, assured, destined to look noble and heroic in military portraits for the rest of his life.

"How are you?" I asked.

He knew I wasn't asking in the casual way of ballroom acquaintances. "I'm feeling much better, now that I've had time to think." He surveyed the dancers and guests spread out across the floor. "I am actually quite content with it all now. I spoke with Ewan this morning, and I told him that if I must learn that I had a brother, I couldn't have been luckier in it being him."

"What did Ewan say?"

Jude shrugged. "Not much, honestly. I got the feeling that he wasn't very excited about adding another gentry person to his family tree."

"Sharing blood doesn't automatically make you family," I murmured, mostly to myself. But then seeing his look, I added, "And I bet Ewan will come around."

"Maybe. Charlie seemed a lot happier about having a new brother." He smiled. "And your uncle is making an effort to reach out, which of course I will honor."

"Have you spoken with Sai yet?"

"That's next," he said. "I hope to see him soon. I'm still soaking it all in . . . to be a Landry—well, you know how much I've wished for that."

I did know, and I held back a shiver at the memory of Jude's ambition on the night of my debut.

"I'm going to get a drink," David announced, and then walked off without another word.

Jude looked after him with a slight frown. "Would you like to dance?" he offered, as if to cover David's rudeness.

"Why not?" And I let him lead me onto the floor, where a lively reel was already in progress. It took Jude a minute to find his feet—for all of his other charms, he was a rather mechanical dancer—and then we spun across the floor so quickly that I was out of breath and laughing by the time the dance had ended.

"I meant what I said, you know," Jude said as the music changed to a stately waltz. "I may not have seemed it last night, but now that I've had time to reflect, I am amazed at the fortuity of all this. I am gratified to be part of your family, Madeline. It feels like my whole future has changed."

I didn't know what to say to that. I didn't even know what to think about it. I'd spent the last year wrestling with my identity as a Landry, and Jude only had to struggle with it one night before he had it all sorted and filed and fitted into his soul like a puzzle piece.

"Jude . . ." I started, but I stopped. There was no way I could warn him against that sense of power, that sense of privilege that came with having Landry Park at your back. And certainly there was no way to warn him without making it sound as if I didn't trust him, as if I thought him weak and susceptible to ambition and greed.

His face was grave. "Don't tell me that you've changed your mind about having me in the family."

"It's not that," I assured him quickly. "It's only that things are about to change and nobody knows how much. I'd hate to see you plan on a future for yourself that may not come to pass."

He held me at arm's length for a moment, silver eyes examining mine, searching for hidden motives and meanings in my words.

"May I?" David stood behind Jude, and I could tell from the flush in his cheeks that he'd already found his drink and possibly a second one. Jude graciously stepped back. I placed myself within the taut circle of David's arms, and we were off, twirling in wide circles across the room.

"I hardly know what to say," David said. "What's the proper etiquette for acknowledging a new addition to your girlfriend's family?"

David was so much lighter on his feet than Jude. Dancing with him almost felt like floating as he led me effortlessly around the room, my dress brushing against the tops of his shoes.

"I believe it's as easy as saying congratulations," I said. And then, because I didn't feeling like playing into his petulance, "What is bothering you tonight?"

"Who said anything was bothering me?" His hand slid farther down my back as he pulled me closer.

We spun again.

I could see the reluctant cant to his mouth. "Just tell me," I said, a little impatiently. "And don't joke about it," I added, sensing that habitual sarcastic carelessness of his about to surface. "Be serious with me. For once."

"I always take you seriously," he insisted, and the irritated tightening of my fingers around his drew out the first genuine grin I'd seen from him in days.

He seemed to debate with himself for a moment then finally ceded victory to me. "Today, I woke up without hope for the first time since Liberty Park," he confessed. "I feel like everything we've worked for is slowly falling apart. The bombings, the burning of the ghetto, the unchanged charges, the unsolved murders . . ." He trailed off, gaze sliding from me to somewhere distant and unreachable, a dark future only he could see.

I cupped my hand around his neck, forcing his blue eyes to mine. There were clouds in them, as if silt had been stirred up, hanging suspended in what were normally vivid, clear depths. "We will work through this."

"But are you and I even still on the same side?"

That stung. And it stung all the more because I couldn't bring myself to reassure him, not at the cost of what I believed to be the truth.

The ballroom seemed to whirl around us as we danced, as if we were the still point in a spinning world, and we were so focused on each other that the drinks and rustling skirts had disappeared entirely. There were only the two of us.

"And whenever I think about it, the murders and the rioting and *us*, I start to feel—" he shook his head, taking a deep breath. "It's not important."

"It is to me."

He leaned down, so that his forehead rested against mine. "I know. And thank you for that."

I lifted my face, expecting a kiss, but it never came. Instead, he withdrew from my embrace and moved easily between the dancers like a fox between trees.

It has nothing to do with you, Madeline, I told myself. But I wasn't feeling self-pity or self-doubt. I was feeling irritation. I was feeling weary of David's demons, jaded by them, well aware that it wasn't fair of me to feel that way.

I left the dance floor, ignoring the curious looks of the other guests, ignoring the whispers. I worried they would have something real to whisper about soon enough.

TWENTY-THREE

"Storm's blowing in."

I glanced up at the gardener, who was helping me carry a solar heater down the wide steps from the patio to the lawn. I'd felt the need to be outside, to be moving and not thinking, so I'd volunteered to help with adjusting the solar heaters. At the very least, it kept me from checking my tablet every five minutes or so, waiting to see if David had messaged me. Though we hadn't fought in the strictest definition of the word, I still felt as if we'd parted badly, as if there was a murky fog of distrust between us—a fog that all boiled down to Smith.

The gardener was right about the storm. The wind had been strong for a couple days now, cold and biting, and there was an ashen cast to the cloudy sky that augured snow.

"News says lots of snow," he said, echoing my thoughts. "Lots of gusting winds. Won't be easy for the folks in the tents."

"Maybe we can squeeze more inside. Just for a couple of days." With so many Rootless defecting back to the ghetto, we could probably manage to have them all indoors now.

The gardener didn't ask why the Rootless were leaving. Given how quickly news spread among the servants, he probably already knew all about the mutation. He probably also knew that no progress had been made on rebuilding the ghetto, despite the number of people still picking a living out of the burned remains. Jack insisted that the sorting yards be shut and real houses built. The Uprisen would only consider erecting the shanties anew—but right now they were barely considering that given the scandal over the charges at Glasshawke. Though Jack had caved and sent the changers, the psychological damage was done. The gentry were now afraid of their own houses, afraid of the latent power that the Rootless had always held.

The idea of trust on either side seemed painfully laughable now.

After we rolled the solar heater into place, I went inside the house to survey what little room we had left. I ran into Jane on the front steps, carrying a basket of food and medicine. "I brought these," she said.

"Thank you. Every bit helps." I sounded tired, I knew I did, so I tried to offer a smile.

She examined me. "Do you need help with anything? You have that look."

I explained the problem of the snow to her. "Honestly, I think the solar heaters would be able to handle the snow, but it would be wet, and aside from that, the wind would make staying in those tents incredibly uncomfortable."

"So you want to find a way to shelter more people inside?"

I nodded. "With the smaller number, they easily fit inside during the day. It's just the sleeping arrangements I'm concerned about. I'm going to do a quick survey of the rooms, see how many people are currently staying in each one. Want to help?"

Jane always wanted to help. Tablets out, we divided up the house, with Jane taking the top floor and the observatory, while I did the bottom two. Most of the Rootless were downstairs in the ballroom, but I counted bedrolls and pillows stacked neatly in corners, and was able to make quick work of the lower level and its larger rooms. Upstairs took me a little longer, owing to the number of bedrooms—almost forty in all. Aside from the blankets and pillows, the rooms were empty, save for one laundress moving through to gather sheets, but she went down the stairs soon after I started looking.

There was something strange about feeling alone when I wasn't truly alone, a sort of cognitive dissonance. I felt as if people were with me, but each room was silent and unoccupied. The maids—so busy with the influx of refugees—had been directed away from the normal luxuries they provided, and so almost every room sported flowers wilting damply in vases of brackish water and white hearths smattered with ash and grime.

I checked my tablet again. Still no word from David.

A crash sounded from down the hall, and I couldn't help it, I yelped, adrenaline pounding through me, the panic flaring and dying just as quickly. I was fine, *I was fine*, it wasn't another bomb, and I was alone. I remembered my fear the night that I'd been alone in the ballroom and a stone had hit the window, how silly I'd felt once I'd gotten to my well-lit room and examined my fears in the safety of my soft bed.

I am alone, I reassured myself. I'd been alone then and I was now.

I was cautious as I stepped out into the hallway, and I went still as I saw one of those neglected vases shattered on the floor. It must have slipped, although the end table it was on was tilted slightly away from the wall, as if it had been jostled by someone moving through the hallway. *The laundress,* I thought. She'd come back up for more sheets. Carrying a heavy basket on her hip, she must have accidentally knocked the vase off the table, and she had probably gone down to get things to clean it up.

There's always an explanation, I reminded myself.

I finished cataloging the rooms on the second floor and went downstairs, where it was lunchtime. I joined in the work, and afterward was cornered by Mother, who was fretful and overwrought by planning the Lantern Day Ball under such conditions.

"How am I supposed to have the cooks start preparing when we're feeding all these people?" she demanded. "The Uprisen are still refusing to come, which is patently ridiculous, the ball is in two days—"

"Maybe it's not that important."

She stopped talking for a moment, appalled at my blasphemy.

"It *is* important. Because it's your eighteenth birthday and you deserve a real celebration!"

Emotion swam in her eyes, floated in her voice. All at once, I realized that this was not about the guest list or even about the perceived snub from her friends. It was about her trying to maintain a semblance of control over her life, and to act as a mother in the only way she knew how—by giving me the things that meant so much to her.

I hugged her. "It will be a real party because you will be there. And Father and the rest of my family."

She sniffed a little. "Sounds like a dull party."

"Sounds like a perfect party," I assured her. Then I looked around the ballroom. "Have you seen Jane?"

"Jane Osbourne? Not at all. Is she here?"

"Yes," I said. "She went to the third floor to survey the rooms in case we have to bring people in because of the storm. I got caught up with lunch and must have missed her coming down."

"Maybe she went home."

"Maybe..." I thought about the top floor, full of dusty unused rooms and the narrow corridors of the servants' quarters. "I hope she didn't get lost." I used my tablet to send her a quick message. She didn't reply, but that wasn't unusual for Jane.

Deciding to go check the house for her, I gave my mother a reassuring sort of touch on her arm and went upstairs. The stairs—made of shallow steps of white marble and bounded by ornately carved banisters—wound up in such a way that it was possible to see the first floor from the third, meaning I could still make out the distant rumble of people moving around on the lower levels. But once I left the stairs, the same muffled silence filled the air as when I had walked through the second floor earlier. I made a quick round of the guest rooms, and then entered into the labyrinth of servants' corridors, comprised of tiny cells all shoved under steeply pitched gables and laid out in awkward, boxy configurations, as if the servants' quarters themselves had been shoved into whatever leftover spaces remained after designing the desirable parts . . . as if they'd been an afterthought.

Jane was nowhere to be found. In fact, I only saw one other living creature—Morgana, who wound around my feet and meowed in the way that signaled she wanted attention.

I bent down to stroke her head, but she dipped under my fingers and trotted away, tail high in the air.

"Fine then," I muttered, standing. Maybe Jane had simply gone home. I turned to go back downstairs.

Morgana made another loud and highly annoying meow and started pacing around the iron staircase that led up to the observatory. I'd forgotten to look there, which was foolish, because if there were any place that someone would linger in this house, it would undoubtedly be the observatory. Even in daylight, the view was astonishing.

I stepped around the cat and climbed the stairs, holding up my dress in one hand and clutching the railing with the other. Even with soft slippers on, my feet seemed to clang on the steps, every noise and rattle captured and magnified by all the metal and glass in the room above. I started casting my eyes about the space as soon as I alighted from the stairs.

There was no one here. The observatory felt just as empty as the two floors below it, just as quiet. A pure absence of breath and movement and thought.

And then I saw it. A pink leather ballet flat peeking from behind a bench, as if it had tumbled carelessly off the wearer's foot. But I knew that flat, and I knew the foot it belonged to, and I knew that Jane was never careless.

Bands of iron-tight fear ringed my chest as I walked toward the slipper; I knew what I would find before I found it, knew it with a vicious, wild certainty. But it still didn't prepare me for the sight of Jane sprawled on the floor, her mass of wild curls cascading around her face, her skin contrasting with the creamy marble. I found myself captivated by her bare foot, the foot that had lost the slipper, wondering if she had tried to run or tried to struggle.

The back of my neck prickled with cold heat as I remembered the shattered vase, realized that someone could still be up here, waiting for me, but I forced myself to look around, examine every corner of the small observatory—there was no place to hide up here. I was alone.

I swallowed down bile as my eyes traced the line of Jane's leg where her fluttering dress had been torn. No, not torn—cut. On her thigh, something savage had been done—it was a mass of blood and ripped flesh.

It took me a moment to recognize it for what it was, but once I saw it, there could be no mistake.

The now familiar slashed atomic circle. Someone had carved it into Jane's thigh.

Carved.

This time I couldn't help being sick. I managed to make it to a wastebasket, and then stayed there for a long moment, my thoughts at once jumbled and unnavigable and also curiously blank, the bands of iron around my chest now too tight for me to breathe normally.

Jane.

Jane.

I realized I was whispering her name out loud, as if I could wake her. I crawled back over to her, past her tablet, which lay a few feet from her outstretched fingers. There could be no doubt that she was dead—her brown eyes stared vacantly ahead and there was no movement in her stomach or her chest. But I felt that I had to be sure, I had to know for certain, for myself. I gently rolled her wrist upward and pressed my fingers against it. Jamie had taught me to take a pulse long ago, when he'd first come to America to study. I'd been just a girl then, only ten or so, and he had quietly amused me at an interminable family dinner by showing me how to check my pulse in my wrist and in my neck.

Jane's wrist was cool to the touch—not as cool as the floor but colder than my own skin. It was still yielding, though, still soft. There was no pulse. She was dead.

I needed to do something. The thought surfaced on a numb ocean of other thoughts, pointless thoughts, but it managed to drift into my awareness. I needed to do something.

Call. That's what you did. You called someone. The police.

I found my tablet and tried to dial, but my fingers were shaky and clumsy, and it took several tries before the call rang through and someone at the constabulary picked up.

"Please," I managed. "My friend, she's dead."

"Where are you?" The voice on the other end was crisp and female—efficient sounding.

"Landry Park."

"We'll be right there."

She wanted me to stay on the call with her, but I let the hand holding the tablet fall to my side. My thoughts seemed so frantic and yet so sluggish, full of a desperate lassitude. This had never happened. I'd always been able to *think*, think clearly—it was something I prided myself on. Logic, order, calm. But even that was deserting me now, deserting me along with any feeling of safety or security or hope.

I looked at Jane, so slender, so beautiful, even in death. Heat and noise and sharp, stitching breaths, and then I was on the floor next to her, something swelling in me, swelling to the point where I couldn't breathe.

I must have cried out, because a moment later, Father and Jack came up the stairs, and when they did, they found me sobbing.

TWENTY-FOUR

At some point, someone helped me up.

I could hear Inspector Hernandez's voice, the voices of many others, and I was guided down the stairs, still crying too hard to really see or speak. I was placed in a guest room on the third floor, and a blanket was wrapped around my shoulders. I heard Jack say, "Shall I get Olivia?"

"No," Father responded. "She'll only get hysterical herself. I'll stay with my daughter—you manage the situation downstairs."

And then Jack was gone.

I was sitting on a stiffly upholstered chaise by a narrow fireplace. Father sat next to me—carefully it seemed, but still there.

Nothing mattered and nothing existed beyond each shuddering breath and each equally shuddering exhalation. Nothing would ever exist besides the shock and the taste of salt on my lips and the memory of Jane's body sprawled— almost elegantly—on the floor. I leaned my head on Father's shoulder, tears dampening the smooth wool of his suit jacket, and I didn't care, it never occurred to me to care, and then

Father tentatively wrapped an arm around my shoulders.

He didn't say anything, but he patted my shoulder every now and again in a consoling manner, and—when the tears finally subsided—he wordlessly handed me the handkerchief from his breast pocket. I stared at the atomic symbol embroidered in one corner and then wiped my face hurriedly, not wanting to recollect the image of the atomic symbol on Jane's thigh.

Father patted his tear-blotched shoulder, inviting me to rest my head there once again. The unexpected tenderness of the gesture made my throat tight and I started crying again, this time slower and quieter.

There was a rap at the door and Inspector Hernandez came in.

"I'm so sorry," the inspector said. "But since you were the one who found Miss Osbourne, I need to ask you a few questions."

I nodded in a numb, uncaring way. The inspector gave me a sympathetic look as he readied his tablet.

Just like with Marianne, he asked me to give an account of my whereabouts for the day, asking if I'd seen anything suspicious, asking if I knew of any reason that somebody would want to hurt Jane in particular, other than that she was an Uprisen heir.

Then he began asking me questions that made me uncomfortable. Why hadn't I looked for Jane earlier? Was I alone when I found her body? How long was I alone in the observatory with her corpse before I called the police?

Luckily, my answers seemed to satisfy Inspector Hernandez, and he finally set down his tablet. Thin lines stretched around his mouth and his eyes, and his hair looked just a little too long, as if he were overdue for a haircut.

"The thing," he said, "is that I don't know if I can justify a lack of arrests at this point. Three unsolved murders . . . and the public outcry is already enormous with the first two. Even if I refuse to make an arrest on the basis of absence of evidence, the chief undoubtedly will do so. And you can imagine he will pursue that end with a recklessness that will make everyone on both sides of the city suffer."

Dewhurst. Just the thought of him made me taste bile.

"What are you saying?" I asked, a prickling worry crawling up the back of my neck.

The inspector looked uncomfortable. "I'm saying that it might be in the best interest of both sides to make a single arrest, to head off any more gentry-incited violence and to protect the Rootless population."

"You mean the man they call Smith," Father said.

"Yes," the inspector said.

"I thought you didn't have enough evidence?" I said. Why did the inspector's words make me so nervous? This was what I had wanted, wasn't it?

Except that this was precisely what David and Ewan had been afraid of, an unjustified arrest, and I had assured them it wouldn't happen, that the police would follow due course.

"I believe we can hold him based on the testimony of what you heard him discussing with your uncle. It wouldn't be enough to charge him in a fair court, but it will be enough to keep him arrested and keep the Uprisen from lashing out. The thing is, Miss Landry, is that it will be your account that we use as grounds for arrest, and so I want to make absolutely sure that you are very certain about it all—what you heard, what you know of Smith, et cetera."

Leaden worry pulled at my stomach. Was he saying that the sole responsibility and burden of this arrest would be on my shoulders? I was quite certain that Smith was somehow behind it all, but did I want him to go to prison on my belief alone?

Was this how corruption began—the best of intentions married with fear?

I looked at Father for guidance. His eyes flicked across my face, reading my hesitation, but before any of us could speak, another knock sounded and a constable stuck his head in the door. "The Osbournes are here, sir."

"Thank you." The inspector stood. "I'll speak to them now." He left.

Father turned to me. "Are you undecided about the inspector's request?"

I rolled the wet handkerchief in my palm.

"I want you to know," Father said in a soft voice, "that whatever you decide, you will have my full weight behind you, whatever it's worth now."

"Thank you," I said. "That comforts me."

It did, in a way, even facing the jagged magnitude of this. If I was right about Smith, then justice would be served and the killings would stop. If I was wrong, then I was condemning a man to a terrible fate, all on the basis of my dislike of him, which was what David had accused me from doing at the start. *No,* I told myself. *It's not just dislike.* Smith had been acting suspiciously since the night of the party. Three people had died, including my closest friend, and it was Jane's vacant eyes that I thought of when I made my decision. It was time— something had to be done.

I looked at Father. "I'll do it. Whatever it takes to have Smith locked away."

Father nodded. "Okay, then. Let's find the inspector and tell him."

I didn't want to go back up to the observatory, not with Jane's body and with her parents. "I don't—"

He understood before I finished. "Of course. We'll wait a moment."

A noise in the hallway. It was one of the constables, guiding a floating gurney, bumping it into the walls. A gurney for Jane's body.

Fighting to keep my breathing even, I kept my eyes on the two parallel lines of superconductors beneath the gurney, the ones that kept the magnets under the bed afloat. The gurney passed, and I knew the constable had reached the stairs when I heard the clang of his boots on the iron steps and heard someone offering to help him with the floating bed.

I turned away from the door. It was an interminable amount of time, but finally I heard the sound of footsteps and the barely audible hissing of the nitrogen, and then the gurney and Jane's body were out of sight.

"Okay," I said. "I can go up now."

We went back up to the observatory. The inspector was directing the constables—they were almost finished surveying and photographing the scene. One was sliding Jane's tablet into an opaque plastic bag.

Surprisingly, Elizabeth Osbourne was still there, not watching the police, but standing with her head nearly against the window, watching the front drive. Waiting for her daughter's—and heir's—body to leave the last house it had ever entered. I assumed her husband had gone down with the gurney.

"Inspector," I said. "I'm ready."

He looked relieved to hear it, but he didn't look happy. Come to that, neither did I. Last week, I would have been ecstatic. Triumphant even. Now I just felt sick. So what if it was Smith? The worst had already happened. Did it really make a difference if he was stopped now?

Mrs. Osbourne drifted over to us. Unlike me, her eyes were dry and her face composed. There was a stiffness to her that suggested buried pain, but the dignified set of her shoulders told me that she wouldn't allow herself to truly grieve until she was alone. "What's happening?" she asked.

Inspector Hernandez met her eyes. "We are making an arrest. Miss Landry has some information that I think implicates a member of the Rootless community."

"Does she?" Mrs. Osbourne looked at me. Though her skin was slightly darker, her features slightly more angular, it was impossible not to see Jane in her face. I looked away.

"It may placate the gentry," the inspector offered.

"I did not realize popular opinion was the concern of the law."

"We know better, Elizabeth," Father said. "You know that the others—Arthur and Harry—will force their will through no matter what, and if they do it their way, it will go all the worse for the city. Madeline is reasonably sure that this Smith is responsible, and his arrest will at least buy the investigation some time."

"Are you?" Mrs. Osbourne asked me.

I had been chasing my own thoughts in circles. "Pardon?"

"Are you reasonably certain that the man they want to lock up killed my daughter?" Her voice was even.

For some reason, I found it much more difficult to look in her eyes and affirm that *yes*, I was sure. I had defended my theory to David and Ewan and Jack, to the police and to my father—but Elizabeth Osbourne, with her gentle but determined Jane-like face, seemed able to peer into all of my flaws and my fears and my guilt, and expose the doubts she found there.

"Yes," I whispered.

Her face relaxed somewhat, though there was still a forced, brittle feeling about her. "Then you and the police have my blessing."

The Rootless had not reacted well to the appearance of the constables, but between the efforts of Jack and Inspector Hernandez, the tension was contained to glares and mutterings and not much more. I went downstairs with Father and the inspector, and together we found Jack. Father and the inspector explained the circumstances to him while I stayed quiet, even though Jack's eyes were burning into mine the entire time they spoke.

"So you plan to arrest an innocent man, based on nothing but a teenage girl's clumsy surmises?"

Any time before today, I would have felt a flare of anger at that. But now it didn't matter. I didn't care what Jack thought of me or of my intelligence—or what anybody else thought.

"You won't deny that this conversation took place, however?" the inspector asked.

"I wish that you would have come straight to me rather than drawing your own conclusions," Jack said, turning to me.

"So it did happen," the inspector repeated.

"Yes," Jack said. "Smith and I did talk that night." He sighed. "But it wasn't about murder. It was about politics. About maneuvering the gentry out of power, which is to say that it was a fairly common conversation had between Smith and me. Nothing as barbaric as murdering teenagers."

Inspector Hernandez gave him a rueful look. "It's your word against hers, I think. And given Smith's behavior the night of Marianne Wilder's death and his past vandalism with the same words: *We are rising*—he is our strongest suspect right now."

"I see that your mind is already made up," Jack said. Red crept up his neck. "And that nothing I say will divest you of your conclusions."

"Do you know where he is, Mr. Landry?" the inspector asked, ignoring his last comment. "It will make it much easier to find him if we know where he is."

"No," Jack said. "I do not. And if you'll excuse me, I am not interested in being a party to this any longer." Jack spun on his heel and left.

My father looked after him.

Inspector Hernandez rubbed at his forehead. "I'll finish up here, and then start the search for Smith. He must still be in the city."

"His shack is pretty isolated in the ghetto," I said. "There's a chance that it survived the fires—he could still be there, hidden in plain sight."

The policeman nodded. "We will most definitely look into that. And as for you—get some rest, okay? You've suffered an extreme shock."

"I'll make sure of it," Father told him.

My tablet chimed in my pocket, and as the inspector went back upstairs to wrap up his investigation, I answered the call from Jamie.

His face was white. "Madeline—my house was broken into . . . all of my notes, all of my samples—trashed or missing. Everything I had about the cure for the Rootless is just—*gone*."

TWENTY-FIVE

"The constables are here now," Jamie said from my tablet screen. "It looks like whoever did it simply smashed in the first floor windows and crawled right in. They found some footprints in the ground below the window. . . ." His voice sounded hollow, rote, as if he were just repeating exactly what a policeman had said.

"Oh, Jamie," I said, unable to process this on top of everything else.

He looked abject, miserable. "Who would want to do this? Who would even think to do this?"

I didn't know, but I did know that whoever did this had just stolen away our best and brightest chance for stopping a war before it started. More, they'd stolen something that would have helped people, something that would have done nothing but ease suffering. "Someone who doesn't want the Rootless to be cured," I said. My mind flipped through the possibilities—Rootless, gentry, Empire.

"Smith?"

I opened my mouth but didn't answer. I thought of Smith—

of his violence and of his ungovernable rage—but I also remembered the way he had looked at Russell, the way his eyes had cataloged every cough and moan from his dying brother. Would he really want to stop the thing that could cure the person he cared most about? Some of the Rootless had been angry about the Landry mutation, but would they be angry enough to actually deny the serum itself? To want to destroy it? I wasn't sure, but my gut told me no. Even hard people have soft spots—even Smith had something, someone, he loved.

A constable moved past me, and I was abruptly reminded why he was here. I swallowed. Suddenly, I couldn't bear it anymore: the navy coats of the policemen, the blue lanterns of their cars vying with the weak daylight. The scent of cleaning solution and blood. I had to leave.

"I'm coming over," I said.

"Why? There's nothing to be done—it's gone and it's not—"

"I'm coming over," I repeated. "Please, Jamie. I can't be here right now. It's Jane. She—" I couldn't say it, I couldn't finish. I took a shuddering breath instead.

He seemed to take in my red-rimmed eyes and splotchy cheeks for the first time. He nodded slowly. "Of course."

Two police cars, glowing blue, idled outside Jamie's town house. Jamie met me on the steps. "They're not allowing anybody in at the moment. They think the intruder might have left fingerprints." He sounded doubtful.

"They'll find him or her, and they'll find what they took." I said that with a surety I didn't feel.

Jamie looked unconvinced.

"Let's go get coffee," I suggested, craving the normalcy of the act. I had a handkerchief balled up in my hand, and I tried to be subtle about the tears that refused to stop welling up, but I knew he noticed.

Jamie nodded, pulling his coat tighter around himself and wrapping a comforting arm around my shoulders, and we walked to a small café on the corner. Once inside, warmer and clutching a wide cup of coffee, he seemed determined to steer my mind away from Jane.

"Most of my research was shared with my partners at the university, so it's not as if it's completely lost. But I was working so fervently, so tirelessly, that I got sloppy. I forgot to duplicate notes and formulas. And the blood samples and the serums . . ."

We stared out of the foggy windows for a while, watching the steel-gray sky spit snow. I wanted a solution for him; I wanted to console him and tell him that everything would resolve itself; I wanted to *fix* this for him somehow, but I couldn't. Jane was dead. Our biggest hope for bringing peace to the city was smashed and stalled for heaven knew how long. I couldn't see how anything would get better. Not now.

"I just wish I knew *why*," Jamie said. "This was going to help people. How could someone not want that to happen?"

"I don't think it was Smith," I said. "I can't see any reason why he would want to prevent something that would help his brother—and help himself."

"Unless he felt like it would help his revolution," Jamie said. There was a hard glint in his eyes that I'd never seen before. "He would do anything to see the gentry smashed, even hurt his own people."

Like Jack, I thought. But I still couldn't see Smith doing this any more than I could see Jack doing it.

Jamie took compulsive, controlled sips of his coffee, his eyes growing harder. Without thinking, I reached a hand across the table and placed it on his wrist. "Jamie," I said, wanting that stony look to stop. It wasn't him—he was gentle, patient, calm—and I needed him to stay that way. The city needed him to stay that way. "I don't know who did this, but the police will find out and they will make sure he or she is punished. Don't drive yourself crazy focusing on what's happened. You need to focus on what's going to happen—how you are going to work on the cure and finish it, despite everything else."

"I know," he said heavily. "I know."

When we got back to his house, he kept his eyes down, plucking at his coat and not saying anything. I got the feeling that he needed to be alone, and I wanted to be alone, too, so I kissed his cheek and left him.

But instead of getting in my car and going back to Landry Park, I messaged Reeve that I would be a few more moments and walked across the street to the small garden that adjoined the Public Hospital. It was narrow, with an uneven asphalt path and thin trees that looked cold and tired; I chose a path strewn with shriveled leaves that rattled unhappily in the wind.

Flurries continued to fall in despondent spirals as I walked over the scattered twigs to a bench. I sat down and the iron bled the cold through my dress, but I didn't mind. I stayed there for a while, thinking of Jane, of her mother Elizabeth Osbourne hugging herself as she watched out the window. Marianne's death had been hard. Mark's death had been shocking. But Jane's death . . . it was something else altogether. An amputation. An evisceration.

I sat until I could take the cold no longer and stood. I spied a small side door into the hospital and tried it—it was mercifully open.

The hospital was completely empty. The lights flickered faintly in the vaulted ceilings above, and the machines hummed quietly to themselves, but there were no men and women lining up for shots, no nurses carrying syringes and bandages between the rows of open beds and tables. The Rootless weren't here any longer now that they weren't handling the charges, and there was no work to be done.

It didn't feel peaceful. It felt lonely.

I sat in a hard plastic chair in the middle of the room and stared at the stained-glass windows. I had been so certain of everything once, and now it felt like all the answers were slipping through my fingers.

The front doors banged open and a gust of cold air rushed through the narthex and into the nave. I turned to see David walking through the front door, peacoat hanging open, hair dotted with snow and tossed by the wind.

I stood.

His footsteps echoed in the nave, off the carved faces of sad-eyed saints and off the stone vaults of the ceiling. And then I was in his arms, smelling wool and snow and under it all, that clove-and-cinnamon scent he always carried with him.

"I heard about Jane," he said. "God, I'm so sorry."

I nodded into the thick fabric, not trusting myself to speak out loud. He stroked my hair, he let me breathe into his chest, let me lean against him as despair washed over me once more. And then he pulled back, his arms dropping to his sides.

"They arrested Smith," he said. It was as if a switch had been flipped, his tenderness gone in an instant, replaced by something flinty and remote.

My chest tightened, but I didn't reach out to him. This time it wasn't pride or anger, but a hollow inertia that made even the thought of reaching out impossible. What was the point of trying, if he was going to draw away even now, after Jane's death?

"They found him in his home and dragged him off in front of his brother," he added, as if this were a particularly damning detail.

He was angry with me. I could see it in the subtle flaring of his nostrils and in the way his lips pressed together in a narrow line, in the way that his fingers flexed and folded at his side. "I know you must be destroyed about Jane . . . but an innocent man was arrested because of you. Now, when things look worse than ever, when we're on the verge of war—you do something that makes us weaker, that divides us. Do you even want the Rootless to be free?"

"Of course," I said. I wanted my words to be vehement, to ring through the hospital with vindication and truth. But instead my voice was soft. Slow. *How could he be so angry about Smith and not about Jane?* I thought, and even my thoughts had become slow.

"So why did you do it?"

"More people would have been arrested—or worse—if Smith hadn't been," I said, my numbness finally stirring into something resembling life.

"You can't know that." He started pacing.

"But I can. How many times have you seen it? The raids?

The arrests? For little to no reason at all? Did you think that it wouldn't happen after three murders?"

"You can't control what they do, Madeline. You can only control your own choices."

"Oh, that's right, it's only about choices. If I just choose to do the right thing, then everything will be *fine*," I said, not masking the sarcasm that curled in my words.

"It is actually that simple, you know."

"Maybe for you. Maybe your choices are easy—in the end what do you have to lose? What do you have to wrestle with? But me—I could lose my home, my family. You would what— maybe have a fight with your mother?"

He paced faster. "I am not even going to engage in this conversation. It's pointless to speculate about who has more to lose."

"Fine, then. How about we speculate about why it's always up to me to make the hard choices. Were you really willing to sit by and watch the Uprisen exact their own brand of justice on the Rootless? Do you know what the Uprisen have been talking about? *Killing them.* To make an example. So I made a calculation: the freedom of one man—who is probably guilty—against the lives of a thousand others. And you know what? It was an easy calculation to make."

He shook his head. "How can you talk about people like that? Like they're not individuals, but units, with a value that you can quantify? That's no better than how your father sees people or Jacob Landry himself would—"

"That's not fair," I said. My voice was beginning to shake. "They were trying to create more power for themselves. I'm trying to help people."

"It's the same thing in the end. You want to be judge and jury for everyone, for the world to be ordered as Madeline Landry sees fit."

"Do you think I like making those kinds of decisions? But ultimately it has to be done. The world is full of difficult choices, David, and if we all just whined about how horrible everything was and never did anything about it, then nothing would change, except maybe to get worse."

"*Whining?* You think I'm *whining?*" His voice was dangerous now. "I am telling you that you are *wrong* and that you did something wrong—"

"Well, it's too late now, isn't it?"

He walked away, his hands lacing on top of his head, and then he turned back to me. "Yes, it is too late."

We stared at each other a moment. I hated this feeling, this feeling of shame mingled with defensiveness, this feeling of David distrusting me, of watching him lose his respect for me. But I didn't have any other choice.

"He killed *Jane*," I said, my voice breaking on her name. "What was I supposed to do?"

He looked away first, jamming his hands in his coat pockets.

"I don't know what you want me to say," I said.

"I don't know either." And he came close enough to touch me now. His voice lowered, and while his face didn't exactly soften, it became less glacial.

He lifted a hand and touched my cheek. I couldn't help it; I leaned into his touch, my eyes fluttering closed. His hands were warm, his fingertips slightly calloused from military drills in the dry mountain air, and he just felt so undeniably and so unequivocally David that I never wanted him to move his hand. I could stand there in the middle of this drafty church for all eternity, listening to portable wall screens humming and the wind cutting past the windows, feeling his skin against mine.

His hand dropped and I looked up at him. The fire had burned itself out in his eyes, leaving behind a dejected blue that spoke of regret and longing.

"Good-bye, Madeline," he said.

"I'm not saying good-bye to you," I said, and even though I thought I had cried all the tears I had to cry earlier, I felt them coming on again, stinging the backs of my eyelids.

"I'm not giving you a choice." He was going to leave. It occurred to me that we'd done this before, this thing where he barbed and stabbed at me with his words and then left me, and I wasn't going to do it again. This time I was going to leave and not look back, even though it would hurt me more than it would ever hurt him.

"If that's what you want," I said. "You were always good at getting what you wanted."

And then I was the one who turned and walked out, and he was the one left standing, staring after me.

TWENTY-SIX

I had no other place to go and so I went back home, my eyes fixed on the glass observatory as the car drove closer. It looked the same as it always did, elegant and ethereal, like a miniature glass castle perched on top of the estate. It didn't look like the kind of place where a girl would be mutilated and left dead on the floor. But that was the way of things, wasn't it? No matter what happened on the inside, no matter what pain and suffering had been borne in those halls, the shell would remain the same. Stoic and unbending and remote.

Not unlike me, I thought. There had been so much pain, so many shattered designs and wishes and longings, and yet my reflection never changed. I still appeared to be the cool, pale girl who stood ready to inherit the most important estate in the country. To look at me, one would never know. . . .

The wind rocked the car as the driver parked, buffeting me in the face as soon as I started for the front door. The flurries had transfigured themselves into thick puffs of white, falling faster and harder, already obscuring the drive and gravel paths around the home. The Rootless would be making their way inside soon.

Inside the house, I was grateful to see that most everyone was keeping to the lower levels and that my room—at least for the time being—was my own. I went in and shut the door, and fell onto my bed without taking off my boots or cape. I considered taking a bath or even just changing into different clothes, but it all seemed too hard. Everything seemed too hard. Couldn't I hibernate until everything was finished, for better or for worse?

My tablet beeped. I took it out of my cape and shoved it under a pillow. I didn't want to talk to anyone. I couldn't talk to anyone. All I could think about was Jane and the serum and David—raveled snarls of memory fraught with pain.

It chimed again. I ignored it, throwing my arm over my face to block out the grayish light filtering in through my filmy curtains.

I finally looked at the tablet screen, where news notifications scrolled frenetically past. After weeks of posturing at the border, sending troops and planes and tanks to the mountains, the Empire had finally issued an ultimatum to the government: America had one week to capitulate to a new set of demands, including paying a tribute of resources, or face the consequences—or rather, the *consequence*, singular, which was invasion. The president still hadn't responded—likely waiting on council from the Uprisen.

It felt incredibly distant somehow, in the shadow of Jane's death.

My door swung open and Cara came in, wearing something bright and swishy and low-cut, looking for all the world as if it were July and she were on her way to swill champagne on an expensive boat. But her face was tired and her dress wrinkled, and there was a faded feeling about her, as if she were a plant that had been without sunshine for too long.

"Have you heard about this?" I asked, holding up my tablet.

She nodded. "Yes. But I'm actually here because I heard all about your fight with David."

"Jane is dead, the Empire wants to go to war, and you want to talk about David and me?"

"I can't do anything about the Empire. Or Jane." A somber pause. "But I can do something about you."

"Since when did you start caring about me?"

She crossed her arms, not answering me directly, but making it very obvious that she wasn't about to leave.

"Sorry," I mumbled, knowing my last comment was out of line. I covered my face with my arm again. I couldn't believe Cara knew about the fight—it had happened only an hour ago. And since when did David and Cara talk about our relationship? "David told you about our fight?" I asked, keeping my voice neutral. She didn't need to know how much the idea bothered me.

"Well, okay, more like he vented to Jude, who tried to call you, and then called me when you didn't answer because we all know that I'm the responsible one around here."

I made a noise at that.

"You know," she said, "you don't seem very upset right now."

"I am," I said, sitting up. "I'm just exhausted from everything that's happened today. If I could cry, I would. But I can't. And with this stuff about the Empire—"

"I know. I saw the news." She shook her head, as if to clear away the gravity of the last hour's events. "Look, if you really believed that things were over between you and David, you would be insensible right now. But you know what I think? I think that you know somewhere deep inside that things aren't really over. You know that there's still hope for you two."

I peered up into her face. She seemed completely in earnest. For Cara, love was just as important as war. After all, she'd dated Ewan despite the politics and violence surrounding them.

"So do you think it's over?" she asked again.

Did I? I thought about that for a moment, turning it over in my mind. Did I feel like there was nothing left between us? After all we'd been through?

No. The answer was sudden, vehement. I loved David. He loved me. We'd spent a year fighting and lying and believing in a cause together. We were entangled now, like atoms at the quantum level.

Cara and I didn't say anything for a few minutes.

"What should I do?" I asked, not directing the question at Cara but at the entirety of my room. "What should I do now?"

She shrugged. "Apologize? Try to talk to him?"

"He won't listen," I said, feeling pessimistic again. "He's done listening to me."

"I guess you'll never know unless you try." She laid herself across my bed, looking like a Pre-Raphaelite painting with her fairy-tale hair and long limbs.

I twisted my skirt in my lap, thinking of all the other things that I needed to accomplish before I could take time to talk to David. "There's just so much that needs to be done. There are five hundred homeless people living in my house and Jane is dead. The Empire is coming. And Jamie's work is gone," I added, feeling the full weight of the robbery once again. "Everything is ruined."

Cara rolled herself off the bed. "If you're just going to brood, I'm leaving."

I tried to muster a glare, but I didn't have the energy.

"You can fix it, Madeline. How hard can it be?"

There was no satisfactory response to that. What excuse could I give to the girl who'd defied her entire upbringing to fall in love with a charge-changer?

Cara left, and I lay on the bed a long hour, staring at the diaphanous curtains of my canopy bed. Again I wondered, whatever had happened to the girl whose worst problem was trying to go to the university? Who had never met David Dana or visited the Rootless ghetto, who had never embedded herself in the center of a brewing war?

The wind blew and the snow fell and eventually I found the motivation to sit up again and start planning.

Cara was right. Enough brooding. There was work to be done.

I didn't find Father or Jack downstairs, so I wandered upstairs until I heard voices coming from the sitting room adjoining Father's bedroom. I rapped gently on the door and then let myself in. I didn't know exactly what I needed to say or do, but I knew I needed to do something, to help us all move forward somehow.

When I came in, Jack stood in front of a small fire facing my father, who sat on a low sofa and was currently reaching for his drink on the nearby table. The atmosphere in the room was grave—grim even—and they both looked at me with expressions so solemn that I almost feared another person had died.

"Madeline," Father said. "You've heard?"

"Yes," I said.

"Close the door, child," Jack said, gesturing impatiently at me. "Come in."

I did as he asked and found myself a seat across from Father. Father indicated a decanter of Scotch, which I declined. Father had never been much of a drinker; the sight of him taking studious, almost medicinal, sips of Scotch was as alien as anything else that had happened.

"The Uprisen are calling an emergency meeting," Father said. "The families from out of state are coming here. I've been invited as well, despite the obvious . . ." He looked at Jack ". . . *obstacles.*"

I turned to Jack. "Please tell me that you didn't know about this. About the Empire's plans to invade." I couldn't keep the pleading out of my voice. I just wanted one thing, one person, not to let me down today.

Jack shook his head slowly. "We had no knowledge of this. The Empire had always indicated to us that they only wanted to help the Rootless overthrow the gentry. I never believed . . ." He trailed off and looked outside. "I won't trade one regime for another," he said after a long moment. "We can't afford to."

"The Empire's demands are untenable," Father said. "Our crop yields have flagged enough that keeping our own country fed is a struggle. We'll never be able to muster such a tribute."

"Do you think they know that?" I asked. "Are they demanding it knowing that they will invade anyway?"

Jack looked at Father. There was something of equals in that look, one leader to another, one Landry to another. "Maybe they plan to keep us busy with councils and decisions while they prepare. Buy them time, sow some fear, make us a riper target."

"Yes," Father replied slowly. "Yes, I think that is their plan."

"But why invade at all?"

"Madeline," Father said, "is a black hole content with only

swallowing half a star? Half a galaxy? No, it wants it all. The Empire won't rest until every continent is under their sway. They need resources on an ever-increasing scale. A large portion of the Empire is nearly uninhabitable—deserts of frozen soil, deserts of baked soil, overcrowded cities where water has to be piped in from hundreds of miles away. We may be a poorer nation on a global scale, but we are more comfortable. They need what we have—more water, more grain, more livable land for their massed people."

"So what can we do?" I asked. "What would make the Empire change its mind?"

Jack shook his head. "I don't know. Stability maybe. A united front." He reached for his own drink now. "I never thought it would come to this. . . ."

The flash in Father's eyes indicated that he was suppressing an *I told you so.*

I tried to move the conversation forward. "So to stop the Empire, we need to become stable and united, and we need to do it fast?"

Father rubbed at his eyes. "It's never going to happen. Not after Jane Osbourne's death. There's no trust on the gentry side."

"Nor on the Rootless side," Jack pointed out.

"Because of Smith," I said. It wasn't a question.

A frown. "He didn't commit any crimes, but now he's in jail. Unjustly."

"What did you want me to do?" I asked tiredly. "You keep secrets, you make plans in the middle of the night—you won't give me a good answer for anything. What was I supposed to believe?"

"You were supposed to trust me."

"I'm done trusting people without good reason," I said. "You want me to trust you? Tell me the truth. What were you and Smith planning that night I heard you talking? Where did Smith go the night of Marianne's death?"

He opened his mouth and closed it.

"Well?" Father asked.

"It's not important," Jack said. "It has nothing to do with Marianne Wilder or Mark Everly—"

"This is what I mean. I know next to nothing about you and your plans for your people. For all I know, you ordered Smith to kill my friends and I'm next."

His eyes narrowed. "You truly don't know me if you believe that I would ever hurt my own family."

"Me excluded, I presume?" Father asked.

"That was different."

"Right, it was different," I said. "And how am I supposed to trust that within the twisted circles of your own logic that the dead heirs weren't any different? That I wouldn't be?"

Father had shifted in his seat, so that we were both angled toward Jack, who now looked down at the carpet for a moment, a small muscle working in his jaw.

"Stephen," Father said. Then he cleared his throat. "Jack. We deserve an explanation."

Jack's face had changed when Father said his chosen name. It hadn't actually thawed, but he'd noticed Father's attempt to reach out, and there was an acknowledgment of that in his expression. It was that concession that seemed to convince him to speak. "The night of Marianne's murder, Smith left early to meet with a liaison from the Empire."

"The Empire?" Father exploded. "So you did know—"

I held up a hand, and to my surprise, Father stopped. Jack went on. "The Empire felt that this new climate between the gentry and the Rootless was an opportunity."

"Yes, yes, we know," my father said.

Jack continued unfazed. "The Empire wants the Uprisen . . . nullified. Smith wants the same thing."

"Nullified?" I repeated.

"He means *killed*," Father said, his eyes on his brother. "And is this before or after they invade?"

"I told you, invasion was never on the table. And I do *not* mean killed," Jack snapped. "How could you think me capable of that? No, I knew the Empire was no longer a true ally after Liberty Park, when they failed to send more help, more supplies. I realized David was right about their true intentions. But forsaking the friendship of the Empire . . . that's not something to be undertaken lightly. With David's advice, I decided to go about it slowly, imparting a gradual distance. In the meantime, Smith—who genuinely wanted to work with them—would convince their scouts and liaisons of our continued adherence to the partnership."

It was actually a fairly canny move, keeping both Smith and the Empire in the dark. And Jack was right, you couldn't simply cross the Empire off your list as if they were an unwanted partner on a dance card; they were not a forgiving entity.

"So David knew," I said. "He knew that Smith was meeting with the Empire that night." I suppressed a flare of temper as I said the words. I thought of times I had sensed that knowledge prowling inside his words, of how I'd doubted my own intuition when it hinted that David knew more than he was letting on. *Why didn't he tell me?*

"I told him not to inform you of our double cross," Jack said, reading my face correctly. "I trust you, but I also know how close you are to your father. I was afraid if the Uprisen knew about the dissolved alliance, they would come after the Rootless more aggressively than ever."

"He still should have told me," I muttered. "But going back to the original topic: How did you know that invasion was off the table? Smith has been out of your control for weeks now. He could have known about the proposed invasion and simply not said anything about it to you."

"You're right, of course, but I am certain that my instincts on this were—and are—correct. Smith would have leaped at the chance to dangle an invasion over my head, along with the reality of losing Landry Park to the East. Concealment isn't in his nature; he doesn't keep secrets, he makes threats."

I studied Jack's face. I believed that *he* believed what he was saying, though I thought Smith was a lot craftier than Jack gave him credit for. I let the point be for now. "So what did they talk about, if not invasion?"

"They proposed using some large event to strike out at the Uprisen. I consented on the condition that I be kept abreast of all the plans. It was my intention to prevent any actual violence from happening while still keeping up the illusion that the Rootless were willing to partner with the Empire."

Realization dawned. "And that's why you changed your mind about the Lantern Day Ball."

"But what was it?" Father demanded. "What did you plan?"

Jack's jaw was tight. "Smith and the Empire felt that a small . . . demonstration . . . was needed. Something to scare people. Something involving Landry Park."

Father didn't answer, but it was clear that any plan that involved the house was little better than murder in his mind.

Jack ran a hand over his face. "It was never going to be anything more than some dramatic vandalism. You have to understand—it wasn't something I was actually going to let happen. But if I put a stop to it outright, then both Smith and the Empire would know of my changed direction and changed opinion. And that wasn't a step I was prepared to take. It was better to let them spin their little webs, and then quietly arrange for enough police or enough loyal Rootless to be present to prevent it."

"So, help me to understand," I said, trying to sift through all this new information. "Smith left the night of Marianne's death in order to meet with someone from the Empire, and you know this for a fact? This is not something he told you— you know it happened."

"I received a confirmation message from the liaison myself afterward."

"And nothing you've discussed with the liaison or Smith involved him killing the Uprisen heirs—only vandalism?"

Another nod. I sat back. So I had been wrong about Smith killing Marianne. And it was like David had predicted— underneath my very real guilt about having Smith arrested without proof was the childish, aching shame of knowing that I had been wrong. My logic flawed, my perception skewed.

I hated being wrong about things. It felt like an indictment of my intelligence, my ethics.

It also made David right, right in being angry with me, right in trying to dissuade me. And I didn't know if I could ever earn back his trust, not only because I'd displayed so much pride of my own, but because I had also wounded his.

God, could this day get any worse?

I looked up to see Father and Jack both staring at me. "I'm

sorry," I said to Jack. "I'll make it right somehow—I'll talk to Inspector Hernandez—"

Father shook his head. "You heard him upstairs, Madeline. This is such a delicate time . . . he needed someone arrested, anyone, so that he could keep the peace. And besides, he was planning a crime anyway. The best place for him is in jail. Unless your uncle can promise us that no harm would come to this house and the gentry if he were free."

Jack didn't answer.

"So we have a man in jail for something he didn't do, but we can't have him freed because of what he *will* do," I said, to clarify. "And we have the Uprisen about to discuss the Empire's mandate, but there's no way we could possibly meet their demands, so an invasion is almost inevitable unless we can get the gentry and the Rootless to work together."

"I can't believe you ever even allowed such a plan to be formulated, regardless of whether it would be carried out," Father said, his mind still on the vandalism. "You were always the gentle one."

"I know. It sounds like something you would do," Jack told his brother.

Father flinched, a tiny, barely there flinch.

"There's got to be a way to convince both sides that continued division will be our downfall," I said, steering the conversation back to the topic at hand.

"You can start by converting every home in the city to solar or wind power and giving the Rootless real homes outside of the ghetto," Jack said. "Immediately. And you can start by making sure every Rootless here and across the country gets Mr. Campbell-Smith's cure as soon as possible."

Jamie's serum. They didn't know yet.

"What is it?" Father asked, catching sight of my face.

I bit the inside of my lip for a moment, knowing they needed to know and yet being afraid to tell them. "Jamie's house was broken into," I said finally. "His lab ransacked, his samples destroyed. He doesn't know yet how far it will set the work back."

"*What?*" Jack and Father said at the same time.

"But maybe it's only the difference of a few weeks . . . ?"

Father shook his head. "We don't have a few weeks, Madeline."

He was right.

TWENTY-SEVEN

"If the gentry are satisfied that the real murderer is caught," Jude said, "they may yet be persuaded to see reason."

Jude had come to offer his help in the aftermath of Jane's death and with the advent of the snowstorm, and I had asked him to join us as we tried to talk through everything. He had looked surprised at my request, but had accepted with a gratitude and an earnestness that made me think that he had been ready for an invitation like this.

When he saw his son, Jack had stood to shake Jude's hand, and Jude had returned the gesture. Jude looked like a young president right then: He had the right bearing, the right handshake—and now he had the perfect pedigree. And he even kept a warm and friendly expression on his face when Jack unexpectedly wrapped him in an embrace.

After he joined us, Jack had invited Ewan in as well. I realized that all of us Landrys—save for Charlie, who was with his tutor—were gathered together in this small room, firelight flickering off our pale skin and Cherenkov light catching in our stone-gray eyes.

"I'm not arguing your point," Ewan said, "but aren't

the gentry willing to believe that the real killer is already accounted for? I don't see how it would help to have someone else arrested."

"Aside from the fact that more Uprisen children could die," Father said. He glanced over at me.

I didn't point out that all the Uprisen children would probably die—and many more—if the Empire invaded. "It's about more than catching the killer," I said. "It's about proving to the gentry and the Rootless that we need to work together."

"If the Rootless resume changing the charges . . ." Father said.

Jack's answer was as immediate as it was flat. "Absolutely not."

Jude cleared his throat. "I've actually been thinking about that," he said. "When Jacob Landry's journals leaked to the press several weeks ago, one of the things they mentioned was his original plan to have a paid workforce change the charges. Has it ever occurred to anyone to revisit that idea, rather than trying to force an immediate conversion to a different power source?"

"But who would ever even think about doing it?" Ewan asked. "It's too dangerous. And none of my people will ever go back to the sorting yards, not even if their lives depended on it."

"It's dangerous as it is now," Jude said. "But what if we proved that the serum was so effective that there was little risk? That, with the right equipment and the right pay, we might show people that it's not nearly as dangerous as it's been historically."

"That's assuming that we have a serum to offer them," Jack said. "Once I tell my people it's been delayed, that the work was stolen—there will be suspicion. Reluctance."

"Jamie will work as fast as he can," I said. "We will have a serum soon. I promise."

"And such work would have to be very well paid," Ewan added. "Where would the money come from?"

"From the gentry," Jude said. "Why not?"

"The stigma is too great," Father cut in. "No one, and I mean no one, would be willing to brave it, no matter how safe we claimed it to be. No matter how effective the serum seems."

"What if we demonstrated that it was safe?" I proposed. "Father, you and I, we could change our own charges. The mutation lives in us, so we could show them how much we believe in the serum. Prove to everyone that the threat is gone—show people that there's no longer danger attached to the work."

He looked as if I'd just suggested that we burn down the estate. "You and me? Change charges?"

"Alexander, I can tell you that a Landry has done it before," Jack said. "And we're doing all this for a reason, remember? To build a bridge, to present a united front."

We all stared at my father, who took a deep breath. "I suppose . . . I could think about it."

"There are more problems besides the charges," Ewan pointed out. "The Rootless want a new government—made up of all classes, not just gentry. Education. Jobs. Homes."

"And what am I to tell the gentry that they are getting in return?" Father said.

"Not having the Empire raze you to the ground," Ewan muttered.

"Why do the gentry feel that they need to get anything in exchange for finally doling out fundamental human rights?" Jack said.

I tapped my fingers against my lips. The idea was faintly distasteful to me, but . . .

"Ewan's right," I said. "I don't like the idea of using the Empire as leverage, but the gentry need to believe that the Rootless will force change on to this country whether they want it or not. The gentry have an opportunity for it to be a peaceful process. Otherwise, they will lose everything." At my own words, that needle prick of a thought returned, a half-formed idea that was too disturbing to allow to fully surface. What if I lost—or gave up—Landry Park?

I shook it off. "On the other hand, the Rootless—all of them, not just you, Jack—must promise to dissolve their alliance with the Empire in order to receive Jamie's formula."

"You are holding our health hostage?" Ewan said. "That's ridiculous. That's unfair."

"Nevertheless, it is necessary," I said. "The Empire can't be invited in by anyone. It doesn't matter if Jack cuts ties with them if Smith and his followers still ally with them. We *all* have to stand against them."

"I know," Jack said. "I know that. But Smith will never change his mind. I will have to cut him off from the community completely. His followers could perhaps be persuaded, however. . . ."

I let him finish ruminating. Jack took a while to complete his thought, staring at his drink. He finally looked up. "We have an agreement."

We all decided that the Lantern Day Ball should continue and that it was vital that both factions be represented. Father felt that the historical significance of the date would make an accord more meaningful, and Jack felt that the two days between now and then was a sufficient span to convince the two groups to work together, without wasting precious time.

We also agreed that the real killer, whoever he or she was, would probably continue to be drawn to Landry Park in the meantime, although I had a suspicion that he would be even more drawn to the Lantern Day Ball, just as he had been drawn to the dinner party the night of Marianne's death. The following morning, I shared my thoughts with Father, who concurred.

"Is this a good or bad thing?" I asked. "To have a murderer

lingering at such an important event?" *And on my birthday,* I thought, knowing it was childish.

"Perhaps it will ensure your safety until then, at least. And we will make sure that a legion of constables is on hand to keep you, and everyone else, safe."

"I just wish there had been someone to protect the others."

"Me too," he said heavily. "But the ball will be different. Trust me when I promise that I'll keep my daughter safe on her birthday."

My fingers plucked nervously at my dress as we finished our breakfast. I hoped Father was right.

Overnight the snow had fallen in low, thick blankets, making everything muffled and serene outside, but wet and crowded inside. News of the robbery at Jamie's had spread, much faster than the initial revelation of the research into a cure, and the mood was bleak. I heard whispers, mutters, blaming the gentry, blaming the constables, blaming my father or even Jack. I kept my head down as I moved past them, wanting to reassure them that it was only a delay, but not knowing if they would resent my intrusion.

As I carried blankets and towels and got steaming cups of hot water from the kitchen, I also wrestled with the fact that I needed to speak to David. I needed to apologize. I needed to tell him that he was right, that he had been right all along. About Smith, about my pride, about everything . . .

But I couldn't. I didn't know why, but the thought of apologizing still galled me, and what was left of my pride balked at the idea. I felt so guilty, but it wasn't a pure guilt, if there was even such a thing. It was guilt wrapped in anger and shame, and I felt as likely to explode at David as to apologize—because he had the nerve to be right when I was wrong, because I felt humiliated by him for that, because he was the one person I wanted to think well of me.

The snow kept falling, slow and steady, large flakes that fluttered under the clouds like moths, and I helped until the smell of rich stew and buttered rolls signaled lunch.

After the meal, we drove in the snow to my uncle Lawrence's house. The Uprisen were meeting there this afternoon, and it was our intention to persuade them to come to the Lantern Day Ball and finally reach an agreement with the Rootless.

The Lawrence estate—Laurel Lake—was set very far back from the road, a tall brick affair with a perfectly circular lake behind it. I'd spent many winters ice-skating on that lake as a girl, trying to avoid getting run over by my cousins, and running inside for steaming cups of spiced hot chocolate in Auntie Lawrence's garishly appointed parlor afterward.

Laurel trees lined the drive up to the house, each with its own discreet warming system wrapped around the base, keeping the Mediterranean flora thriving in the midst of the Kansas City winter. The house gave the impression of enlightened refinement, but there had always been a darkness to it. Not the damp, environmental darkness of Sai Thorpe's house, but a darkness shaped by the impatient taps of Arthur Lawrence's cane and the oversized paintings of the Last War that lined the halls, all depicting the most gruesome things— bleeding rioters, burning churches, gibbet cages. Even now, no longer a child, I felt a shiver of unease just approaching the place.

We stopped in the drive, a footman already emerging from the front to take the car.

Father didn't move.

"Is everything all right?" I asked.

He took a minute to answer, his eyes fixed on the front door. "They won't be easy to convince," he said. "This will be difficult. It will be a miracle if they even bother to listen to me."

"They will listen," I said with a confidence that I in no way felt. "They are out of options and they know it."

It had been almost a year since I'd been to Laurel Lake— the last time I'd come was for a dinner party and I had spent it watching Cara and Philip Wilder flirt, counting the seconds until Jane and I could leave the dinner table and find a quiet corner to pass the time. The house was as unsettling as I remembered; dark, dark wood paneled the walls and the floors were a bloodred granite. Large brass chandeliers and narrow windows studded the shadowed halls, but it was a failed endeavor. The house seemed to eat light.

Father guided me to the Lawrence library, where the Uprisen were seated around a table.

"It's the Landrys," Harry Westoff said drily. "What a surprise."

Arthur Lawrence fairly glowered at my father and me, but Elizabeth Osbourne stood. For a moment I thought she was angry, but then she came forward and hugged me tightly. I could feel her anguish just under the surface, gnawing and grasping, but when she stepped back, her face showed nothing of the sort. "Jane's funeral is tomorrow," she said quietly. "It will be small, just the family . . . but I wanted you to know."

I nodded, blinking back the sudden emotion.

"Well, shall they stand forever or are you going to offer them a seat, Arthur?" a woman from Denver asked.

"*Fine,*" Uncle Lawrence said, and rang a bell on the wall behind him.

The woman winked a dark eye at me, and I smiled back at her. There were only four women in the Uprisen at the moment, and even though female gentry had historically held seats on the council since its inception, there was still a feeling of solidarity at seeing another woman in the meeting.

A few seconds later, a servant emerged and found chairs for Father and me. As we sat, Uncle Lawrence rapped his cane against the table a couple of times. *Rap, rap.* "Why are you here, Alexander?" he asked. "We told you last week that we are not interested in helping with your little refugee scenario. Especially after what happened at Glasshawke with the charges."

"They have finally exhausted our patience," Mr. Glaize said. "My family could have been made ill, my house made unlivable—"

"Not to mention their vicious and causeless murders of our children," Harry Westoff added. "Alexander, you sit next to your own heir, but the Everlys and the Wilders and the Osbournes will never be able to do that again."

"I'm here for the same reason as you," Father said. "To discuss the Empire's demands and the possibility of war."

Rap.

"I want to hear the girl," Arthur Lawrence cut in, preventing my father from continuing and turning his reptilian eyes to me. "You brought her here, so let's have her speak."

I blinked for a moment, surprised and unnerved.

Rap.

"Well, girl? Speak!"

TWENTY-EIGHT

I was only silent for a matter of seconds. But in that matter of seconds—in the way that only happens when a room full of people are looking at you—months and years unfurled, stretching time into an infinite band of silent anxiety. I felt certain that nothing I could say would sway them, that my attempt to do so would be laughable, and that I'd harm our cause much more than if I remained mute.

I cleared my throat. "Father and I have come here because we believe that we might have a solution to our problems with the Empire and here at home." My voice sounded frail, even to me.

"The only solution," Mr. Westoff said coolly, "is for the Rootless to rescind their ridiculous demands and return to their rightful place in this world."

"Agreed!" another man—this one from New Chicago—shouted.

The rest of the group rippled with assent, although Elizabeth and the woman from Denver remained quiet and impassive. I looked at Father, looking for help or a word of encouragement or anything at all, but there was nothing save for a flicker in the depths of his eyes. *This is what I raised you to do.*

But it wasn't that simple. These people didn't want me to lead them. They didn't want anything to change, ever, and how was it possible to reach people like that? I thought of growing up with Father, learning how to run the estate with him, how to tell when a creditor was bluffing or when a farmer was hiding his true profits. Father had showed me that every person had a weakness that could be leveraged somehow, that each person was a mix of fears and angers and hopes, and with acute judgment and a deft twist of words, you could bait and leash them with their own secret troubles. So what was that for the Uprisen?

Their greatest fears involve land and money, I realized. Not watching their loved ones die, not dying a terrible death themselves, not watching snow blow in through the chinks of their shanties . . .

Just like that, my unease ceased. How could I be intimidated by people with such limited perspectives? I straightened my shoulders and leveled my gaze at the Uprisen across the table. "Do you think the Rootless will really just return to the way things were? Do you really think they will go back to the shadows? They won't give up easily . . . and they won't forget."

"And that is why we must crush them now," Arthur Lawrence said, "before this disease corrupts any more of our country."

"It's more complicated than that," I said. "The Rootless may have been quiet these past few years, but that doesn't mean that they haven't been busy. They've been preparing, and they've prepared by making an alliance with the Empire."

There was a silence thick with shock.

"How would they have the means to do such a thing?" Mr. Glaize demanded after a long minute. "This cannot be."

"It's a bluff," Mr. Westoff said, narrowing his eyes at me. "A bluff calculated to make us capitulate to their whims."

"It's no fiction," I said. "It's absolutely true. You can ask Robert Smith. I'm sure he would love to put you in touch with his friends in the Empire."

Mr. Westoff didn't respond, but neither did he look away from me. I thought of Cara standing in front of the Uprisen heirs last week, tossing her hair and telling them off when they insulted her. I summoned her confidence and kept my voice even and my face as still and Landry-like as possible. "The Empire is ready to finish what they started two hundred years ago. Why wouldn't they see the Rootless as the easiest avenue to making that happen? They are poised to invade, and if the Rootless fight against us as well, we are finished."

"We stopped them in the mountains," Arthur Lawrence said. "And if they come again, then we will stop them again."

I shook my head. "You underestimate their strength. They

have tens of thousands—if not hundreds of thousands—of soldiers to fling at us until we break. They have aerial weapons and we have none. When they are ready, they will smash us—unless we refuse to play into their hands, and we keep our country strong."

Rap.

Everyone looked at Arthur Lawrence. "I will not allow this idle, specious reasoning to sway this discussion. The Rootless and their emissaries"—here he looked at Father and me—"are *lying*, plain and simple. They want us to entertain our worst fears, to conceive of the worst possible scenarios, all so that we can be robbed of our rightful place in this world. But I will not allow us to be so misused; we will *shatter* them—"

"Enough," I snapped, and my voice rang out across the room. Uncle Lawrence actually stopped talking, his mouth still open, his eyes wide, as if he were so unused to being interrupted that he couldn't even process what had just happened. "You do not get to use violence, Uncle Lawrence. Not this time. And neither will they. This time there will be no police, no gibbet cages. Because if we continue trying to force an entire population back into indenture, then the Empire will come and we will lose everything."

I paused, but no one spoke, not even Mr. Westoff or Arthur Lawrence. I went on. "My uncle Lawrence is asking you to ignore the very real probability of Eastern invasion, but I'm asking you to envision it. For only a moment, envision what it would feel like to watch your estates bombed, your land stripped away, your very country subsumed by the Empire. They will come. They will spill over the mountains and when they do, they will not be merciful."

They were shifting now, uncomfortably.

"But we have one thing, one weapon, and that is that we are not easy prey. United and calm and ready, we would make it so difficult to be invaded that they would turn away, discouraged, even if they could eventually win. They do not like to do things at great cost, and that is where we have the power. They have planned on us weakening ourselves. We do not have to oblige them."

Four or five of them were nodding now, and even Mr. Glaize—lackey to Mr. Westoff in most things—looked thoughtful.

"Everybody has a rightful place in this world," I said. "And it's not under the heel of somebody else. We won't be subjugated to the Empire and the Rootless won't be subjugated to us. We have this chance now to work together. It may seem like we are losing something, a way of life, a way of tradition, but in the end, we are saving ourselves from losing *everything*. Come to the Lantern Day Ball tomorrow. Sign a treaty with the Rootless—give them homes and education and access to the serum. Pay for your charges to be changed. And keep your farms and industries and livelihoods. In exchange, the Rootless will disavow all contact with the Empire, the country will remain whole and unmarred by riots and violence, and the Empire will have to go back to biding its time."

I took a deep breath and sat back, still trying to channel the air of magistracy that Father had always so effortlessly exuded. When I glanced over at him, he was looking down at his hands, but he made a small nod, something like approval in the lines of his face. I looked back at the table of pensive Uprisen, and a contentment unfurled within me.

I had done it.

It took two more hours of bickering and protesting, mostly from Arthur Lawrence, but in the end, it was settled ten to two. The Uprisen would attend the Lantern Day Ball and they would sign a treaty with the agreed-upon terms—the serum in exchange for a disintegration of the Rootless-Empire alliance. The charge changing would be on a volunteer basis only, and it would be paid and safe, and those who wished to adopt wind or solar power would be encouraged to do so. But nothing was certain until things were signed and hands shook and agreements announced, and the contentment I had initially felt had already melted away, even before we drove away from Laurel Lake.

"I am so proud of you," Father said. "What you did in there— standing up to Arthur Lawrence, speaking so authoritatively—I know that wasn't easy."

"Thank you," I said. But my voice sounded distant, even to me.

Father didn't look over, his eyes on the snow-covered road, but I knew he was taking in my malaise all the same. "Madeline, all you have wanted for the past two months—if not longer—is to find a way for the Rootless and the gentry to come to an agreement. You just did it—almost single-handedly, too. Isn't that what you wanted?"

"It is . . . you're right," I said, trying to shrug off my anxiety. "Now, all we have to do is make it to the ball."

TWENTY-NINE

The mood leading up to the ball was mildly optimistic. Mother finally had the help and the guest list that she wanted, Jack had good news for his people, and Jamie and the scientists at the university had been able to regain almost all of their lost footing, after Father and I had donated more blood. Jack had donated as well, and he shared the good news with the Rootless, sleeve still rolled up to show the bandage on his arm. *The serum will be ready in a matter of weeks.* . . . The news flooded the city with optimism.

The tendrils of assurance and brightness began to arc and helix within me, too, slowly at first, and then as crates of Cherenkov lanterns and plum wine began to arrive, faster and faster until I felt something like cheer and hope.

It was infectious. The Rootless who were still on the estate—free of their freezing shanties and poisonous sorting yards, with the prospect of the serum and a real life ahead—had become downright happy. And I even saw two families returning to stay with us. The snow stopped and everyone worked to shovel the layered drifts and move the solar heaters around the grounds, and by the day of the ball, the entire lawn was clear and dry.

It was my eighteenth birthday. Any other year and we would have celebrated with a succession of sumptuous food and extravagant gifts, but this year was different. After a small breakfast of tea and toast, Father and Mother gave me a present—my grandmother Genevieve's tiara, sparkling silver and diamonds with an atomic circle set in the middle. Charlie gave me a picture he had drawn, a detailed crayon portrait of me standing by the gates, and Jack gifted me a dusty copy of *The Little Prince* in its original French, which I vowed to read right away.

My birthday was different for one other reason: Today was the day that Father and I would change our own charges. The eyes of the country were already on Landry Park, on the historic ball tonight that would host both the Rootless and the gentry and that would hopefully witness the signing of a historic accord. What better time than this to demonstrate the safety of the job?

Serum aside, we'd also pledged to invest in modifications to make the job safer: new suits, additional protective gear for the sorting yards, and water and cooling systems for the packers who would shepherd the waste to Florida for disposal. The new equipment would be ready within a week or two. Once the aim of the job was not to degrade the Rootless, it was all too easy to improve the conditions.

We invited journalists and wall screen presenters—already in the city to report on the ball that evening—to come to Landry Park to watch. Father was hesitant, I could tell, but I never wavered, and strangely enough, that seemed to reassure him. As the late morning sun peeked weakly through a haze of March clouds, we dressed in the old protective suits that Ewan had brought us from the sorting yards. Pictures were snapped, questions were asked, and then we went downstairs together to find the charges.

Jack had talked us through it all, but Father still fumbled with the charge boxes, trying to slide them out of the generator, and I finally stepped in to help. He looked at me gratefully, his face half hidden by the protective mask. We pulled it out together, and replaced it with one of the new charges that Ewan had also brought. I remembered long mornings of playing with porcelain dolls at Father's feet, afternoons of serving him imaginary tea from a miniature, filigreed tea set that had been custom-made just for my small hands.

"Thank you," I said to him. I wanted to thank him for everything, not only for the lessons and for the love of this house that he had bequeathed to me, but for all of his mistakes, and mine, too. If he hadn't denied me the university, I might never have fallen in love with David or gotten to know Jack and Ewan and Charlie. If he hadn't tightened his fist around the Rootless, I wouldn't have stepped forward. If our past choices hadn't lined up in this precise constellation, then we wouldn't be here, now, carefully sliding the charges into their lead-lined carriers, waiting for the world to change for the better.

I could barely make out the lacework of scars that were still fading from Father's face, but I knew they were there, and even if they shrunk and faded and vanished entirely, they would always be just under the surface, haunting him. Much like all of the people upstairs—the serum might expunge the sickness from their bodies, but nothing would ever erase the memory of it from their hearts. There would be bitterness and nightmares in the years to come. But still, Father's hand was steady as he carefully placed the carrier strap on his shoulder, even though he was only a few thin layers away from the thing that had poisoned him. He was being brave—perhaps more for me and the sake of stopping the Empire than any actual conviction to help the Rootless—but it still counted.

Two rows of silent Rootless greeted us as we emerged from the basement, a parade of quiet watchfulness, of caution without hostility. The rows stretched from the hallway out into the foyer, and then beyond the front door, all the way down the drive to the wrought-iron gates at the end. Some inclined their heads at us as we passed, some offered watery smiles, and some simply stared, not angrily, but patiently, as if waiting to see if we were really going to do this and bring the charges all the way across the city.

The silence pressed in on us, not oppressively, but watchfully, and there was only the sound of my own breath inside the mask and of my boots scraping across the wet stones of the drive. When we passed through the gates, I turned to look back, not at the Rootless, but at the house, wondering if it would look any different from this perspective. Any different now that I had been its caretaker in an entirely new and strange way.

It didn't.

We drove to the ghetto in one of the new vehicles we'd bought especially for the purpose. Father drove us, slowly; it had been years since he'd driven himself anywhere. We stopped the truck at the entrance, barred from driving any farther by the unplowed streets, and when we stepped through the stone gates of the old park, I realized that we were not alone.

We walked through the burned ghetto, the shacks and streets still in a dispiriting mess, although the latest foot of snow had covered over the worst of the char and rubble. People emerged from the ruins to stare at us, faces unfriendly and harsh, marked by cold and distrust. I didn't know what I could say to them to change that; I didn't know how I could convince them that the serum really would help them and that it wasn't some elaborate trick on the part of the gentry.

An idea came to me then, and I pulled off my hood and dropped it on the ground. No one reacted, except for Father, who seemed alarmed, but remained quiet. I removed the suit gloves and then reached into the lead-lined satchel where I'd placed my charge. I removed it from the bag and held it in my bare hand.

The charge itself was cool to the touch, smooth like glass but incredibly heavy, ringed with blinking red lights signaling its expiration. I wondered how long it would take for the radiation to do its work, to maim parts of me that were invisible to the eye, and how long it would take for my body to repair itself.

The crowd said nothing as I started walking again, cradling the charge in my bare hands, but something had shifted. It might not be enough, but it was something.

The tang of metal still hung in the air around the sorting yards, but when we opened the door, there was no crying, no vomiting. There was only the heat and the *whoosh* of trains passing through from other cities where the Rootless were still changing charges, where they were still waiting for hope and freedom. *Tonight,* I thought. Tonight things would change for everyone everywhere.

We descended, the dark steps still only barely lit by Cherenkov lanterns. The vast charging floor was completely empty, save for several lead bins, ready to receive their radioactive cargo. The faint bluish light created long eerie shadows, as if we were in the depths of a winter night, a feeling at odds with the sweltering temperatures.

"It's entirely too hot," Father said from behind his mask. I agreed. The heat from the nuclear-steam hybrid trains made the yards broil like a sauna. I had forgotten how sapping it was, the wet heat and the heavy suits. We both knelt and started opening our cases, searching for the tiny hearts of the charges—the small fragments of dull metal that had caused two hundred years of sores and cancer and early death. Those went into the deceptively heavy bins, which had to be laboriously dragged across the floor.

By the end, Father's face was slick with sweat, and I could hear his labored breathing as we moved the new boxes to a loading dock. There were no trains at the moment, and no packers anyway, so we left the boxes with the spent uranium inside and walked back out into the world, the feeble early spring light almost blinding after the dim yards, relishing the bite of the cold air on our flushed faces.

"They did all of that in that heat?" Father asked incredulously.

"Yes. And they didn't have enough suits for every worker, so many of them were working without any protection at all. Children too."

He pressed his lips together and started walking. We didn't say anything more, but I could read the pensive set of his shoulders well enough without words. Now I knew why Jack had insisted that I go down to the sorting yards all those months ago. It was one thing to hear of suffering or even to watch it from afar. But to be in the middle of it, inches away from someone coughing up blood or throwing up or collapsing from pure exhaustion, was different. Father might not have seen the Rootless at work, but now he had done the work himself, in the heat, and so now maybe he was experiencing the same spiral of realization that David and I, and Jack all those years earlier, had gone through.

It was late afternoon by the time our truck passed through the iron gates once more, and the servants were hard at work laying out flowers and lining up trays of Cherenkov lanterns for the Lantern Day celebration. The Rootless didn't applaud or cheer when we walked back through the house, my hair now tangled and sweaty and Father's face grim. But there were more nods, touches on the shoulder.

It was only a step, but it had been a good one, at least.

Father said nothing as we parted at the top of the stairs, but he did open his arms, offering a rare paternal embrace. I closed my eyes and hugged him.

THIRTY

Elinor drew a bath for me while I peeled off my sweaty clothes, and she made a bigger fuss than normal about steeping rose petals in the water and about washing my hair for me. I had been insisting on doing it by myself for the last few weeks, now that she had to wait on Cara and help with our Rootless guests as well, but I was tired and she refused to back down, and so I found myself almost asleep in the bath as Elinor's strong fingers rubbed the ivy-scented shampoo into my scalp.

After I'd toweled off and slipped into a long silk robe, Elinor began pressing me for dress choices. Gray? Ivory? Scarlet? Lavender? And my hair—down or up? Tiara or comb? Diamond bracelet or the amethyst ring?

"I don't care," I told her after every choice. "I honestly don't care."

Her eyes narrowed. "Tonight is important. For the country and for *you*. How can you not care?"

"Because things are going to happen the way they will regardless of what I look like." I glanced at her. "Is there a reason you are so intent on the state of my apparel tonight? Do you know something I don't?"

331

"No," she said vaguely, and then disappeared back into my closet. A second later, her head popped back through the doorway. "And I definitely haven't talked to Captain Dana today. And he definitely doesn't have an amazing gift for you."

My chest tightened. If he had talked to Elinor, if he had a gift for me, that meant that he would be here tonight, which meant that we would need to talk. I would need to apologize.

As if there wasn't enough going on tonight.

Everything had to go smoothly—the gentry needed to be respectful and calm, the Rootless needed to remain patient. At midnight, after the dinner and the dancing, after the lanterns were hung and the annual fireworks display had taken place, the gentry and the Rootless—represented, respectively, by the Uprisen and Jack, who had managed to win the majority of his people over to the plan—would sign a formal accord, granting freedom and aid to the Rootless and disavowing any more contact with the Empire. Waiting until midnight had been Jack's idea, perhaps to have the added aesthetic of the gleaming lanterns about them as the two factions made history, but I had disagreed from the beginning. I wanted the accords signed as soon as possible; too much could go wrong between dinner and the signing.

Not for the first time, I pushed down a worry that the Empire's influence would find a way to slip into the night's events. But Smith was in jail, and I had no choice but to trust that Jack did not actually work with the Empire any longer.

It will be fine, I reassured myself. I was worrying over nothing—everything was already decided and agreed upon, everybody was convinced that this was the right course. The signing was simply a formality.

Elinor dressed me in the lavender gown, which had a high collar and one lacy sleeve, leaving the other arm completely bare. The bodice—silk with a lace overlay—clung to my frame until it reached my waist and then was belted with a wide silk sash. Below that, the skirt tumbled over onto itself, decadent layers of silk and tulle, with hidden clusters of jewels that flashed in the light when I moved. Elinor pinned my hair up into elaborate crimson coils, finally inserting a tiara into the masterpiece.

It was the Landry family tiara, the one my parents had given me for my birthday. I rested my fingertips against it, but I didn't pull it out. "Do you think this could be potentially problematic?" I asked. "Given the circumstances of the night?"

She leaned down so that her cheek rested against mine as we looked into the mirror together. "Are you proud of your estate, Miss Madeline?"

"Yes," I answered without hesitation.

"And of your family?"

That was a more difficult question to answer. I thought of Jacob Landry, of my grandfather, of my own father standing in front of a gibbet cage, his cold voice ringing throughout the park. But then I thought about that same father, walking into the sorting yards with me, a charge slung across his shoulder, willing to abandon all of the prejudices that he'd been raised with. I thought of Uncle Jack, willing to leave behind every comfort and commodity in order to live among his chosen people, to live with a free conscience. And I thought of Mother—tremulous but lovely—and of brash Ewan and sweet Charlie and determined, stoic Jude.

"Yes," I finally answered. "I am proud of my family."

Her skin moved against mine as she nodded. "Then you should wear it. The world should see tonight that you are making history as a Landry, not despite being one."

I reached up and squeezed her hand. "Thank you."

"Of course. Now you should head down—it's almost five thirty."

I stood, pausing when I passed by the full-length mirror. I looked so much older. Maybe it was the dress—more dramatic than the sort I usually wore—or the hair, which I rarely allowed to be put up. Or maybe it was the gravity of tonight that made my face so serious and so contemplative.

"You look lovely," Elinor said, a little impatiently. "And of course you do, because I dressed you. Now hurry or you'll be late. And I'll be late helping Miss Cara, and nobody wants that."

Downstairs, the house still bustled with activity, the smell of rich food and sweet desserts hanging in the air. From the long windows, I could catch glimpses of navy-coated constables roaming the grounds in the fading dusk. I wondered how the

Rootless felt, sharing the same space with the very people who had beaten them and torched their homes. What an inverted world it had become when the Rootless were inside the estate as guests while the agents of the gentry looked on from outside. *What a much improved world.*

Once I walked into the foyer, I saw the whole family assembled: Father and Mother, Uncle Jack and Ewan and even Charlie, dressed in a stiff tuxedo and relentlessly fiddling with the collar. And Jude. Jude, who stood apart from the others, with his hands behind his back and his shoulders straight, as if awaiting orders. He lit up when he saw me.

"You look beautiful," he said, taking my hand for a quick kiss. Our eyes met, and I looked away, reminded of another night like this only two months ago. A night where it had seemed very possible that I might marry Jude, not for love, but for the safety of my own future and of my friends.

"You know," he said with a smile, "it's not uncommon for cousins in the gentry to marry."

He said it like he might have been joking, but his eyes were silver pools of seriousness and I knew that he wasn't. "Jude . . ." I didn't know what to say. It didn't matter that he was my cousin. My heart had been David's from the beginning.

He shook his head, indicating he didn't want me to say more, indicating that he knew David and I belonged to each other. And in that rueful gesture, I realized his heart would be pulled in two directions for a very long time, no matter how much he claimed to accept it, no matter how stoically he bore it to the rest of the world.

"You have the Landry connection that you wanted," I said, in a stab at levity. "You don't need me anymore."

"I know I'm bad at expressing my sentiments," Jude said, "but I didn't know I was so terrible at it that you would think that was the sole reason I wanted to marry you. I did want the estate and the family. But it was always with you by my side."

"You're family now," I said, and took his hand. "I will always be by your side."

We were interrupted by the first guests arriving. It was the Wilders, led by Philip, tall and handsome as ever, although his normally laughing demeanor was absent. When he made his way down the row, shaking hands and thanking us for inviting him, he reached me and leaned in close, so that Jude couldn't hear. "The heirs are gathering together during the dinner to talk. Where is a good place?"

I raised my eyebrows. "To talk about what?"

He glanced around, as if to say *not here*.

"Philip?"

"It's about the person who killed Marianne," he said. "We all need to talk, but away from everyone. I don't want to stir up a panic."

"The morning room," I said, making sure he understood that I was still doubtful. "Even with the Rootless here, it's usually empty."

I wanted Jude to come, too—he'd been party to everything else about the murders so far and I knew he could be trusted, but he'd already slid off to greet some of his gentry admirers. Before I could go after him, more guests arrived in a parade of silky clothes and even silkier manners, and I found myself once more swept up in greeting them. Some families—the Osbournes in particular—seemed happy enough to be here. Others, like the Lawrences, made no secret of their disgust for the situation. The footman opened the door once more and David walked in.

My breath caught.

He wore a simple tuxedo, which highlighted his narrow hips and lean body as tuxedos always did, but it was his face— intent and stormy and raw—that did me in. It was a face I saw only in between kisses, a face I saw only when he was at his most passionate. I swallowed, politics and treaties temporarily eclipsed by this army captain. My army captain.

His mother was by his side, looking stunning in a thin scarlet gown, narrow and filmy, the fabric hanging from the angles of her frame in such a way as to make her look more like a painting of a woman than an actual woman. Mother stepped forward to take her hand, effectively cutting her off from greeting Father. Mother was also beautiful, her dark hair shining and studded with jewels, and for a moment, I could see them as teenage girls, both dressing and dancing to impress one man.

That man now stepped forward as well, and I thought he might reach out for Christine or speak to her, but instead he slid his arm around Mother's waist. Father and Christine exchanged a look, and from the way Christine turned away, offering a falsely bright smile to Ewan and me, I could tell what the exchange had meant.

David strolled up to me, his hands in his pockets.

"Hello," I said quietly.

"So you convinced the Uprisen and the Rootless to come here together," he remarked. "That's quite an achievement."

"Is that really what you want to talk about?" I asked. "The treaty?"

He ran a hand through his hair, looking down. "Not really," he said.

Worry and hope, love and pride and the last dregs of guilt, all of it fluttered inside me, like a flurry of birds taking flight, like leaves tossed in a storm.

He looked up, meeting my eyes, and there was nothing uncertain or fidgety about him now. For once, he was completely still. "I want to talk about how you will always be the one I can't live without. I want to talk about how I said that I would leave because you had Smith arrested, about how I said good-bye, and about how I'm here to swallow those words, in the most painful way possible if necessary."

I was already shaking my head. "Don't. It's me who needs to apologize." I took a breath. "I'm sorry . . . you were right. About everything—about Smith and about me and about my reasons. I should have listened to you in the beginning, but

I chose not to, and so everything that's happened because of that choice is my fault."

He took a step forward, my skirt now pressed against his legs. "It's just that I know you are capable of so much—and of so much more than me. If it seems like I expect too much from you, it's because I believe that you can do it."

"I know."

His hands circled my upper arms just above the elbow, and his grip wasn't tight, just warm and thrilling and a tiny bit possessive. That cinnamon-and-clove scent hung in the air.

I tilted my face toward his, my heart stuttering in irregular and frantic beats as our eyes met. Aware that we were now drawing stares, I murmured, "This is an intense discussion to have in a greeting line."

"Then let's have it somewhere else," he said urgently. "Right now. Before the dinner even starts."

"I'm supposed to go meet the other heirs in the library. But you're more than welcome to come with . . ."

He gave me a look that was part disinclination, part defeat.

"Philip said it was important," I assured him, and just then a bell rung, signaling that the food was ready. "And it will only be a moment. If we slip out now, no one will notice."

It was true. The sheer size of the ball meant that the guests were eating buffet style, around small tables and in corners and even in the parlors and the library. Mother had fretted over this—it wasn't done, really, not to have a sit-down dinner at such an important event—but there was no way around it. There were almost thirteen hundred guests and every room was bursting at the seams.

While the crowd in the foyer began to push for the ballroom where the food was laid out, I took David's hand and guided him closer to the hallway, waiting for an opening in the crush.

David made an exasperated noise, but I ignored it, darting into a gap and taking him with me, pulling and weaving until we made it down the hall and into the silent morning room.

Philip was already there, as were the Lawrence boys, and Sai and Cara, who had brought Ewan with her. Too late, I realized that I'd forgotten to get Jude.

"Oh, should I have brought my boyfriend, too?" Tarleton sneered, seeing David.

"He's with me," I said firmly. "Anything you want to discuss, he will be a party to."

Frank Lawrence rolled his eyes. "And the Rootless one?"

Ewan looked ready to snap his neck, but Cara looked even angrier. "I'd like to see you try to make him leave," she said dangerously.

"Okay, okay," Philip interjected, hands up. "Let's all take a deep breath. We're all here for the same reason."

"Which is?" I asked.

"Smith has escaped from jail."

THIRTY-ONE

"What?" Cara and David said at the same time.

"I heard it from one of the constables just as I was walking in," Philip explained, "but when I asked them about it, they said that they aren't telling anyone at the moment. They don't want to cause panic at the ball."

That was understandable—most of the gentry believed that Smith was the murderer. Word of his escape would not be conducive to the spirit of negotiations.

But . . .

"Look," I said. "I've learned some things since we last talked and I think that he had nothing to do with the murders. I think he's innocent."

Sai and Philip raised their eyebrows in surprise and Stuart snorted. "He escaped from jail," Tarleton said. "That doesn't sound very innocent to me."

"My uncle says he is, and I believe him," I insisted.

"Okay," Philip said slowly. "So if he didn't kill the others, then who did?"

"I don't know," I had to admit. God, I hated not knowing things. Even more, I hated admitting it.

"There you go, then. I happen to think that he did do it, and I think that we should try to catch the bastard tonight," Philip said. "Once and for all. We know he likes killing Uprisen heirs and we know he likes doing it here at Landry Park. Well, we're all here, one big cluster of targets. He'd have a big audience. This is the perfect time to draw him out and expose him. With all the constables around, we can have him locked back up in seconds, and remove any shadow of a doubt that he's guilty."

Philip spoke with a grim intensity, and I knew there would be no dissuading him. I remembered his tears over Marianne's body, all of the times he had lingered around Jane, had fetched drinks for her and danced with her. He'd lost much more than I had these past three weeks—I couldn't fault him for his zeal.

"What are you proposing?" I asked. "That we expose ourselves somehow? Use ourselves as bait?"

"That's exactly what I'm suggesting," he said.

"That doesn't sound safe," David said. He looked at me and Cara. "If you and Sai and Stuart want to go play vigilante, that's fine. But leave Madeline and Cara out of it."

"Are you saying that I can't defend myself?" I asked, turning to David.

"He was able to kill Mark," David said. "Whoever he is, he's strong. And clever. Maybe you think that you would be fine, but the people who care about you might not agree."

"Actually," Ewan said, "I think both girls *would* be fine.

Cara's strong. We could make it so that I'm nearby, ready to jump in any sign of trouble, and she'll have her tablet. . . ."

"Are you really willing to take that risk?"

"It's not my decision to make," Ewan said. And he looked at me. "And I feel the same about my cousin, if you want to know."

I smiled at Ewan. "Thank you."

David looked incredulous. He didn't say anything more, but I could tell that the thought of letting me walk into danger was deeply antithetical to him. As it would be to me, if our positions were reversed. "However we may feel about our various strengths," I told Philip, "I think this is unnecessarily dangerous. The constables are on alert for Smith and for any other suspicious characters. If we want to remain safe, then we should stay with one another and stay indoors."

"If he's as clever as you think," Stuart said, "don't you think he'd find a way to kill again no matter what you do?"

"I have to agree," Sai said. "There might be a moment when we're stepping out for a cigarette or where we're returning from the coat room, a moment when we are alone anyway. We won't be safe as long as he's at large."

"We might as well meet him on our terms," Frank said. "Be waiting for him, with a plan."

I worried at the inside of my lip with my teeth. I saw their point—the idea of meeting the killer while prepared and in a trap of our own seemed smarter. But the foolhardiness of the scheme was undeniable. "What if we tried to work with the constables?"

"We don't *need* to work together," Stuart said. "They're all around the freaking building. If one of us lets out so much as a shout, they'll come running."

Philip stepped in. "Stuart's right. We need to do this ourselves—if we involve the police, then they'll swarm the grounds and scare off the killer." Seeing my expression, he added, "We'll only be alone for as long as it takes to draw him out. And we'll never really be alone—there's a house full of people and police."

"A house full of people didn't protect Jane," I pointed out, but I knew that I was close to agreeing. I didn't want to see my friends place themselves in harm's way while I stayed safely indoors. The others looked at me for a minute, and I finally caved.

"They'll be finishing dinner soon," I said. "There will be some dancing and then they'll hang the lanterns. That will be the best time to slip off—people will be coming in and out and going outside anyway. And then there'll be the fireworks— noise, distraction. Maybe he'll come find one of us before the signing even begins."

It was decided that Ewan would shadow Cara and that David would shadow me, so as to always be within earshot, and we all agreed on different parts of the house and grounds. I took the maze—it would need someone who knew it well.

I didn't mention that its distance from the house and lack of cameras would make it a very attractive place for a murder. David was anxious and twitchy enough as it was when we started down toward the ballroom.

Downstairs, the dancing was in full swing, music thrumming through the floor, guests jostling elbow to shoulder, the air hot and thick with the smell of perfume and alcohol. I looked for Jude, but it was nearly impossible to identify anybody in the crush—I wouldn't have been able to find David if he hadn't been right next to me. I sent Jude a quick message as we tried to make for the doors that led out to the grounds: *The heirs want to draw out the killer. David and I are going to the maze.* I didn't know if he would see it or not, if the chaos and noise and inevitable glad-handing would make it difficult for him to check his tablet.

It took us almost forty-five minutes to push through the crowd, and by the time we made it to the patio doors, servants were dimming the lights and rolling in carts and carts of covered lanterns, some on the ballroom floor, some out on the patio. The gentry guests crowded around them, pulling on coats and scarves and chatting animatedly while they waited. For the gentry, this was just another Lantern Day—a celebration mostly devoid of its original meaning and an excuse to drink and play in the snow. But for the Rootless, this was something entirely new—something that had always been an insult to their suffering but would now be a reminder of the night that they'd been freed. The Rootless were largely silent and were the last to take up their lanterns.

One by one, the lights around the house clicked off, and everywhere outside, everywhere around the country, streetlights and bedroom lamps and candles fell into darkness. The doors opened and people began unhooding their lanterns, suffusing the world with a sapphire glow.

As the blue light filled the hall, David and I moved past the others to get to the ballroom doors and onto the lawn, grabbing two lanterns as we went.

The solar heaters were on, making a path of mild air all the way down to the end of the lawn, keeping the grass unfrozen and dry. The skirt of my gown rustled and brushed against the brown blades as we walked, both of us now holding our lanterns high. I looked back to see the guests spreading across the grounds, the Cherenkov beams like blue sparks in the penumbra of the evening, and I could hear the faint laughter and shouts of guests as they began to scramble into the trees to hang up the lights.

I scanned the grounds as we walked, noting that no one else seemed to be walking this far back. We'd be in the maze alone. Even though I knew this maze like the back of my hand, even though I had David and my tablet and constables all around me, I still felt keenly aware that I was wandering into a dark and lonely corner of my estate in order to be approached by a killer.

The large red door wasn't locked, and I was able to push it open easily. The door gave a creak, but other than that, the maze seemed totally devoid of sound. Even our footsteps on the crushed gravel were almost imperceptible.

We walked, David taking in every flicker and shadow, his body loose but alert. Sometimes I forgot that he was a soldier, used to crawling through hostile territory on his own.

"There are a series of half doors in the shrubs," I told him as we went. "They are on the west walls of the maze on the other side of the mausoleum. They lead straight out—for gardeners, so they don't have to risk getting lost every time they need to trim a hedge. If either of us needs to get out of here quickly, those doors are our best bet."

David nodded, his face still in its soldiering mask, but he did put a hand on the small of my back as we walked, as if to reassure himself that he was close enough to me.

"Should we hang the lanterns?" David asked.

I didn't much like the idea of shedding what little light we had with us, but if we wanted to continue the illusion that we were normal partygoers, we didn't have much choice.

"The mausoleum," I said, and led David to the center of the maze.

The mausoleum was made of marble and covered in ivy, once the meeting place for Jacob Landry and his associates.

It was the place where it had all started, every event that had tumbled and crashed together to make tonight into a reality. One wrought-iron hook extended on each side of the mausoleum door and we hung the lanterns, watching shadows swing and sway until the lanterns finally came to rest.

"Well," he said. "I guess now we wait. And what are you doing?"

I had walked over to the east wall of the clearing, where a clever eye could pick out the ordered lines of a ladder built into the shrubbery. It had been there for as long as I could remember, meant to give the maze-wanderer a chance to get their bearings from the center.

I started to climb up, almost immediately entrapped by my dress, which was perfect for dinners and historical events but somewhat less conducive to climbing ladders. The skirt caught on the branches and it took some frustrated tugging and an alarming amount of ripping, but I finally had my head above the maze walls.

David came to stand beneath me. "See anything?"

I shook my head, squinting into the darkness. I could see the house—blue light streaming from every window—and clusters of lanterns in the orchard and gardens, but it was impossible to pick anything out of the darkness of the lawn. There was a quiet, though, that suggested that the revelry was dying down and people were beginning to return to the house. The fireworks would begin soon.

Almost as soon as I formed the thought, a rocket of light flew into the sky and exploded. I chewed my lip. I really did not want to miss the signing.

"Madeline . . ."

I looked down at David. With the lamplight behind him, his hair and skin looked almost blue, like an illustration of Krishna in the old manuscripts we kept under glass at the library. I remembered that he had wanted to finish our talk.

"Yes?" I asked.

He took a deep breath. He looked nervous. It wasn't the same kind of attentive anxiety that had kept his eyes sweeping over our path as we had walked down here, but an intimate, personal sort of nervousness.

"Everything that's happened over the last month—it's made me realize how much . . ." He shifted his feet. I stared. I'd never seen him at such a profound loss for words. "I thought tonight—your birthday—would be the perfect time to tell you—"

A firework shot into the sky and flowered into thousands of golden sparks, the gold for a moment chasing away the blue and gilding every curve and line of David's sharp face—no longer Krishna, but Apollo. The sparks fell and he was reaching into his tuxedo now and my heart was beginning to pound as a rushing wave of understanding surged in my chest and I thought, *really, now, after the fight two days ago?* and at the same time: *yes, yes, yes.*

And then there was the creak of the door to the maze.

I put a finger to my lips and David shut his mouth, his eyebrows rising, and then I pointed toward the front of the maze. "Someone else is here," I mouthed.

He was all business immediately, pulling his hand out of his jacket and plucking me from the ladder with an ease that reminded me of how deceptively strong he was. "Stay close to the ladder," he said quietly. "I'll be in the next row over and I'll be watching the entire time."

"Remember the doors," I said, and then I was in an embrace so tight I could barely breathe, my lips pressed to his. I reached up to twine my fingers in his hair, and he broke the kiss, burying his face in my neck.

"I'll be fine," I whispered. "I've got you and my tablet is right here. I'm not scared."

He let go of me, searching my eyes with his own. "You never are, are you?"

I gave a laugh that sounded hollow, even to me. He brushed a knuckle against the corner of my mouth and then he was gone, melding into the dark recesses of the maze with practiced fluidity and speed.

I withdrew my tablet out of the deep dress pocket to make sure that it was on and that the battery was fully charged. I also made sure that a video call was all ready to be placed in case I needed help. I had meant only to call the police, but, on a whim, I added Uncle Jack and Father and the other heirs into the addressee list. If I were actually confronted by the killer, I would need all the help I could get.

I straightened my shoulders and turned toward the opening in the maze that faced the front. It was impossible to see anything outside the circle of lantern light—the blue haze making everything outside of its glow that much darker. I thumbed at the edges of my tablet, openly chewing on my bottom lip since no one was around to see.

I have the tablet, I have the tablet, I have . . .

And then I slowly registered the fact that the other victims had tablets, too. Inspector Hernandez had found Marianne's by the road, and I had seen Mark's in the crime scene in the garden, and Jane's only few feet away from her corpse. They all had the ability to call for help . . . so why hadn't they? *They probably didn't have time,* I reasoned. But there was another possibility. . . .

I heard footsteps, saw a shifting in the darkness that could be movement, could be the pale reflection of lantern light off of a white dress shirt. I took a deep breath, my fingers pressed against my tablet screen, ready to shout or scream or run, but when the figure emerged, it was somebody I knew, somebody I loved, but he had a gun in his hand and it was aimed at me.

THIRTY-TWO

Another firework exploded, throwing the maze into blinding light, illuminating the broad shoulders of Jude MacAvery.

Jude stepped closer and my brain signaled danger. I took a step back.

He lowered his gun, blinking. "Madeline?"

I didn't say anything, keeping my hand tight around the tablet, my knees slightly bent, ready to run. Jude wasn't a killer, he wasn't a killer, I knew he wasn't, he couldn't be, so why did every part of me feel tense and suspicious?

"You weren't at the fireworks display, and then I saw your message that you had come down here. . . ."

I still didn't answer. He looked down at the gun, which was still slightly raised. "Sorry—the lantern light is so bright—I couldn't see who was actually in the clearing."

"Why do you have a gun?" I asked, glad that my voice sounded more stable and sure than I felt inside.

"It's a very sensitive event. Even without you trying to hunt murderers." He slid the gun back into the holster inside his jacket and held out his hand. "Let's find David and go back up. Let the constables worry about everyone's safety. This is your big moment—you helped do all this. Don't you want to see it?"

I let out a breath. I was being stupid. Jude wasn't going to hurt me, of course he wasn't. But before I could absorb that thought, another figure stepped out of the darkness, and before I could lift my hand or utter a warning or even see exactly who it was, there was a thick, wet-sounding smack and Jude fell.

Stuart stood behind him, panting, forehead stippled with sweat, a garden spade dangling from his hand.

"Jesus Christ," I said, breathing out suddenly. "*Jesus*, Stuart!"

I rushed over to Jude, kneeling beside him and fumbling with his wrist, trying to take his pulse.

"I'm sorry," Stuart said breathlessly. "I knew you were out here and I came to check on you and then I saw Jude. I thought maybe he was trying to hurt you."

"No," I said, shaking my head. "He wasn't, he just came back to check on me, same as you."

Stuart didn't bend or kneel to see if Jude was okay. He kept standing. He examined the spade instead, wiping his brow and licking his lips.

I finally found Jude's pulse, thready and maybe too erratic, but there. "We need to get him up to the house. Maybe I should call up . . ."

Stuart flipped the handle of the spade so that the blade was pointed down, and then flipped it back up.

"Aren't you going to help?" I demanded.

He didn't say anything. But he smiled.

Something inside me, deeper inside than conscious thought or feeling—the part inside that was shared with all other animals—told me to stay very, very still.

"No," Stuart said. "No, I don't think I will."

And then it came to me. I knew the reason why the others hadn't used their tablets, why they hadn't tried to call the police or anyone else. They hadn't used them because they knew the killer. Because they had thought that the killer was their friend, or at least their peer.

Or their cousin.

The prey animal inside of me told me to stand, very slowly. I did, for a moment grateful for the wide, tumbling skirt that hid my legs and feet under yards of tulle and silk. I slowly—*oh so slowly* so as not to make my skirt rustle or move—wriggled a foot out of its low heel. David had said he was near, had said he was watching, but he wasn't here, he wasn't helping. And that wasn't David at all—something must have happened to him. He was hurt or trapped or something.

So I'd have to run.

Stuart smiled again, spinning the spade in his hand, watching the blade rotate.

"I thought you were going to be up at the front of the house," I said, and God bless my Landry demeanor, because I sounded as unperturbed as ever. One foot was now out of its heel. The gravel was freezing but luckily crushed so finely that it didn't hurt my feet. I started on the other heel.

"You know, I was. And then I thought, why not go see where Madeline and her boy of the month went off to? It's so dull to be alone when we could all be together. So where is he, Madeline?"

My mouth was dry. "He left," I said. "He went back up to the house."

"Hmm. Now why don't I think that's true?"

My other foot was free. Now for my tablet . . . I slipped my hand into my pocket, hoping to look casual, and my fingers brushed against it. I felt a small vibration, meaning that I had activated it, but just as I was about to take it out, Stuart clucked his tongue.

"Let's not go for our tablet yet. We're just cousins, having a little chat . . . aren't we?"

I slid one last finger across the screen before I pulled my hand out, hoping to God that I had hit the right buttons.

We stared at each other for a moment, and I took in every twitch of his fingers, every drop of sweat, every flick of his eyes. And so I knew—in the half instant before he swung the spade—that he was about to attack. I threw myself backward, the blade of shovel missing my face by inches, and I could feel the wind from it, feel the breeze of it swinging back behind his shoulder and knew that he was about to swing again. I scrambled to my feet, the awful dress tangling between my legs and tripping me, and I heard the shovel swing again, ducking, even though it missed. I was on my feet for real now, my skirt gathered in my arms, pounding across the clearing toward the south opening.

"David!" I screamed. *"David!"*

"Oh, I'm sorry," Stuart said from behind me. "I forgot to mention something. My brothers are here, too."

Tarleton and Frank emerged from the opening, pushing David in front of them. I came to a standstill as I watched my boyfriend being hauled in front of me like a prisoner, a rag tied firmly around his face, gagging his mouth.

David had a bloody lip and a bruise blooming dark and large on his cheek, but his eyes glinted and his body was tensed in that soldier's way of his, and I knew he hadn't been beaten, not really. He wanted to be near me, to protect me. We met eyes, and he canted his head infinitesimally, in the direction of the hidden ladder.

He wanted me to run, and I knew he thought he could hold the Lawrence brothers off while I did. But I wasn't so certain.

"Why?" I turned to face Stuart, stalling for a better opportunity. "I don't understand why."

"Because, cousin mine, the few pure Uprisen left need to take a stand. Against this"—he waved a hand toward the house—"this *travesty*. It's disgusting, what you and your family have done. You've taken a good thing and sullied it, dirtied it. Someone had to stop you."

"How is this stopping anything? The treaty is going to be signed. Your sick game didn't stop anything."

He spun the spade in his hand again. "I thought that killing the heirs would ensure that the Uprisen wouldn't trust the Rootless again. I thought attacking those families that were growing weak and sympathetic would show them what monsters they were ready to make peace with."

"Stuart, *you* are the monster," I said, voice shaking now. "*You* killed our friends. Not the Rootless."

"We are," he stepped closer, "so much *more* than them." The blue light carved strange shadows across his face. "We are *better* than them. How can you not see it? How can you not *feel* it? I feel it, Madeline. I feel it every day. They are worse than animals, and you want to just let them roam all over the city, living in our houses and marrying our girls? It's *disgusting*."

"And Jamie's serum?" I asked, voice shaking. "Did you steal that, too?"

"Well, obviously. Did you really think that the gentry, what's left of the real gentry, would let them have something like that? I mean, why don't we just turn over our estates and all our money while we're at it?"

"It was going to help people," I said.

"No, it was going to make them more like us. But they need to be different. They can't have all the things we have. Otherwise nothing makes sense, does it?"

"And the bomb in my father's room? Was that you, too?"

He grinned. "That one was all your Rootless friends. Although I know of a few gentry that wouldn't have minded putting the fear of God in old Uncle Alexander. It was his weakness, after all, that allowed all this to happen."

Frank cleared his throat behind me. "Come on, Stuart. Let's just take care of this and get out of here."

"Yeah," Tarleton echoed. "I don't really want to miss any more of the party. Let's finish up."

I looked back at them. "Did you guys know? Did you help him?"

Tarleton stared at me, uncaring, but Frank looked away. "What brave boys you are," I said softly. "Holding down your friends so that your brother could kill them."

"It's not like that," Frank said. "You heard Stuart. We had to do something, we had to make sure that the gentry remembered how much they hated the Rootless."

"Yes, like I said, you really succeeded. All this worthless blood on your hands, and nightmares in your mind—you do have nightmares about it, don't you, Frank? I can see the circles under your eyes from here."

Frank squeezed his eyes shut.

"Be quiet," Stuart warned me.

"Why? You're going to kill me either way, right? And David? And Jude? And it still won't matter. I'll have won. I'll have beat you, Stuart, because that treaty is still going to be signed."

"Are you so sure?" Stuart asked, still looking at the spade.

There was a beat. "What do you mean?"

"I mean," he said deliberately, "that there is someone else here tonight who agrees with us. And he has no intention of letting the signing happen."

Smith. Oh, God.

Smith was here, just like he'd planned to be all along.

"It was tricky, a bit, freeing him from jail. But I find that a little distraction and a lot of money can go a long way toward befuddling those poor, overworked constables."

"He wanted to help us," Tarleton added. "Even though he was in jail because of what we did. He was happy to go along with us if it meant he got to come out and play tonight."

"So we get Madeline Landry," Stuart continued. "And Smith finally gets to be the wild revolutionary he's always wanted to be. I'd call that a win-win, right, boys?"

I didn't look back to see if the brothers agreed. I just kept staring at Stuart. "What is he going to do? Where is he now?"

"Well, that would spoil the fun, don't you think?" Stuart said. "Let's not do that. But oh wait—you won't get to see it happen anyway. So sad."

He stepped toward me, and I slid the tablet out of my dress, brandishing it like a weapon.

I only needed the barest of seconds. "One more thing," I said, tapping the screen, bringing up what I had just recorded.

The sound was surprisingly clear. *David!* the tiny tablet version of my voice shrieked. *David!*

I could see the moment that Stuart understood, the moment his face went from arrogant to alarmed, and I wanted that, that one small victory for myself. I wanted him to know that no matter how brutal he was, how depraved or how strong, that I had bested him.

And then using the video call I had already prepared, I pressed *send,* almost feeling the pulse of the file as it left my tablet and rocketed to the stars and then back down to Landry Park, to the police and Jack and Father and the other heirs. "Now everyone will know."

He looked at it and then up at me. His eyes glinted.

And then I knew that he didn't care about getting caught. Not really. Whatever darkness ate away at the man inside had eaten away at that fear, too.

"Maybe they will know in a few minutes," he said. "But everyone is watching the display now, not checking their tablets."

He flung himself toward me, and I knew there was no way I could run from him, not in this dress. I wasn't a fighter—I never had tussled with the boys like Cara had loved doing— but I did know one thing and that was where men were the weakest. I waited until Stuart was almost on top of me and then I fell to my knees, slicing up with a forearm and burying my elbow into his groin. The tablet tumbled out of my hand

and crashed onto the ground right as he toppled, heaving. I tore off toward the ladder, seeing David fighting with the other two Lawrence brothers as I went. I stopped at the ladder, one foot on the rung, and looked back at David, wanting to go help him.

David yanked the gag down over his chin. "Go, Madeline!" he roared, fending off Frank and Tarleton. He was faster than them, lighter on his feet, quick and slender as a dagger, but there were two of them and they were burly, with years of boxing training behind him. David noticed me hesitating. "I'm fine! Just go!"

"I'm going to get help," I said.

Stuart rose unsteadily to his feet behind me and I started climbing.

He came toward me and I was almost at the top of the ladder, but my dress had snagged, and then he had a hold of it, a handful of silk, and he yanked down. My foot slipped off the rung and I nearly fell, but managed to cling to the ladder with my arms. I kicked out wildly, blindly, until I connected with something, and then I managed to squirm my way to the top of the ladder. The shrubbery stabbed and pricked and buckled under my weight, and then, with a great tearing of tulle and silk, I tumbled the six feet down to the ground.

I landed on my hip, hard, and the breath was knocked from my chest. I was covered in scratches and my dress was in tatters—but I was on the other side. I could do this—I'd grown up playing in this maze. I could find my way out in a matter of minutes.

"Oh, Madeline," Stuart called from the other side of the shrubs, his voice lilting in a singsong rhythm. "I'm coming to find you. . . ."

I took off in the other direction, making for the west walls and their hidden doors. I could hear Stuart climbing the ladder and then landing on the other side. I'd already turned the corner, so I tried to run as silently as I could toward the west end of the maze.

Stuart was whooping now and it sounded as if he was running with his hands along the branches as he chased after me. I turned another corner, dodged a dead end, and then found myself finally in the right part of the maze. My feet dug into the gravel and I nearly tripped myself trying to stop at the door. Like the ladder, it was cleverly hidden inside the leafy walls, but I found it.

"I'm coming for you, Madeline!" Stuart shouted, almost gleefully, and my stomach turned over. Through the next door, and the next, but now I could hear him pushing through the doors as well, following my trail. *Only three more to go.* There was a small gardening shed outside of the maze, hugging the very back wall. Maybe I could hide there.

He was gaining on me, I could feel it. I could feel it in the prickling of my neck, of the silent screaming of the prey-brain inside of me, screaming at me to run faster, run harder. I could no longer feel the gravel chewing into my feet, nor the cold—all of my energy and thought was on breathing and pumping my legs. The dress dragged and tore every time I contended with one of the hidden doors, but I finally emerged from the maze during an explosion of fireworks, pain woven into every breath. I knew I had only seconds.

The snow was not cleared back here, and I sank into the drifts, fumbling pointlessly for the shed. There would be no hiding, I recognized, not with these deep footprints of mine, as clear as any signpost. But I had to hope—for something, anything. I made it behind the shed just as Stuart emerged from the maze.

His footsteps crunched in the snow. They were slow, methodical, the measured steps of an animal that knows its quarry is helpless.

"This has been fun, hasn't it? More fun than the others, let me tell you."

I slid along the wall, my snow-covered feet now burning and biting with the cold. I stepped on something hard underneath the snow. I raised my foot. It was a garden stake—metal, with a viciously sharp end, meant to dig into soft earth.

"Marianne was so easy. You wouldn't believe how easy it was. She barely made a sound. I killed her too early though—I had trouble dragging her in the house when no one was looking. And you wouldn't *believe* the mess she made on the patio. It was a good thing I had Tarleton and Frank to help—Frank was the one who found the paint after we realized the blood wouldn't work. He was at a luncheon at the Yorks' and there were gallons and gallons of red paint just sitting right there."

I picked up the stake, breathing hard.

"That symbol—you've got to admit, that was some artistry. I wanted to make sure that you would see, Madeline, that you would see that this was all your fault, really. If only you'd kept your mouth shut at Liberty Park, none of this would have happened. Things would be just like they were."

Painstaking step after painstaking step, sliding my foot into the snow, trying to keep my dress from rustling over the top of the drifts.

"Mark was harder. He was strong. And it took a couple tries to kill him. I did that one mostly by myself. My note was a little hasty, I admit, but I thought it was a nice touch—no way the police wouldn't think it was the Rootless then."

I kept moving, finally rounding the other corner. We were on opposite sides of the shed now. I needed to figure out when to make my move.

"Jane, though. Jane Jane Jane. She knew the minute I came up to the observatory. She was always smart, wasn't she? You were the top of our class at the Academy, but she was right behind you, you know?"

I wanted to scream. I couldn't do this—this chase, this hunt, listening to him talk about Jane like she was nothing, nothing at all.

"I remember the look on her face when I smacked her tablet out of her hand. She was so defiant, so insolent. And then I got to watch all that insolence fade out of her eyes." He took two quick steps forward—I could hear them, *crunch crunch*—and then he was around the back of the shed. Only one more corner separated us.

"Come out, come out, wherever you are," Stuart sang.

I adjusted my grip on the stake, trying to stay calm, trying to see everything the way my father had taught me—taking in every movement, every sound. Only this time it wasn't about reading people in a ballroom or at a council meeting. This time it was to save my life.

Crunch. A breath.

Crunch. A sniffing breath. I shuddered.

Crunch. No breath.

Now, I ordered myself and ran toward him just as he rounded the corner. His arms circled around me, and he brought me to the ground just as I stabbed upward with the stake, catching him right in the upper thigh.

He howled, rolling off me. I jerked the stake out of his leg and pressed the point against his throat, scrambling to get to a kneeling position. The point of the stake made a divot against his skin, dripping the blood from his leg along his neck.

"You wouldn't," he said. And then he licked his lips and smiled. He brought his hand up and wrapped it around mine.

A rocket of red and green exploded in the sky, throwing our grisly tableau into a relief of sickly, unnatural colors.

"Come on," he said. "Let's do it together. You know you want to, don't you?"

I sucked in a breath. Stuart had killed three of my friends, he had hurt Jude, and he'd tried to kill me. What else could be done, really, but to make sure that a monster like him was never allowed to hurt anyone ever again? I saw Jane's face, slack and cold, that ballet flat abandoned on the observatory floor.

My hand pressed the stake in deeper. Fresh blood pooled around the point, spilling over like a flooded lake.

He should die. He was a danger to everyone, he was warped, he was guilty, and he was evil. Why on earth should he be allowed to continue to live when Jane was in a plot of cold, lonely earth?

And then I remembered David's words to me in the cathedral. *How can you talk about people like that? Like they're not individuals, but units, with a value that you can quantify? That's no better than how your father sees people, or Jacob Landry himself. . . .*

I sat back, shaking, wrenching the stake out of Stuart's hand and flinging it across the snowy expanse. David emerged from the maze, looking sweaty and bloody, but victorious. He ran to us.

"Are you hurt?" he asked breathlessly.

I shook my head.

He looked down at Stuart, who was still smiling, with blood on his neck and a gaping hole in his thigh. "Damn," he said in wonder. He glanced up at me, his face full of admiration.

"You must be so proud," Stuart said. "She couldn't do it. She's weak, like the rest of the gentry have become. . . ."

David knelt, almost thoughtfully, and then just as thoughtfully cocked his fist back and rammed it into Stuart's face. He went slack, blood running from his nose.

"That was satisfying," David observed.

I nodded. And then I remembered.

Smith.

THIRTY-THREE

"I'll call the constables down here and then I'll be right after you," David said, noticing me looking back toward the house. "Go."

"Okay," I said, and I went.

I ran up to the lawn just as the finale began, loud spitting pops and whistles of smoke and heat, exploding again and again, one on top of the other. As I reached the top of the lawn, I could see the people congregated on the patio, faces upturned to the white and blue lights. They paid me no mind as I ran up the stairs to the patio, bloody and barefoot, dress shredded beyond all recognition. I pushed past them, looking for Father or Uncle Jack, someone who could help, but the guests were crammed so closely together and the flickering lights of the fireworks made it impossible to identify anyone. . . .

I pressed my hand to my forehead. The adrenaline was beginning to drain out of my blood, and I realized that my hands were trembling violently, and that my feet were red and raw from the snow. I needed to sit down. I probably needed a doctor. I definitely needed help—the police or my father or *someone*.

I finally emerged from the crowd on the patio and walked into the empty ballroom. Crumbs and napkins littered the floor, but there were no servants clearing them away. Lantern Day was one of the few celebrations that they got to partake in as well, and so they were all presumably outside, clapping and cheering at the fireworks, too.

I turned one way, then turned the other, completely undecided. Should I check the front? Try the back again? Go ahead and call the police from a wall screen?

Police. Police first. David was still back there with Stuart, and Jude needed help, and I didn't even know about the other Lawrence brothers, whether they were hurt or whether they were hunting.

I started hobbling over to the wall screen, and then Morgana darted in front of me, streaking from the hallway, tearing past me as if I weren't even there. She disappeared outside into the sea of legs and skirts.

Strange. Morgana was the very definition of desultory. Unless Charlie was chasing after her, her preferred mode was slinking, not sprinting. I looked back up to the hallway. What had made her run like that?

And then I smelled it—sharp and acrid and wrong. Some innate and fundamental part of me knew what it was before I could even name it, a smell that had been braided with human history for millennia.

Smoke.

Smoke.

I ran through the ballroom and into the foyer, down the hallway, following the smell and the faint gray haze that was wreathing itself on the ceiling.

It was the library.

Flames licked at the shelves, crawling up the wood and the crimson leather spines, framing the glass cases scattered across the room. It crept along unlikely routes and seams, following the hand-knotted carpets and reading tables, shying away from the marble floor. But it raged hot and virulent, a virus that had long passed its tipping point. It didn't matter how much stone and metal barred its way—the fire would eat it all. Eat it all and still be hungry.

But the books—

I ran into the furnace of a library, blasted by heat, red blotches dancing before my eyes, but I had to save at least the manuscripts. Some of them were over six hundred years old. . . .

A crash sounded from above, and a row of shelves on the second story fell, spilling books and flaming splinters of wood onto the first floor. I reached a case, fumbled with the searing latch, knowing that scarlet was welting across my fingers, but not caring. These were *my books*, the things that had kept me company for years, had kept me sane and content and curious. I finally flung open the lid and gathered the manuscript to my chest.

There was a roar and another crash, and another row of

shelves collapsed, this time sending the embers showering onto my shoulders and neck.

"*Madeline!*"

It was David, slipping easily out of his tuxedo jacket as he ran toward me, throwing it over my head and trying to pull me out of the room.

"No!" I screamed, jerking my body back toward the books.

"Don't be an idiot," he yelled in my ear, his voice hoarse from the smoke. "You can buy new books. You can't bring yourself back to life." He wrapped his arms around me and hoisted me up, carrying me out of the library as I fought him, squirming.

I can't live without my books and then as he carried me into the hallway, coughing but still strong, still focused, I realized that what I meant was *I can't live without my house.*

My house was on fire. Landry Park was burning.

David carried me all the way to the ballroom, and we stumbled onto the patio, where the partygoers were still reveling, still clapping enthusiastically for the fireworks. This time, though, they stopped and stared at the sight of David and me, covered in scrapes and blood, faces blackened from the smoke, my dress in complete tatters.

Father's voice boomed over the crowd as the last magnificent firework fizzled to the ground. "Where is she? Where's Madeline?" He pushed through the crowd as David set me gently down.

"I heard that the constables were called down to the maze, and then I saw the recording you'd sent . . ." Father trailed off as he took it all in, my shaking hands still wrapped around the manuscript I'd saved, my bare feet, my eyes, which I knew must have looked wild and frantic.

"The house," I said. "The library." I meant to say more but I couldn't choke it out.

"We have to call the fire department," David said. "The library is burning. It will take the whole house with it. We need to get people clear in case the fire reaches the nuclear charges in the basement."

Father looked unbelieving, but desperation and fear still blossomed in his eyes, and he ran into the house. I made to follow him, but David was too fast.

"Everyone onto the lawn!" he bellowed. "Away from the house! Away!"

Without the fireworks, the orange glow coming from within the house was easier to see. One scream echoed out, then several others, and suddenly there was a stampede, people tripping down the stairs, people crying out in fear. David kept one arm around me, the other relentlessly fending off the terrified guests who crashed into us in their frenzy to escape the fire.

"I have to get my father!" I yelled.

David shook his head. "He'll come back out."

And he did. Just as the flames began waving out of the

second story windows, I saw Father's tall frame silhouetted against the fire and the smoke, and he found me easily, since David and I had stopped at the bottom of the stairs. He didn't say anything, but his face said it all, a mirror of my own face, a mirror of my own shock and empty horror and of the word *why* etched in blood and char onto my very heart.

I could already see the skeleton of the estate, black and flaming, as the walls began to tumble down around it, and I didn't need to see inside it to know what was happening. The silken drapes, the thick carpets, my bedspread with the atomic symbol embroidered in silver. And the library—oh, God—the library.

It was me, this house. Its struts and supports my bones, its walls my sinews, its paintings and statues my skin. I was as much a part of the house as it was part of me, and it was like watching my entire life—triumphs and anguishes and all— disintegrate.

It was the single most perfect, stable, beautiful, and mean-ingful thing in my life. And it was lost.

David was still behind me, and with the smoke and heat stinging my eyes, he was nothing but white hair, blue eyes, and smears of blood marring his lips and cheeks and chin. He reached for me, but I stumbled forward and then fell to my knees, unable to do anything but watch as Landry Park continued to burn, burn, burn.

Smith had done it. Or Smith and Stuart, or Smith and the

Empire, or Smith and somebody else. But I found that I didn't care who at the moment. Did it matter who destroyed my life? Only that it was destroyed. What possible vengeance or anger or sorrow could I muster that would be equal to this? This wanton malice?

"Madeline," David was saying. "Madeline, we can go. We don't have to watch this."

I shook my head. I had to watch it die. I had to watch the flames lick at the observatory and I had to watch the roof collapse and I had to watch the snow melt at its foundations. And for now, I wouldn't be an heir or the girl with the plan. I would just be Madeline, just a girl watching her childhood home burn and tumble to the ground.

THIRTY-FOUR

Things take on a life of their own, a momentum, and continue after the initial impetus is long gone. Not unlike fire.

A treaty was signed by the Rootless and the gentry a few days later in a quiet meeting at City Hall. The wheels of peace had turned too far to be denied now, and the exposure of Arthur Lawrence's sons as the murderers was deeply crippling to his cause. I saw his face as the constables climbed into the ambulance beside Stuart while the house smoldered in the background, and I knew for certain that he hadn't known. He may have been power-hungry and prejudiced and cruel, but he at least wasn't a psychopath. And in one fell swoop, he had lost his heir and two of his other sons to prison, not to mention all of his credibility. After the recording of Stuart went viral, the opposition to the treaty crumbled.

The fire raged all night. Perhaps Smith had expected praise, or perhaps he had known better. But when the Rootless gathered shoulder by shoulder with the gentry to watch the building being devoured by flames, there was no joy, no happiness or cheering. Landry Park had been home to many of them for the past several days and it had been good to them.

And they knew how it felt to watch their homes burn.

They found Smith a couple days later and they put him in jail, for the crime he'd actually committed. He had no visitors, not even Jack, who was as shaken and sickened by the arson as Father and I. In the end, it had been the three of us left watching the house. David had gone to the hospital with Jude, Mother had thoughtfully taken Charlie away, and Cara and Ewan had melted into the crowd long before.

It was fitting, really, that it should be the three of us. The three people who had been formed by Landry Park and, in return, had hoped to form its future. We hadn't touched, hadn't spoken as the firefighters sprayed the charred stone walls, and when the faint pink of dawn began to blush at the horizon, we left without a word, making our way down the drive and walking the short distance to the Osbournes, where we were received with kindness and efficiency.

It didn't take long to determine that the fire had indeed reached the basement, and that the charges had been compromised. Radiation had leaked everywhere, seeping into the blackened foundations and the soil. The remains of the house and the surrounding grounds were quarantined for the safety of the public; it would be five years before it would be deemed safe for habitation again. Jamie reassured me that the estimate was a very conservative one—likely the thick walls of the basement had contained a large amount of the radiation and that it would take less than a year for levels to be brought low enough for human activity. But it was cold comfort. One year, five years—what did it matter? The house was gone. It had stood for two hundred years; it had been perfect for two hundred years, and now it was gone.

David and Jude, having been granted a special dispensation to stay until the signing of the treaty, had left for the mountains. They were going to keep an eye on the Empire, which had formally accepted the new united government and had withdrawn its demands. But peace with the Empire would always be a watchful, wary peace, and the army was making sure that the Empire knew that.

Jude and David had left me with tight hugs and lingering kisses, and nothing made me feel emptier than watching the car drive away, one dark head and one blond one visible from the back window, knowing that months would fall between this and seeing them again.

That night, we sat around the Osbournes' dinner table, discussing what to do about the estate, Jack and Father no longer talking like enemies or reluctant allies, but brothers.

"We could build it again, you know," Father said. "Once the radiation clears."

"We could build an even bigger house," Mother said.

Jack, Father, and I looked at her.

"We would build it exactly the same way," Jack said. "It was perfect as it was."

I thought of the strange and bitter notion that had occurred to me more than once this past month. Even the diaphanous ghost of the idea had been too terrible to entertain before, but now that feeling seemed childish and clingy.

"What if we gave it up?"

Father raised his eyebrows. "Pardon?"

"The grounds, the ruins—the entire estate. What if we donated it? To the city or to the university? We've never had a public library in the city before, but the treaty is opening up voting to every citizen. There will be millions of people who've never voted. The children might have education provided for them, but the adults won't . . . what would be a better way to support them than to open a library? A place where anyone can come and learn?"

"That's very civic-minded of you," Jack said.

I wished it were because I was so noble. I didn't tell them about the nightmares I'd had, watching the house burn down, running into the library, and then standing trapped as I watched the flames kiss the leather spines of the books. How I'd wept and wept that night when David had finally pried the thick manuscript from my hands and I saw that it was *Le Morte d'Arthur*, the one book out of them all that I would have saved, and I had grabbed it only by chance.

"But . . ." Father began, clearing his throat and trying again. "How can you suggest that we give it up? The land? The estate? We could build another house there as soon as it's safe. There's no need to let our shock push us into something so rash."

I could smell once again the burned leather, hear the crash of the shelves as they fell. I could feel the cold air whipping around my shoulders as we had watched every room burn until there was nothing left but scorched stone.

But my voice was as steady and reasonable as ever. "It's not rash. I've been thinking about this for a long time. Smith did a terrible thing, but I understood why he did it. Landry Park was always going to be the paradigm of gentry life. It was founded by the man who created the Rootless in the first place. As long as it stood, it was only going to be a reminder, to both sides, of the past." I turned to Father. "And how long have you labored to keep this family solvent? Without the burden of the estate, our expenses will be greatly reduced and our accounts can once again be in the black."

"You are suggesting that Victory Lodge become our permanent home?" Father asked. Mother wrinkled her nose. I ignored her.

"I'm suggesting that we give a gift both to the city and to our own future. It's not easy. But we've never done the easy thing when another path was more logical, have we?"

Jack and Father looked at each other.

"No," Father agreed. "I suppose we haven't."

The next week, Jamie announced to the city that the prototype was ready for human trials, a formula combining the scope of the Landry serum with the modality of the fertility vaccines. A formula that might not rewrite DNA, but would do enough so that an entire population could finally live without sickness. The gentry clamored for it, too, and so it was decided that all citizens, regardless of caste, would be offered the shot. No longer would the Landrys be the only ones with nothing to fear when it came to radiation.

Rootless men, women, and children filled the Public Hospital, standing in lines that stretched several blocks in either direction, all waiting for their turn. While they waited, I walked up and down the lines, asking the now-enfranchised people to help me sign a petition for Dewhurst's removal. To my surprise, once the gentry heard about the petition, they wanted to sign it, too. They were angry that Dewhurst had failed to protect their heirs, that he'd persecuted an innocent group of people while the real killer still stalked and planned and attacked.

I didn't bother reading the stories or watching the videos of his fruitless attempts at appeal, and I certainly didn't listen to his self-pitying resignation speech, but I did hear later that he knew it was me who had started the petition, the little girl he thought he could so easily intimidate. I didn't even feel guilty taking pleasure in that.

I moved to Victory Lodge with Mother and Father soon after, but only for a few months, because finally, finally, *finally*, after years of dreaming, I was going to the university.

Father and I had taken a walk late that April, into the thick woods that surrounded Victory Lodge, the latest litter of hounds bounding playfully around our feet. It was almost warm, the thawing breaths of spring blowing through the trees and targeting the clumps of snow that lingered in shady groves and in hidden corners of the grounds. Father was content, at least as content as he ever seemed to get these days, with the ghost of the estate trailing behind him.

"I want to go to the university," I said abruptly. "And I'm going to go, whether you object or not."

"This is quite a change in tone from the last time we had this conversation."

"Last time I was asking," I pointed out. "This time, I'm telling you. I would like your support and your blessing, but if not, then I'll find a way to pay for it on my own."

He stayed quiet, his head turned away, but when I caught a glimpse of his face, it was on the brink of a smile and not of a frown.

"Well?" I asked, feeling a slight ray of hope.

"I admire your initiative and your assertiveness."

"So . . . you don't object?"

"Why would I? Everything else has changed. I suppose there's not much point in denying you the university when I have failed to provide you with an estate to inherit."

"I'm not turning my back on the family," I said. "There's still Victory Lodge and all the farmland, and who knows?

Maybe there will be more. It's only a handful of years, and when I'm finished, I will have so much more to offer this family and this city."

He touched my shoulder. "I always knew that you were destined for greatness. All the things you've done . . . it's only the beginning."

"Thank you," I said. "And I do have one other favor to ask."

EPILOGUE

There was a hill a quarter mile away that overlooked the empty grounds of the estate. It had only been five months since the fire, but five months of neglect had already taken its toll. The gardens were unkempt riots of color, punctuated with sprawling bushes and leaf-choked fountains. The shrubs grew tall and wide and shaggy, and the grass of the lawn looked like it was already doing its best to return to its natural prairie state—light green and knee-high, with rabbits and chipmunks darting around and birds circling up above.

I sat on the soft, warm grass of the hill, happy to watch the August breeze blow through the grass and through the ruins of the house. I couldn't set foot on the land, but I could still watch it, still recall the vivid, clean memories of my girlhood and still dream of the library that was to be built there one day. Soon, in just a few years, everybody would come to Landry Park, not for a party or for a dinner, but to read and to learn, to chase their curiosity to the dustiest, most obscure ends. They'd asked the Landry family to name the new library, and we did. We named it Jubilee Manor, after the ancient tradition of returning land and freeing slaves.

Normally, Elinor came up here with me, but she had gone to an extra lecture this afternoon. At my request, Father had released her from her service to the family and offered to pay her way through school, and so for the first time, we were no longer mistress and maid, but friends. It was new and strange, but everything was new and strange these days. Several of the estates had switched to solar and wind power, while others now kept private crews of contractors to manage their charges. Schools had been built and filled, and everywhere you looked, you saw new faces, healthy faces—faces free of lesions and sores, skin tinged with all manners of clean tans and browns and pinks, without jaundice, without the ashen cast of the nearly dead.

"I thought I might find you here."

I looked up, squinting into the bright daylight. A man stood next to me, a tailored scarlet uniform emphasizing the tall, narrow lines of his body. He had a strikingly angled face, with cheekbones that looked carved from stone and a jaw much the same. Light blond hair framed his face, shorter than I remembered, but still too long to be properly military. And all of it was overshadowed by eyes a color usually only seen in Cherenkov lanterns.

I bit my lip, trying not to smile like a schoolgirl, trying not to reveal the way he made my pulse race and my face flush. Trying not to show how happy I was that he was home, for however short a time.

"You're delighted to see me," he observed.

"I am no such thing," I insisted.

"You are, too! You liar."

I didn't answer, but I pulled my legs up to my chest and smiled.

He sat down beside me, his long legs stretched out. "Nice view."

"Yes," I agreed, looking back to the tangled wilderness that used to be my home. "It is."

"Jude would have come, too, but he's doing some sort of diplomatic thing for the general. I think he's got his eye on the White House sometime in the next decade."

"He would," I said. "He's a Landry."

"My dream is to one day watch you two fight it out in an election. Landry to Landry."

"I'd win."

"I know."

A few minutes of peaceful silence followed—not true silence—but the kind of summer quiet that has wind and birds and voices carried from far away.

"You know, on your birthday I was going to ask—"

"I know," I said.

David stood and offered me a hand, and I stood as well. "And what would you have said?" he asked, running a finger along my jaw, and then leaning down to press his lips against mine. I slid my arms up his chest and around his neck, pulling him closer, thinking of every kiss we had shared—the tender and the turbulent—and of the way he kept me sharp and smart. Of the way he had risked arrest or worse to save Charlie, of the way he had never allowed me to think easy thoughts or live an easy life, of the way he had saved me from fire and held me as my world burned down.

Love warred with logic—as it had for five months as I'd thought it over. I knew what I had to say, and I had to hope that David wouldn't hate me after I said it. "I would have said that I'd like to finish my time at the university. That I want to wait until I'm older and know what I'm going to do with my life now that the estate is gone. That I want enough time to make sure that we wouldn't kill each other if we were married."

He smiled at that, but then his face went serious. "You want to wait to marry?"

I nodded, feeling his cheek brush against my forehead as I did. "It's not because of you," I whispered. "Part of me wants to marry you right now. But for the first time, I have complete control of what I do with my life—there are no longer plans for me to marry a certain way, to live in a certain place. And I want to be a fully formed person when I marry. And I'm not that right now."

"What would you say if I told you that I was willing to wait as long as you wanted?"

Relief swelled in my chest. "So you don't mind?"

"I never mind anything when it comes to Madeline Landry."

"Who's the liar now?"

"I'm not lying," he said, and then he kissed me until I believed him. After several moments, he pulled away, breathless and eyes shining.

"Shall we?" he asked, gesturing down the hill in the direction of his car.

He laced his hand through mine and together we walked away from the estate with its stone ruins and abandoned gardens, and when I looked back, I saw in my mind the house as it once was—tall and perfect—and myself as I had been living there, quiet and uncertain, without agency or direction. They were ghosts now, that Landry Park and that Madeline. They had been transformed and refined, and now the future was limitless for the estate and, for me, messily triumphant and terrifying and open. Freedom hadn't come only to the Rootless this year.

Jubilee indeed.

Acknowledgments

I hear second books are hard for authors to write, but I'm positive *Jubilee Manor* had an exceptionally difficult birth into the world. That's why I'm so grateful for my tireless agent, Mollie Glick, and saintly editor, Nancy Conescu. Without you two and your Job-like patience, this book would not exist. Whenever we meet in person, the first round is on me. (And the second.)

Kate Harrison, my new caretaker, thank you so much for all you've already done for these books (and for taking me on!) I promise to behave.

Thank you to Emily Brown and Ellen Cormier—you guys do so much of the heavy lifting that makes my job possible. Whenever we meet in person, I will shower you with chocolates. To Cara Petrus, who gave my books beautiful covers, and to Elyse Marshall, who's done such fantastic things for this series (and who also has a fantastic Tumblr). Thank you.

Laura Barnes, your acknowledgments are always so eloquent and I never know what to say in mine. So I'll just say that none of my books or stories would exist without your book fairy dust, and that I need you in a borderline-obsessive, definitely codependent way. So don't go anywhere, okay? Gennifer Albin, thanks as always for the hard words and the business advice. You're the smartest cookie. Robyn Lucas, thank you for reading every single draft of *Jubilee Manor* (there were thirty-seven, I believe) and giving me feedback on all of them. You are the most encouraging cookie.

Kayti McGee, Melanie Harlow, and Tamara Mataya, talented and hilarious ladies. Thank you for the snark and the blackheartedness when I needed them the most. To Nadine Long, who made me an amazing website and who fantasizes about moors with me, thank you. To the WrAHMs, who kept me flush with Tom Hiddleston pictures and dinosaur romance books, and to the women who Order me around—thank you from the bottom of my heart.

The best part of being an author is being friends with other authors, so thank you to Natalie Parker and Tessa Gratton for making sure Papa gets her drinks, to Julie Murphy for (innocently) sharing my bed for a week, to the girls of the Hanging Garden, the extraordinary people of the League, and my fellow debuts, the Valentines.

Thank you *thank you* to Ashley Lindemann for meals and babysitting and Internet videos and whatever else my quantum-entangled heart needed. And thank you *thank you* to Ritu Nanos for wisdom, whiskey, and shadow staff. To the librarians in the Johnson County Library system, the most supportive coworkers a girl could ask for: thank you. And to my AKKA family, for reminding me that the system is the solution.

Thank you to Sandra Whitman, Milt and Kathie Taylor, Eddy Bisceglia, Dana Hagen, and Doug Hagen. I hope that one day I can deserve you all. Josh Taylor, your support and love and time on the couch with me is what keeps me going. And to Noah and Teagan, thank you for being so patient with Mommy's stories. And yes, we can build LEGO sets now.

And finally to Renee Bisceglia. Thank you for being a wonderful and devoted mother, and I hope that you knew that I would not have been an author if it weren't for you (and our biweekly trips to the library). I miss you. I love you.

About the Author

BETHANY HAGEN (www.bethanyhagen.com) was born and raised in Kansas City, Kansas. She grew up reading Charlotte Brontë, Jane Austen, and all things King Arthur, and went on to become a librarian. *Jubilee Manor* is her second novel.